I0692378

The Red House on the Hill

By

Timothy Vincent

W & B Publishers
USA

W & B Publishers

For information: W & B Publishers
Post Office Box 193 Colfax, NC 27235
www.a-argusbooks.com

ISBN: 978-0-9862808-6-3
ISBN: 0-9862808-6-0

Book Cover designed by Nadine M. Smith
Printed in the United States of America

Chapter One

Later, after she was in the ground and the pain was finally, mercifully over, he remembered the red house on the hill. He pointed it out to her once on a trip through the Appalachians. She pronounced it too small, too lonely, and too out of the way. She didn't care for the looks of Torview either, for that matter.

In those days her every whim or mood was law to him: a glorious, benevolent, and wanted necessity. Now that necessity was gone, taken by a terrible and unforgiving reality found in her breast on a cold Wednesday morning. Three months later she was finally free of the pain, even if his still persisted and took on new and deeper realities.

It was not hard to absent himself from the day to day process of being. He simply cut all the inane and un-important ties he once believed so significant. In truth they were significant to her, and so by consequence important to him as well. Now she was gone, and they held no more meaning than useless bric-a-brac.

There were no close friends to say goodbye to, just acquaintances, and most of those were hers. No children to watch over or comfort, or be comforted by. He declared it a blessing. They were enough for each other, he insisted, and she smiled.

Over the course of their marriage he would see that smile again and again. He wondered at times if he ever really understood that slight ironic curve of her lip, the dolphin-like profile that hinted at other levels, levels playful and knowing, and yes, maybe even sad.

Now it didn't matter. Now she was gone. And everything else was just useless bric-a-brac.

The house was the easiest thing to let go. Their home for twenty-five years was not just suddenly empty, it was full: full of ghosts and memories and countless echoes of familiar events never to be heard or felt again. It became almost physically painful to crawl beneath the cold sheets of their bed, to reach out for the warm leg that should be beside him, to wait for the whispered goodnight that never came. He took to sleeping on the couch for a time, but still the unfilled expectations remained.

* * *

He took a temporary room in a local hotel while the real estate agent showed the house. His possessions were reduced to the contents of two boxes and a carrier bag (everything else went to Goodwill or the trash). It was while he was waiting for a buyer that he remembered the red house and asked the real estate agent to check on its availability.

The agent called him back the same day. "I had to do a little digging, but if I have the right house it's still there and I think we can get it. Your timing is good. It was tied up in some crazy town proprietorship for the longest time but the bank owns it now—an out of town bank—and wants to sell. The listing's not cheap, but it's a fair price. You want me to make an offer?"

"Just give them what they're asking for."

"Are you sure? I think we can come in a little under..."

"Just get the house."

Frank couldn't say why it was so important for him to have the house. He was certain there was no rational or financial motivation behind it.

Two days later the house was his, the paperwork signed and witnessed, the funds transferred, and the deed passed. It was all of a moment for Frank, with no intrinsic pleasure or sense of accomplishment. Like paying his last utility bill or registering at the hotel, or putting her in the ground, it had to be done.

His reaction, or lack of one, must have bothered the agent. It didn't stop him from making the sale, but he did appear to suffer a moment of conscience outside the lawyer's office on the day of closing.

"Well, congratulations," he said, offering a hand and his best smile. Frank shook the hand mechanically. The agent searched Frank for signs of pleasure, shock, or even regret.

"You should know," he continued, his smile firmly in place, "I heard some grumblings from the town about the sale. The bank doesn't care of course, as long as they get their money and everything is in order. And it is. I assure you. You own the deed, free and clear. Don't let anyone tell you different."

He looked to Frank again for some reaction, appeared slightly puzzled but relieved to see none. He handed Frank two keys.

"This one is to the gate at the end of the drive," explained the agent, pointing to a common lock key. "And that old man is to the front door. You can probably change it later if you want."

The 'old man' was a heavy piece of iron work from a different age. Frank rolled the key over in his fingers, feeling the weight and admiring the odd teeth and ornate bow.

"As you know there's no electricity," said the agent, "so you don't have to worry about that."

Frank didn't rise to this, or the ironic wink that accompanied it.

The agent nodded as if this was all perfectly normal. He padded Frank on the shoulder, glanced briefly at his watch, and pushed the selling points one last time.

"Running water and ten acres of land. Great outdoors, huh?"

Frank put the keys in his pocket and walked away.

He packed his car the next morning, checked out of the hotel, and left without a word to anyone.

* * *

The road was a twisting, ever rising blacktop that lay like a discarded ribbon amid the heavy pines. It was a lonely stretch. He had the roadway to himself most of the time with only the occasional farm houses or rest stop to break up the running line of trees and hills. He remembered to fill up in a gas station about an hour out of Torview.

He knew he was close when the road started to dip and rise like a coaster. The woods to either side grew heavier, and the shadows longer and somehow more permanent. It was almost four when he passed the small bent white sign, *Torview 15*. He assumed it was fifteen miles and not the population.

The exit was little more than the size of a driveway and nearly hidden behind a copse of overgrown pines. He drove up the tarmac and out of the trees, stopping at a crossroad to overlook the valley of Torview and the hills that surrounded it. He was the only car on the road and he took a moment to look around.

It was still there: a flash of red, visible in the late afternoon like some secret doorway to another time, another place. For a fleeting moment the lonely ache in his chest was replaced by bittersweet excitement.

And then the moment passed.

Now what? Crossing the intersection and going straight would take him back out to the small highway. The road to his right led down to the town. He assumed the way to the house was to the left.

He rolled his window down, letting the cool night air brace him, in no hurry to make a decision. He caught his reflection in the rearview mirror. At fifty two, he had always looked ten years younger, a gift of genetics and regular exercise. Now it was closer to the truth to say the opposite.

He turned around, glanced at the boxes in the back seat of his car: his worldly possessions. He ran through their contents in his mind: a few books, his overnight bag, fresh linen, and some winter clothes. With no electricity there would be no need for his computer or entertainment devices so these had gone the way of the bric-a-brac. What was in the house? Certainly no food. He was hungry, and would be hungry again. He should buy some things for the night and morning.

He looked to the right and the shallow skyline of block buildings that was Torview, a scar of humanity sitting among the tree-lined hills like an abandoned car on the side of the road. *My new home,* thought Frank.

He turned right.

Chapter Two

It was advertised as *Sol's*, with a hand painted "fresh tacos" sign under the marquee. It sat between a hardware store and a municipal building, looking lost and out of place. Frank parked against the curb in front and climbed from the car.

There was no traffic on the street, foot or otherwise. No flashing lights or screaming speakers, no stained sidewalks or careless litter. There was a hint of snow in the air, and the distant smell of burning leaves.

Walking to the diner, Frank saw a man watching him from the hardware store window. His hands were tucked down the front of his pants, and he rocked on his heels like a schoolboy waiting for the last bell of the day. He pulled a hand from his pants and casually saluted with two fingers. Frank nodded in return, and for no justifiable reason hated the reflex. He rushed deliberately to the diner's entrance.

A tiny bell rang as he stepped through the door, and an aproned man behind the counter looked up from his paper. Frank stood a moment just inside the doorway, blinking in the bright light and getting his bearings.

The eatery had a simple, timeless layout: all light and chrome and tile, smelling of fresh coffee, fried ground beef, and a hint of warm bread. The white Formica counter ran almost the entire length of the diner and was framed in polished chrome siding, a series of vinyl padded pedestal stools bracing the counter like a row of chess pawns. A cut-out in the back wall exposed portions of a stainless steel kitchen, and another, smaller serving counter with a coffee stand and register ran along this same wall.

To Frank's right, and just inside the storefront window, sat a row of four red and white checkered tables with plastic lawn chairs for seating, all empty.

Two small Mexican children played a video game in the far corner. They gave Frank a curious once-over and returned to their game.

Directly across from the entrance and with his back to Frank was a large man in a calfskin coat and greasy ball cap. The man didn't bother to turn around at his entrance, but as Frank's eyes fell on the reflective back wall he saw two hard black eyes looking back at him. Frank turned away quickly, feeling awkward and unsure.

The aproned man behind the counter put his paper aside and nodded to Frank. He was dark of skin, and the boys were conscious of his presence even when he wasn't watching them. "Sit anywhere you like," he said.

Frank hesitated a moment, torn between a table and relative isolation, or a stool and convenience. In the end he chose a stool, somewhere between the hulking figure at one end and the boys at the other. The man behind the counter wiped his hands down his apron and walked over.

"How can I help you?" he asked.

"Coffee," answered Frank in kind.

"Menu?"

"Yes, please."

The apron-clad man reached under the counter, produced a white porcelain cup and saucer and placed them carefully in front of Frank. A laminated one-page menu soon joined them. He then took one of two coffee pots from a burner, filled Frank's cup, and put the pot back without looking. He glanced at Frank and moved a dented tin of cream and a bowl of sugar packets next to the menu. The ritual finished with a well-placed paper napkin, stainless steel knife, and fork. Everything was done with care and muted investment, like a jaded shaman going through another season of rituals. He then retreated shyly to the register, leaving Frank alone.

With his departure, Frank felt suddenly exposed. Despite the occasional noises from the boys over their game, the diner was full of pregnant stillness, as if he had inadvertently walked in on someone who had just been talking about him, and not in a kind way.

He took a sip of the coffee and studied the menu to distract himself. Tacos, eggs, steak, and other Mexican-American cuisine were listed in tiny brown script, no pictures. The prices were less than the city fare he was used to. He wondered about the quality.

When he set his cup down the tiny clink against the saucer rang out, like a dropped plate in a funeral parlor. Embarrassed, and knowing he had no reason to be, he brusquely signaled the man in the apron over to take his order.

"Steak and eggs," he said, sounding harsher than he intended.

The man took his order, topped off his coffee, and disappeared through a swinging half-door. Soon the familiar sounds and smells of cooking emerged from the back and, for a brief moment. the unnatural stillness retreated and Frank was just a tired, hungry customer in a slightly over heated diner in a small town, and the world, if new and unfamiliar, was again behaving as expected.

He glanced down the reflective wall of stainless steel. The large, hairy man in the calfskin jacket was now staring into his coffee.

He turned back, saw a folded paper by the register and remembered some newspaper boxes out front. He hesitated. and then walked outside. He grabbed change from his car and bought the local paper for fifty cents. It was all of four pages, with hardly an ad on any one.

He took the paper inside, ignored the man at the end, and climbed determinedly back onto his stool. In his absence the unnatural stillness had descended again. He picked through the paper and read everything of interest or importance before his food was ready.

The man in the apron brought Frank his food, and retreated again to the register where he picked up his own paper. It was thicker than Frank's, and in Spanish.

Frank turned to his plate. The food was simple, but good. The condiment rack featured a variety of spices. He settled for salt and steak sauce and ate in silence, staring at his plate or the well-used paper, ignoring everyone.

When he was finished, the man in the apron came by, took the empty plate to the back, then returned and topped Frank's coffee off again.

The man noticed the paper by Frank. "I use that for the fireplace." He nodded to the small weekly.

The wry confession broke some of the tension, and Frank found himself answering in kind. "Yeah; it's a little light. And not very heavy, either."

The other chuckled. "Passing through?" He stopped for a moment, coffee pot in hand, clearly ready to move on if necessary.

"Not exactly," answered Frank. "This is good, by the way. The steak."

"Thanks."

The pot found its way back on the burner. The man in the apron stayed.

"We sometimes get visitors," he said, leaning back against the small serving counter. "For the fall," he explained. "Though not as many as I hoped or expected. They come to see the leaves. That's why I ask if your passing through. Little late in the season."

"I might be staying awhile."

The man in the apron raised an eyebrow. "That happens even less than the tourists." He offered a hand. "Sol."

"Frank. I came here once before. A long time ago. It was a coffee shop I think."

Sol nodded. "That would be when Philo Mundt owned it." He dropped his eyes but not before glancing at the big man in the brown jacket.

"I don't remember the shop very well," continued Frank, "but I like what you've done with the place."

Sol sighed, looked around the nearly empty diner. "I thought I was smart. Got it very cheap. If things worked out, some of my cousins were going to come out here and help me." His mouth twisted in regret. "That didn't happen. No one is coming to Torview. Not since they closed the mine."

"Mine?"

"Copper mine. Torview was built around it. The Mundts..." he stopped, shrugged. "The mine's all played out. No one is coming."

He looked again at Frank with renewed interest. "Except you. What brings you here?"

"Retiring."

"Oh." Sol's temporary hope vanished. "Somehow I don't think Torview is going to be the next big retirement community."

"Probably not."

"You building a home? I don't remember hearing anyone selling recently, except..."

His voice trailed off. This time his eyes strayed to the man at the end of the counter and stopped. "You want some more coffee?" he asked quickly, his voice rising.

"Maybe some water."

Sol turned to get the water. Frank thought he looked tense, like a man expecting a beating.

A hard, raspy voice filled Frank's left ear, "You bought the house?"

Frank turned as far he could in his swivel chair.

The man in the calfskin coat was now standing behind him, glaring down at Frank in a black cloud of tangled hair. Up close, the coat was as rough and weather-stained as the man's complexion, what could be seen of it behind the heavy beard and greasy hair.

Frank started to answer, then almost gagged at the foul, sticky-sweet odor of tobacco pouring from the stranger's loose lipped and slightly crooked mouth.

"Not right, you buying that house," said the man in rough, broken dialect, spraying Frank with tiny flecks of tobacco and brown spit. His black pig-like eyes bore into Frank, demanding some response.

Frank didn't answer, couldn't answer. In another time and place he would have spoken, would have tried to make peace...for her.

But now she was gone. Now, he simply didn't know what to say. He simply didn't care.

The hard eyes contracted. For a moment, Frank thought the man actually might hit him.

They were interrupted by the return of Sol.

Frank turned around, giving the other man his back. But he could still hear and feel the heavy breath of anger against his neck, could almost taste the stale chewing tobacco and coffee erupting from that crooked, oversized mouth. He casually picked up the remains of his own coffee and buried his nose halfway down the cup to kill the smell.

"Thanks," said Frank, putting the cup down again and nodding to the glass of water forgotten in Sol's hand.

Sol started, then set the glass of water down carefully by Frank. A moment later the bell over the door rang. Frank looked to the reflective surface of the kitchen. The big man was gone.

"Well, you've met Henrik," said Sol, staring at the door.

"Henrik Mundt," he continued, turning back to Frank. "Not the most sociable of the Mundt clan, though it's not much of a competition."

"Who are the Mundts?" asked Frank.

"You don't know?" asked Sol, eyeing Frank. "I guess that would explain a lot. You bought the red house on the hill, yes?"

"That's right."

"Uh-huh," said Sol, leaning on the counter. "You bought it through the bank."

Frank nodded. "Yes. What's that matter?"

"That was Henrik's great grandfather's house," explained Sol. "Or maybe it was his great-great grandfather. No one knows, outside the Mundts, and they're not saying.

Anyway, he was a big name around here, Captain Mundt.
Still is. Moved here after the Civil War. The Mundts say he
was a Captain—on the Confederate side. They're proud of
that."

Sol leaned in closer, dropped his voice. "But my boy,
Hector," he nodded to one of the two boys with the video
game, "he looked it up on the Net. There was a Mundt in
the Confederacy, but it wasn't a Captain. Everything about
the...*Captain* is like that. One time he's from Germany, the
next time St. Petersburg. The next, a bastard from a New
England whaling village who took the name of Mundt
after the War."

He leaned back. "But I wouldn't go saying that last
to any of the Mundts."

"So, Henrik thinks I stole his inheritance," said Frank.

Sol nodded. "It's been in their family a long time
now." He pulled out a rag and idly wiped down the counter.
"Could be trouble for you."

Frank met his eyes. "I'm not looking for it."

"That won't matter. More coffee?"

"No."

Sol pushed the rag around the counter top some
more. He seemed to be considering his next words
carefully. Finally, he looked to Frank and said, "I guess you
got the house like I got this place."

"How's that?"

"Philo Mundt."

"I've never heard of him."

"Philo, Henrik's oldest brother, inherited the coffee
shop and lot of the town, including your new house. Philo
was unusual for a Mundt in that he didn't really like being
in Torview. He was always going out of town. He liked to
drink and gamble, apparently. That's how they say he lost
the house and this place to the bank."

Sol leaned in close again. "The rest of the family
didn't know about the shop until I showed up with my
deed. I got the same welcome as you, and I only got the
shop. They must be really mad about the house."

"What can they do about it?" asked Frank.

"What can they do about it? I'll tell you what they did to me. I can count my customers on two hands since I opened. I think the Mundts warned everybody off, but I can't prove it." Sol snorted. "Hell, Henrik's my best customer. I think he's here to make sure everyone stays away."

"They have that much power?"

Sol looked bitterly to the rag in his hand. "The place should be called Mundtville." He looked away, brushed something from his eye and stared at his boys. "Of course, I didn't know any of this when I bought the place. I was told I had to act fast."

Frank reached for his water, took a long sip, his eyes on the glass in his hand. By the time he put the glass down, Sol was wiping the counter again, his expression back to normal.

"So," continued Frank. "Philo was living in the house before I bought it?"

"No. Philo lived in town, mostly at Claire's. Claire's Bed and Breakfast. Claire was his wife."

"Was?"

"Philo disappeared just about the time he lost everything to the bank."

"So who did live there, if not Philo?"

"No one's lived there for a long time as far as I know," said Sol. "You know of course it was built on the mine shaft."

"No," said Frank slowly. "I didn't."

"Guess you had to act fast, too."

Chapter Three

He found Henrik waiting for him outside. The man from the hardware store had joined him.

Like Henrik, the other was tall and stout, though not as large, and like Henrik his lips hung at a crooked angle. A tower of crinkly black hair framed the back of his head like a dark halo. The rest was bald as a scoop of vanilla ice cream. The hands were down the front of his pants again, and he bounced on his toes when Frank stepped out of Sol's.

"Morning, friend!" he said, the heels coming down with a smack. "Emil Mundt. Please to meet you. This is Henrik, my brother."

"We met," said Frank, with a glance to the Henrik. He ignored Emil's extended hand, freshly taken from the front of his pants.

"So I heard," said Emil, looking to his hand and then putting it back down his pants. "Sorry if he was a bit gruff. Henrik's a little short on temper at the best of times, but his heart's broken just now, you see, and he tends to speak right from it. The heart, that is."

"I see," said Frank. He had little interest in Emil or his brother's broken heart. "Well, good day to you." He moved toward his car.

"Well, just a second there," said Emil with a frown. Quicker than Frank would have thought, the hand was out again and now on his shoulder. It was a big hand and it stopped Frank short. "I don't think you introduced yourself."

"He's a leach is what he is," muttered Henrik.

"Now, Henrik," said Emil. "Let the man talk."

"My name is Frank Henning."

Frank looked down to Emil's hand. The other man smiled, as if they were sharing a joke, and put the hand back down the front of his pants with a wink.

"Listen," said Emil, his brown eyes dancing. "It's cold. Why don't we go inside the store and discuss matters." He nodded to the hardware store.

"What matters?" asked Frank.

"Well," said Emil, "Henrik may have made a hash of the message but basically we want to talk about rectifying the..." He seemed to search for the right word, his bright red tongue rolling and retreating over the even white teeth like a fat worm over sandstone.

"Confusion!" he said, rocking on his heels again. "Over the house. You see, the bank shouldn't have sold it to you. We got an injunction against it."

Frank looked at Emil. "The bank received notice of this injunction?"

Emil's high forehead erupted in wrinkle lines, the heels ground to a halt, and the fat-lipped smile fell away.

"It's in our courthouse," he said, with a nod to the building on the other side of Sol's. "You can see for yourself. There it sits...on Judge Mundt's desk." He added this last with eyes popped in feigned surprise, and gave Frank another wink.

"I think I'll wait to hear from the bank," said Frank. He took a step around Emil and toward his car.

"The bank will just tell you what you want to hear!" whined Emil. He stepped in time with Frank to block his way again. Frank could feel Henrik crowding in on the other side.

"You know how they are," continued Emil. "They're only in it for the money."

He looked hard at Frank, as if the word money were some kind of code.

"And if this is about that," he went on carefully, "I don't know why we couldn't come to some agreement without bothering them. Save you a lot of trouble. When that injunction goes through, good luck getting your money

back from the bank then. They'll tie you up in all kinds of
paperwork, till your blue in the face like a hanging pig."

"Leaches," muttered Henrik again.

"That they are," agreed Emil, still watching Frank
carefully.

"I'm sure you're right," said Frank. "If you will excuse
me now, I'm going to my house. If you or the judge has any
problems with me calling it my house, I've got the deed in
the car. No injunction, just a deed, legal and clear. I
believe the bank has one, too."

Emil's mouth opened to one side, the red tongue
falling out now like an old tired dog lolling on a porch
step.

"Well, Henrik," he said, staring at Frank. "There, you
see, is what comes of living in the city. No manners at
'tal. Might as well be talking to a goddam bank teller."

Frank ignored him, tried to head to his car again, but
this time was blocked by Henrik.

"I really think we should go into the store now, Mr.
Henning," said Emil, his voice as soft as smoke.

Henrik put his big belly on Frank, forcing him in the
direction of the hardware store. Frank got another bitter
whiff of stale tobacco, and the greasy brim of Henrik's hat
poked him in the forehead like a duck snapping at bread. He
met Henrik's eyes, so close to his own. The pig-like black
irises were hard with anger and expectancy.

They all turned at the sound of a car pulling up. A
brown, four-wheel drive SUV with big gold stars on the
doors, stopped just behind Frank's car. Out of the corner of
his eye Frank saw Henrik and Emil step back a pace.

The man who climbed from the car was easily as tall
as Henrik and Emil, but built along different lines. Broad
shoulders and a thin waist made a V of the heavy brown
coat, which hung open over a flannel shirt and jaded jeans.
He wore a sheriff's hat, and his gun made a slight bulge
under the coat at the hip.

It was hard to see the face under the low hanging
hat, but Frank took a little heart in the thin-lipped mouth
that showed no signs of crookedness.

"Boys," said the sheriff in a soft drawl, nodding to the Mundts.

"Sheriff," replied Emil, the crooked smile firmly back in place.

There followed a short, pregnant silence. The sheriff didn't say a word, or indicate in any way what he wanted, but the Mundts took another step back from Frank. The sheriff considered Frank for a moment, then turned back to Emil.

"This about the house?" he asked.

He had sad blue-grey eyes that complimented the voice and seemed to suggest passivity and quiet. But as the brim of the hat lifted to get a better look at Emil, Frank got a good look at the profile. There was no softness in the rigid lines of the jaw or weathered cheekbones, only stubborn patience.

"Of course it's about the house," said Emil with a touch of petulance.

The sheriff sighed, looked off to the right. "We talked about this."

Emil fidgeted. "We're not causing any trouble. We just wanted to talk."

The sheriff ran a big hand along the back of his neck. "You go on now. I'll be in to talk in just a minute."

"Cal..." started Emil.

"Go on now."

"Ain't right," muttered Henrik. "You takin a stranger's side."

"I'm not taking any sides," said the sheriff, but he turned to stare at Henrik. "Emil, take your brother and get inside now. I've got to talk to this gentleman alone for a bit."

Emil looked like he wanted to argue as well, but then thought better of it.

"C'mon, Henrik," he said sarcastically. "The sheriff wants to have a talk."

The Mundts moved off and entered the hardware store. They watched Frank and the sheriff from the window, Emil's hands once again taking shelter in his pants.

The sheriff looked up to the sky, as if Frank had commented on the weather. Slowly he returned to Earth, only to stare sleepily at Frank's feet. Apparently he was in no hurry to have his talk. The big hand found his ear lobe and massaged it between his thumb and forefinger.

"So, you met Emil and Henrik,' he said at last, still staring at Frank's feet. "And they made their pitch."

"I guess you could say that, Sheriff."

The sheriff frowned, scratched his chin. Finally he looked up and met Frank's eye. "I'm not going to lie to you, Mr....." He left it hanging there.

"Henning. Frank Henning."

"Cal Miller." He offered his hand, which was warm and brown from long exposure to the outdoors. A strong hand thought Frank, shaking it, like hard leather.

"I'm not going to lie to you, Mr. Henning," repeated the sheriff. "Your purchase of that house is not very popular here."

"So I gathered. At least, not with the Mundts."

"And you can't throw a stone in this town and not hit a Mundt," said the sheriff. "You mind me asking, Mr. Henning, why that house?"

The blue-grey eyes glanced briefly in Frank's direction again. There was no hostility or officiousness in those eyes, just curiosity.

Frank didn't answer right away. He hadn't expected to defend his purchase, at least not here on the street, and so soon. He didn't want to go into specifics, wasn't sure if he understood all the reasons himself. He searched for an answer that would suffice and finally settled on a half-truth.

"I drove by here once when I was a young man, saw the house on the hill and wondered about it. I'm at a place now that I can afford to retire, and it seems like as good a place as any."

The sheriff surprised him with a soft chortle, pushed his hat to the top of his forehead with his thumb.

"Here?" he asked in disbelief. "Torview? That house? Have you ever actually been inside the house, Mr. Henning.?"

"No."

The sheriff shook his head in wonder. "You married? She know what she's getting into?"

"I showed it to my wife long ago," answered Frank. "She didn't like it much."

"But she likes it now?'

Frank sighed. They'd gotten here without even trying.

"She's..." Frank couldn't bring himself to say dead. It was too blunt, too crass. "She passed away," he finished.

The blue-grey eyes rested briefly on Frank, took their measure and looked away. "I'm sorry to hear that."

And Frank felt certain that the sheriff was sorry, but not just for Frank. If Frank read those knowing eyes correctly, the sheriff now understood, or suspected, the real underlying motivations behind Frank's sudden purchase and presence in Torview. But if the sheriff did understand or suspect, he had the grace to let it be. For now.

"Anyway," continued the sheriff, his eyes now looking steadily at the hardware store window. "Give me a minute."

He turned, and walked in the store, his steps, like his voice and every gesture, slow and deliberate, infinitely patient and resolute.

Frank got in his car and started it up, letting the heater blunt the cold. After a time, the sheriff returned, bearing a small box. Frank rolled the passenger side window down and the sheriff put the box gently on the seat.

Frank glanced down, saw the dull flash of a nickel-plated flashlight sitting prominently on top of an assortment of odds and ends.

"You might need these," said the sheriff, leaning through the window. He waved Frank's protest off. Then, as Frank reached for his wallet, he added, "No need; compliments of Emil."

Frank frowned.

The sheriff chuckled. "Oh, don't think it was his idea. Take it. Emil needs some lessons in humility." He stood up, took something from his pocket, and leaned back in. "Anyway, I reckon you're going to need them. There's no electricity up there, did they tell you?"

"They did."

The sheriff grunted, shook his head again, and handed Frank a key. "This is to the lock on the gate."

"I got one from the bank."

"Yeah, but not to the lock I put on. That bank lock wasn't worth a damn."

He handed Frank two more keys.

"This one is to the woodshed," said the sheriff, "and this one is to the cellar." He looked as if he wanted to say something more about the last key, but changed his mind. "You follow me out, and I'll take you up to the house."

"That's not necessary, Sheriff."

"It is. Those roads are complicated, especially if you've never been there before. Plus, this will save me a call from old Granger Mundt. He borders your property. Better if he sees me escort you."

Frank met his eyes. The sheriff shrugged.

"All right," said Frank. "But do you mind if I stop somewhere to get some food first?" He looked down at the box. "I guess I didn't plan this out very well."

The sheriff nodded. "We'll hit Claire's. She'll fix you up. Follow me."

They drove the entire length of Main Street and turned right at the small crossroads. On the corner was a quaint three-story house with two poplars in the front, and a stone walkway running to the porch entrance. A wooden sign in the front yard read, *Claire's Bed and Breakfast. Rooms Available.*

The sheriff climbed from car, beckoned Frank to follow him, and walked up the sidewalk and through the front door like he owned the place.

A woman met them in the foyer, the echoes of the vacuum cleaner in her hand still in the air. She tucked the vacuum cleaner in a nearby closet, turned and put a thin arm on her aproned hip.

"Cal," she said, looking to the sheriff. Her hair was pulled back up in a bun, a mix of faded yellow and gray, tucked in with haphazard hairpins. Frank thought she might have been pretty once, but the years and something tragic had left a deep worry line down the middle of her brow and set her mouth in a perpetual scowl of doubt.

"This is Frank Henning," said the sheriff. He turned to Frank and introduced the woman. "Claire, the owner."

"How do you do?" said Frank.

"Pleased, I'm sure," answered Claire with a perfunctory smile.

"Frank bought the Captain's old place," said the sheriff.

"But..." started Claire, the smile falling away and the deep worry line suddenly growing to life.

"Free and clear," said the sheriff, speaking softly, but firmly.

Claire looked from one to the other as if she were a victim of some poor joke.

"Wondering if you could fix him up some dinner for tonight?" continued the sheriff. "And maybe some necessaries for breakfast."

"I'll gladly pay whatever you ask," said Frank, wondering if everyone in Torview would react so strongly to his purchase of the house. Then he remembered Claire was Philo Mundt's wife, maybe widow.

Blushing, he glanced to the sheriff at his right. What was the man thinking, bringing him here, of all places?

"I've got some fried chicken," said Claire, pulling at a hairpin distractedly. "It's left over." She looked again at the sheriff, then turned abruptly and left.

"Thank you," called Frank to her retreating figure.

A moment later they could hear Claire's voice talking from the next room, apparently on the phone. Her words were indistinguishable, but there was a heat in to her end of the conversation.

"C'mon in," said the sheriff, taking Frank gently by the elbow, much like an usher in church, and moved them into the living room.

"Claire has been running the place for some time now," said the sheriff, releasing Frank. He waved him to a seat. "Nice, isn't it?"

Nice would not be the first word Frank would use.

The room was old, but well-built and maintained, with high ceilings, arched passageways, and lots of polished wood and ornate molding. It might have made a *nice* room, but the decor was somehow off. Everything fit, but nothing mattered. Even the air seemed overly contrived, the well-placed cinnamon candles on the fireplace mantel giving off a tired scent long since grown jaded by time and lack of use.

A giant fireplace, empty and closed, dominated the back wall. Two overstuffed chairs and a matching sedan faced it, but like everything else, the placement seemed stilted, awkward. It was as if a vital element had been left out, reducing the room to pure display, like the floor of an Ikea. *Maybe a lit fire would warm the things up a bit*, he thought. *But probably not.*

"It looks comfortable," he said, taking a seat in one of the chairs.

"Reason I show it to you," explained the sheriff, taking the other seat. "Is to give you options. It's offseason now, of course. She'll have a room available."

Frank sighed, shook his head. "Sheriff."

The sheriff nodded. "Okay. Okay, Mr. Henning. But, I'm not trying to run you out. I'm trying to do you a favor. That house isn't really a fit place to live, if it ever was. Even Philo didn't live there."

"Of course," he added, looking to the fireplace with a wry grin, "Claire didn't give much of a choice."

"So why didn't they stay there?" asked Frank, curious.

The sheriff thought about it a moment. "It's not what you would call a very comfortable house, by anyone's definition. The Captain was an eccentric man, and a tight-fisted one. He didn't care much for comforts. Hell, he built the damn thing over a mine."

"Yes," said Frank. "I heard that."

"It will be a mess now, too. Kids use it for various things, if they can get in."

"Why do Emil and Henrik want it so bad, if it is such a mess?"

"Well," said the sheriff slowly, "it's their heritage, isn't it? It's like that ugly painting your great uncle or aunt did that gets passed down from generation to generation. Nobody really wants it but they just can't throw it out. I assure you, Claire's will be much more comfortable."

"I appreciate the thought, Sheriff, but I'm going to give the house a go."

"You change your mind, you know where to find Claire's," he said kindly. "And if you really want to live in Torview, well, I imagine Emil will make you a better offer on the house than you paid for it. With that kind of money you could make a nice place out here. I'm sure the Mundts will set you up with a good piece of property, in exchange for getting the house back."

They sat for a time in silence then, looking at the empty fireplace and tired candles on the mantle place. The sheriff seemed quite comfortable with the silence, but Frank felt awkward, as if he let the sheriff down somehow.

"So why did the Captain build a house over a mine shaft?" he asked.

"Don't know," answered the sheriff. He tapped his finger on a jean-covered knee. The awkward room revolved to silence again.

"They sealed the shaft openings off some time back," he continued abruptly after a time. "But you still feel the draft sometimes. Some say the house was built with a lean toward the shaft. Makes the house feel like it's moving at times, or falling." He paused. "You'll hear things too. Part of the reason some of the local kids go up there, for a lark. They think it's haunted."

"Are you trying to scare me now, Sheriff?" asked Frank with a half-smile.

But the sheriff seemed to take the question seriously. "No," he said, rubbing a hand across his chin. "I wouldn't do that."

"I appreciate that." Frank tried to catch his eye, but the sheriff was staring at his knee, thinking.

"You met, Sol," continued the sheriff finally. "Nice guy, Sol. I'd be sorry to see him go. Torview needs new blood, and it's coming whether the rest of them like it or not. The Emils and Henriks of this town don't understand that. The Sol's of this world are the right kind, so why not welcome them." He raised his eyes to Frank. "No," he repeated. "No, Mr. Henning, I'm not trying to scare you away. I'd just wish you'd picked a different place. There is something very wrong about that place."

"Is that your way of saying the house *is* evil?" asked Frank with a laugh. "I thought you weren't going to try that."

The sheriff shook his head sadly. "No, the house is a house. It is men that are evil, and they bring their evil with them wherever they go. The Captain..." He trailed off, looked to the empty fireplace, listened for a moment to the sound of clinking cutlery from the kitchen.

"Anyway," he continued a moment later, "houses might not be evil, but ones like that can be dangerous." He leaned forward slowly, catching Frank's eye. "Which reminds me about that cellar. I'd ask you to be careful with that. If you don't mind just leave it locked for now, at least until I can come out there and help you with it."

"What's wrong with the cellar?"

"Sinkholes. One opened right up under the Thomas boy a few years back. That's what I suspect happened, anyway. I found a hole in the cellar when we were searching for him. It runs straight down to the shaft, I think. When you drop something down that hole, you ain't ever going to hear it land. Never found that boy's body."

"I'll leave it alone," said Frank.

"I'd be grateful."

"Here it is," said Claire, coming into room with a picnic basket and a thermos. The men stood. Claire put the basket and thermos on a coffee table by Frank. She didn't look at either man. "Half a chicken," she said, "and warmed-up mashed potatoes, peas, and some corn on the cob. I also put in two boiled eggs, half a loaf of bread, and some butter and jam for tomorrow. There's a knife, fork, and plate as well. The thermos holds coffee. Should be still hot tomorrow if you keep it closed."

Frank could smell the chicken from where he stood and tried to still a rumble in his stomach. "I'm very grateful. How much do I owe you?"

"Just bring the basket and thermos and such back tomorrow." She still refused to look at him, staring instead at her floor as if to bore a hole in it.

"I insist on paying you something."

"Just bring 'em back," she repeated, and walked out of the room before Frank could argue.

"Claire's hometown version of marketing," said the sheriff with a smile. "You eat that chicken, you'll be taking most of your meals here from now on. She'll charge you in time, don't worry. Shall we go?"

"After you," said Frank.

Outside their cars, the sheriff told him to stay close, then climbed in his SUV and pulled slowly onto the main road.

Frank followed him, glancing in his rearview mirror as he left the driveway. No shadowed profiles stood in the doorway of the bed and breakfast, no thin hands pulled back a curtain to watch them leave.

But somehow Frank knew he was being watched.

* * *

The red house looked to be a straight shot up and to the left from the town, but it was a good fifteen minutes of cutbacks and winding road before they drew close enough to see it clearly.

Just before they ascended the hill proper, they passed a well-tended field on a rare stretch of flat land. A fat, square farmhouse sat to one side of the field, framed like a child's abandoned lunch box by the hills around it.

As they drove slowly by the house, Frank saw a bearded man in overalls watching them from his porch swing. The sheriff tapped his horn twice, and the bearded man nodded in his direction. Frank hesitated over his horn, decided to wave instead. The man didn't return the wave, but casually turned his head and spat over the porch rail.

They turned a corner and left Frank's nearest neighbor and field behind. The road grew smaller and less defined and the next cutback was almost straight up. Frank felt and heard the car shift down a gear to compensate.

Signs of the past littered the view to either side. Large, rusted iron buckets and broken bits of tools lay like abandoned beetle shells in the verge growth. The foundations of a ruined brick building, riddled now with saplings and wildflowers, sat above and to Frank's right, looking like an open tomb.

The road made another steep switchback and all signs of the past—of human presence of any kind—disappeared, swallowed up by a thick line of pines.

Though it was only just past the dinner hour, and the sun still up, the light outside Frank's window grew noticeably dimmer. The heavy, close tree line hung over his car like a shroud. The atmosphere was almost primordial. Frank turned on his headlights and pulled closer to the sheriff.

They soon came to a branch in the road. The turnoff to the right was little more than a sliver of blacktop, rising at a 90 degree grade. The other branch continued along the hill line, presumably going back down eventually.

The sheriff slowed to almost a stop, and turned up the steep grade. Frank followed, feeling his heart race as he experienced the odd sensation of having his car nose elevated higher than the back end.

At the end of the blacktop, almost at the very top of the hill, was a car-port of sorts. A small circle of gravel, covered by a wooden awning, provided just enough room for a car to turn around. But not without an adrenaline-spiked view of the drop where the port extended from the hillside. Across this hillside was a locked gate. It blocked the final, short run up to the very top of the hill, and the red house.

The sheriff turned his car around in the gravel, signaling Frank to stop in front of the gate. They both climbed out of their cars and met at the gate.

"You're going to have to watch the weather carefully," said the sheriff without preamble, nodding to the steep incline. "When the Mundts lived here, they would just run some men down to clean the road of snow and ice, but I wouldn't want to tackle the task by myself." He looked to the sky. "Should be clear for the next few days, but we do get the occasional surprise snowstorm."

Frank glanced up, then back down the hill. If his car went over that he would probably get hung up on a tree...eventually.

"I'll keep an eye out," said Frank, trying to sound cheerful. "Maybe I'll get a shovel and put it down here. I can always use the exercise."

The sheriff grunted. "Just the same, you should park at the bottom of the incline in the winter proper." He turned to Frank's car. "And get some chains for those tires."

"Right," said Frank.

The sheriff chewed his lip slowly, his thoughts unspoken and, to Frank, unreadable. "Well, let's see if you can manage those locks." He stood back.

Frank released the locks and let the heavy gate of three galvanized steel beams, swing open. That done, he returned to the sheriff and handed him back his Yale lock.

"You keep that," said the sheriff. "I got spares keys to all the locks—for ease of access in an emergency. You okay with that?"

"Sure," said Frank, not sure he was, but not prepared to take issue with it just then.

"And here's my number." The sheriff handed Frank a business card. "It won't do much good up here. There's no phone, and you can't get a cell signal most of the time. But a little ways down you can call if you need anything. If you like I'll come by tomorrow and walk you around your property. You own everything from Granger's place up."

Frank took the card. "Thanks. I think I can manage for a time. I'm sure you have other things to do."

The sheriff shrugged, looked as if he might have a different opinion on the matter. "It's not too late, Mr. Henning," he said with a sigh. "Claire..."

"I'm going to stay in the house," interrupted Frank, meeting his eyes.

"I can see you're determined to try."

The sheriff put a foot on the bottom beam of the gate, leaned into like a farmer coming to rest after a long day.

"Don't get me wrong, Mr. Henning," he said. "I got nothing against you. It would just make my world a lot easier if you take Emil up on his offer and leave this house to the Mundts."

"You think there will be trouble?"

The sheriff hesitated and then shrugged, looked off to the house.

"Emil will lawyer to death," he said slowly. "You can be sure of that. And I'd stay out of Albert's Bar and Tavern for a time. That's the local hole where Henrik spends his nights, and most his days to tell the truth." He paused. "But I reckon they'll be none of that kind of trouble here. I was pretty clear about that."

He frowned at the house, as if expecting it to disagree, then dropped his head, shoved his big hands deep in his coat pockets.

"I'm more worried about you," he said, turning to Frank. "It's not easy living alone up here, especially in a place like this. Especially alone."

He turned deliberately to the house again, as if not to make too fine a point or cause offense.

Frank looked there as well. A small rutted car path led from the gate to the house. His new home sat tucked in against the hilltop, surrounded by a crown of pines and a few poplars. From here, it looked like an ugly red cinder block. There were no signs of the warm light he'd envisioned from the road so long ago.

He turned back to the sheriff, thinking of his wife, wondering if that was on the sheriff's mind as well.

"I'll be all right," he said.

"Do you own a gun, Mr. Henning?" asked the sheriff, tilting his head up slightly and looking at Frank directly.

He was caught off guard by the question, and smiled in confusion. "I thought you said there wouldn't be that kind of trouble?"

"Just want to know what I'm dealing with here," said the sheriff, measuring Frank with his eyes like a carpenter studying a length of fresh cut board.

I can dance around the questions all day, Frank thought. *But there will be no hiding from those eyes, or the mind behind them.*

"Stranger," continued the sheriff, not waiting for Frank's answer, "buys a house not worth living in, and says he is determined to anyway. A man who just lost his wife. It raises questions. At least, it does for me."

"No, Sheriff," said Frank, fighting to keep the blood from his face. "I don't own a gun." Then, he added almost peevishly, "You think I should get one?"

The sheriff didn't answer right away. Finally he turned again to the house. "Most people around here have one."

The two men stood in silence, the house the only witness to the tension generated in those simple words. Frank searched for some response, some way to show the sheriff that he not only understood the implications of his questions, but was still determined to stay, to make his stand anyway.

But before he could find the right words, the sheriff surprised him again and offered a hand.

"Good luck then, Mr. Henning."

He took the hand slowly, unsure if he was shaking the hand of a new, concerned friend (or at least a fair public official), or if he'd just been given another message that he was not welcome.

The sheriff tipped a finger to his hat, turned and headed to his car without another word.

"Just a minute, Sheriff."

The other man stopped, one leg in the door of the car.

"You said Sol was the right kind of change for Torview. What did you mean by that?"

Again, the sheriff took his time answering.

"Sol's not looking to shake things up," he said finally. "He keeps to himself, not looking for trouble or bringing any." Then he climbed into his car and drove away.

Frank watched him leave. He didn't have to ask what kind of change the sheriff thought he was.

Chapter Four

With about an hour worth of light left, Frank drove through the gate, closed and locked it behind him, then inched his way up the rutted path. The top landing was a rough duplicate of the car port, only smaller and covered in grass not gravel. To his right, and cattycorner to the house, stood a rustic woodshed. There was just enough space between the house and the shed to turn the car around, but it was a frightening process of stop-and-go, forwards and reverses. When he had the car facing downhill again, he pulled the emergency brake handle up as far as it would go.

He climbed from the car, feeling the cool air along his neck and cheeks. He grabbed the box with the flashlight from the passenger side, but left the food in the car. He turned to face his new home.

Apparently the Mundts (or the bank for that matter) hadn't bothered to keep the grounds up. The short path leading to the concrete steps of the front door was covered in weeds.

Standing up close did not improve the house's appearance. Built of heavy red stone, the front presented a flat, listless face, with two fixed second-story windows. The red color of the house was not from paint, but the presence of iron or some other ore in the stone and mortar. In places, condensation or drainage made the rust run in dark oily patches, possibly the source of reflection he saw all those years ago.

The roof, viewed from the front, looked flat. But he knew from the drive up it was actually slanted, running at a downward angle to the back and stuck like a doorstop in the hill. A big, square-topped chimney rose from the right of the roof (his left), with smaller stove pipes scattered on either side of the house.

The first floor once held a massive front entrance, which was now bricked in but for a small wicket door in the center. The concrete steps, four of them, ran to this door.

He shifted his box and climbed the dirty gray steps to the wooden wicket. The door, once painted black, was now faded with time and wear, the paint chipped and cracked. Somewhere behind him an angry Blue jay scolded him from the safety of the pines.

He set the box down and tried the ancient house key on the wicket door. The thin wood panel door swung open with a fuss of rusty hinges. He picked up the box and stepped carefully inside, leaving the door open behind him.

From the real estate agent, Frank learned the strange slope of the house was based on an old saltbox design. The inserted tongue in the hill presumably allowed for easier access to the mine, the emphasis being more on facilitating work then residence. Only later, when the mine went dry, did the house become a true home. The mine was sealed off from the tail end, the rooms converted to fit a more traditional family environment.

Because of its sloping nature, the house had two floors in the front half, and only one in the back. *And somewhere there's a cellar, he* reminded himself. *a cellar he wasn't to bother with until the sheriff said so.*

The first floor of the front half was divided into three sections: a central hall, and two wings. A kitchen made up the left wing, and a sleeping annex the right. The upper floor was reached by a twisting stairwell in the right corner of the central hall. The second story contained a master bedroom, a smaller bedroom, and a bath.

The single room in back was more like a long hallway, apparently once used for dining. It was hidden behind closed doors.

Standing now in the central hall, an empty foyer of hard angles, flat ceiling, and bare wood floors, more suited to a warehouse than a home, Frank could see the house held stubbornly to its industrial origins – and was badly in need of repairs.

The hall was long since empty of furniture or decoration, the white plaster interior walls chipped in places and stained with streaks of black, he hoped was not mold. The bare wood floor showed signs of rot and turning at the edges, and was riddled with stains of various colors. The ceiling was a crazy quilt of water stains and cracked paint.

And it was cold, he thought. The house was cold in every sense of the word. A box of wood and stone to hold things in a perpetual state of preservation, lifeless and still. The stillness almost physical, tangible, like a funeral parlor.

Despite the frigid stillness, chipped paint and turning floor, the infrastructure looked reasonably whole. For all the years and inattention, for all its impractical design, the house remained a solid shelter.

It may not be welcoming or pleasant to look at, he thought, *but it had endured. And it was home.*

He then shattered the stillness with a sneeze.

He put the box down, searched for a handkerchief or tissue in his pockets, and finally settled with rubbing his sleeve across his mouth and nose.

The air was thick with dust and long years of neglect, and smelled like the underside of a river rock. He felt another sneeze coming on.

He would have to open the windows upstairs, air the place out. He looked to the front of the foyer; why on earth where there no windows on the first floor?

He left the box of odds and ends on the floor and walked to the kitchen, the wood creaking and bending beneath his feet.

The hall was divided from the left wing by an archway with two swinging doors, one of which was nearly off its hinges. Stepping through this arch, he was brought short by an unexpected vision.

Two roundel windows, built on either end of the outer wall and just under the ceiling, caught the last minutes of day. At this hour, the light was little more than afterglow, but in that half-light tiny dust motes fell in a slow shower like living bits of gold, turning the kitchen into a wondrous promise of peace and comfort.

For the briefest of moments the stillness and cold were forgotten, the hard, deep ache of the recent past replaced by timeless distraction. Then the moment passed, and Frank turned reluctantly to the rest of the kitchen, the ache, the cold, the stillness once more in place.

A large wood burning stove sat at the front end of the room, directly across from the entry. The stove was built against the far wall, a soot stained chimney pipe running off into the ceiling above it. Next to the stove was a sink and cutting board station, followed by a series of storage shelves.

The shelves were surprisingly intact, empty but for cobwebs, stains, and debris. Built to fit the sloping ceiling of the back half of the wing, the open faced boxes of gray wood grew smaller and smaller until they were little more than the size of a shoebox in the farthest corner of the kitchen. Frank had no idea why someone would want a shoebox sized shelf in a practically unreachable corner. Maybe it was aesthetic.

The stove looked functional, but like everything else needed a good cleaning. A rusted fork stood on the cutting board. A broken oil lamp hung from the ceiling. Judging from the lamp's appearance, it had been some time since it was used. Otherwise, the kitchen was picked clean.

To his right sat two large wooden cold lockers. The heavy lids were rounded smooth and stained were countless hands over the years had gripped them, and some of the sealant was peeling, but they looked functional.

He lifted the lid closest to him, and almost gagged. A terrible stench, like rotten meat, spewed out of the empty locker. He quickly closed the lid again, but the smell hung in the air like a draft from a slaughter house gutter. Desperately Frank looked to the high windows, but there was no relief there. They were fixed shut.

The second one was little better. It, too, was empty, and had a smell. Not as pungent as the first, but still unpleasant, like wet rags left too long in a plastic bag. He closed that lid as well, stepped out of the kitchen for a time to let the air clear.

With a little cleaning, he thought, (a lot of cleaning), he could use the kitchen. He imagined mornings filled with frying bacon and weekend chicken dinners, but it took some effort as the rotted air sat in his mouth like a bad aftertaste. He braced himself, and reentered the galley.

This time he discovered a small trapdoor in the flooring, near the very back. Bent over because of the sloped ceiling, he ignored the mouse gnawed rope handle and pulled the rusted ring latch instead. The trap lifted with a god-awful groan, revealing a circular hole about the size of a laundry basket.

More fetid air assaulted his senses and he quickly covered his mouth and nose with his free hand. What he could see of the top portion of the hole was bordered in tin, suggesting a chute of some kind. Dark stains, some of them clearly dried blood, lined the rim. There appeared to be no visible bottom to the hole, and the foul air was cool and damp, as if it came from deep below the earth.

He guessed the chute to be some kind of refuse dump, perhaps taking advantage of the mine or a natural fissure. He closed the trapdoor and inched his way back to the front of the kitchen where he could stand up again.

He left the kitchen and crossed the foyer to the right wing. It was closed by a heavy plank door with a busted lock and loose latch spring, which opened outward.

Presumably like the kitchen, this wing ran the full length of the house. But unlike the kitchen there were no windows and beyond the first few feet everything was lost in darkness.

He went back to his odds and ends box, picked up the flashlight. The beam was surprisingly strong even with the light from the front door. He was quickly losing the sun. He decided to retrieve his basket of food before it grew too dark, and put them on the floor just inside the doorway.

He returned to the right wing, the door having swung shut again on its own, and shone his light down the

long sloping interior. Sections of rusty iron bedding and
rotted planking leaned against either wall. The floor was of
hard dirt, countless footsteps making it smooth and level
over time. The width of the wing was roughly the same as
the kitchen. It would be a tight passage if the beds were laid
out. The air had a stale, musty quality, long unused.

There was a fat, square panel door crossing the back
of the wing where the ceiling was nearing its final descent.
A simple hook latch kept it closed. Frank lifted the hook
from the eyehole catch and then pulled the door toward
him.

Behind the panel door was a small room, the ceiling
slanting uncomfortably closer until it ran to ground in the
very back. In the short space that was available to stand
up, sat an iron hospital table with castor wheels, a moldy
sheet rolled up on top of it.

Stepping inside and pushing the bed against one wall,
he discovered another wooden trapdoor in the flooring.
This time he was not surprised by the stench that
erupted from the dark maw, but almost gagged just the
same. This hole was bigger than the kitchen's, perhaps
because the refuse that went down it was of larger quality. He
looked again to the hospital bed. There were also more stains
along the rim of the tin-topped chute. Dark smears of
something sticky and viscous.

He hesitated, then reached out to touch one of the
stains with his thumb, sickened by the hard, tarry
substance but also relieved that it didn't run fresh and red
when he pressed down.

Something raced across his hand holding the
trapdoor up, the never-forgotten many feathered touches of
something chitin and multi-limbed. He saw the roach run to
the board even as he dropped the trap in revulsion.

With a shudder, he turned and left, putting the panel
latch back in place behind him and returning, happily, to
the back room.

Two enormous oak doors, twins in dimension to the
front bricked section, closed off the rear of the house.

Another wicket door, again similar to the one outside, was set in the right hand door.

Looking to the front bricked entrance, he imagined both sets of enormous doors open and the countless mineral laden carts that must have passed through them in the past.

He turned a rare knob handle in the wicket door and stepped through. Beyond was a large, open dining room. A fireplace made of black stone sat to the left, and a lengthy wooden table ran down the middle. The room was dark. Again, there were no windows. It was also colder than he expected.

He took a few tentative steps inside, using the flashlight to pick out pieces among the shadows. A small number of dilapidated wooden chairs sat around the table, many turned over, one lying near the fireplace with two missing legs. The table itself was long and heavy, made of oak, the edges scratched and chipped with time and use.

The walls to either side were lined with shelves. They were bare, but for a few rusted candleholders and a dozen worm-eaten books that fell apart when he tried to pick them up.

He walked past the long table, and to the back wall. The rough, yellowed plaster was obviously a newer edition, and gave the impression that the wall was there to cover, not support. A broken blister line ran down the middle from ceiling to floor, giving the false impression of wings in the limited radiance of the flashlight. Scraps of rotted tapestry at the wall's base hinted that the blister was covered in the past. He ran his light slowly down the line, as if he were tracing a long scar.

Stepping closer to the wall, he felt the cold emanating from behind the plaster like a block of ice, and small beads of condensation ran along the blister as if the wall were crying. Slowly, carefully, he leaned his ear against the wall.

At first there was nothing. Then, so distant and faint it could easily have been his imagination, he heard what sounded like a cry, a cry of something lost and angry and hurt. It rose from deep, deep behind the wall, grew in intensity but no more distinct, then stopped as suddenly as it started.

Wind in the mine, he told himself, pulling his head away from the wall. What he heard was nothing more than an accident of acoustics, wind, and hollow spaces.

He turned away, satisfied with his answer, but also relieved to put the ugly wall behind him.

Facing the front, his light tricked out a rusted lamp similar to the one's hanging in the kitchen. It was sitting on one of the few chairs standing upright around the dining room table and only visible from this angle.

He put his flashlight of the table, picked the lamp up carefully, and fiddled with the rusted accelerator. After a time he detected the faintest hint of oil, but it was impossible to tell if it was just residue or something in the tank. He put the lamp on the table.

I'll have to buy some new lamps and more oil, he thought. He didn't relish sitting in the house in the dark every night. He would make do with the flashlight tonight, and whatever else was in Emil's gift box, but buying lamps was high on the priority list of things to do tomorrow.

Standing in the doorway, he played the light one last time across the empty blackness, trying to reach the back wall. He could just make out the rise of the blister line, the occasional twinkle of a water bead. For reasons he couldn't say, the wall called up unpleasant memories and implications. He shut the door with a shudder.

He stood a moment with his back to the door, gathered himself, then crossed the foyer and took the stairs to the second floor.

The stairway was a bit close and twisted, giving him a vague sense of claustrophobia and making it difficult to see what was ahead. The steps tended to dip in the middle from years of use, and there was one that creaked ominously near the bottom, but otherwise were solid.

The second floor was made up of a short landing at the top of the steps. To the left were two bedrooms, one leading to the other, and eventually, a bath. The first bedroom, the smaller of the two, was missing a door, the broken hinges still hanging on the frame. The room was roughly rectangular, with four plain walls and a low ceiling. The walls were done in plaster like the rest of the house, and the floors of wood. It was empty, except for some garbage piled in the middle of the floor, and cobwebs along the ceiling and corners. Another doorway, this one with a door, separated it from the next room.

Stepping through this door, Frank entered what was obviously the master bedroom, judging from the big four poster taking up most of the floor. This room was brighter than any other in the house, including the kitchen, having both of the fixed upper story windows in its front wall.

Each window had a pair of indoor shutters. The right window with both shutters intact, and open. The left with one shutter dangling precariously across its pane like a lazy eye. The fourth shutter was on the floor, and was missing some rails.

Frank stepped to the right hand window, and took in the view. The scene that stretched below him was colored in darkening greens and browns, the pines heavy and huddled, the ground bare and hard. Only the setting sun, a fleeting splash of burnt orange just above the horizon hilltops, offset the stark shades of approaching winter.

Not approaching, he thought, winter is here.

He turned from the view to the massive four poster bed sitting in the middle of the room.

And my house is a wreck.

The bed's ornate canopy frame was still up, but the canopy was hanging in shreds like bits of skin. The mattress looked as old as the house, lumpy, and probably infested. Someone had put a modern sheet across the middle. The sheet was stained to the point of stiffness, and a small pile of used condoms lay on the floor beside the headboard.

Next to the bed was a small wood stove, its pipe running up and out of the ceiling. Soot and grime covered the wall next to the stove, and a bad burn mark ran along the floorboard behind it.

Disgusted, disillusioned, wondering how he could sleep here tonight (and thinking seriously about Claire's), Frank turned to the final room, the bath.

It didn't help matters. Little more than a walk-in closet, the toilet, sink, and short tub that comprised its fixtures were stacked almost on top of each other. The toilet was filthy, and the enamel on the sink and tub, gray and chipped.

He tried the sink faucet, and was surprised to see clear water after a brief spurt of brown. The water was ice cold. He would have to heat it up on the stove, or face some tough mornings. But it was running water, and that was something.

A broken vanity mirror hung above the sink, glass shards scattered in the basin and along the floorboards. Something plastic lay among the shards in the sink.

Frank reached in and carefully retrieved a headless doll's body, blackened and melted in parts where someone tried to set it on fire. It was absent of clothing or arms, looking not just broken, but ruined. Something tugged at the base of Frank's exhausted mind, a discordant reminder of another mess left unattended and ignored. He pushed it down again before it could take root, tossed the doll on the floor, and went back to the main bedroom.

After a long moment of staring at nothing, he stepped deliberately to the bed, found a relatively clean and unstained part of the sheet, picked it up by two fingers, and tossed it over the condoms.

Downstairs, he retrieved the rest of his boxes from the car and set them inside the foyer. It took him two trips.

He shut the front door, and locked himself in.

* * *

The air was getting very cold now, and the house was starting to become uncomfortably dark. Frank looked to the fireplace, thought about the wood shed outside, but couldn't bring himself to go out again. It wasn't laziness or reluctance that held him back. He was simply too mentally exhausted to care.

He would need to sleep soon. And eat.

He took his boxes upstairs, one at a time, so he could hold the flashlight. He then found a candle and some matches in Emil's box. He set the lit candle in its own wax on the wood stove, and turned off the flashlight. The room traded some of its stark obscurity for half-light shadows and the occasional flicker.

Bracing himself, he tore a lid from one of his cardboard boxes and tried to brush the years of filth from the mattress. He raised a storm of dust and twice had to stop to sneeze, and once to keep from gagging.

Finally, his piece of cardboard reduced to a crumpled, pulpy mess, he rolled his sleeping bag out on the bed. In the candlelight, with the sheet off and the sleeping bag in place, it didn't look so bad.

He blew the candle out to save it for later, and used the flashlight again to go downstairs for his late dinner.

The sheriff was right about one thing: Claire could cook. The chicken was particularly good. He mixed his peas in the mashed potatoes, and washed everything down with an ice cold cup of water from the kitchen sink.

He ate by candlelight in the dining room, sitting in his winter coat. The house was so still he could hear the flicker of the candle flames. He looked occasionally to the ugly wall with its broken, weeping line down the middle, but mostly kept his back to it. If he was going to take his meals here in the near future—a big if, he decided—he'd have to do something about covering that crack. Maybe the whole wall.

When he finished his dinner, he quickly rinsed his plate and silverware by more candlelight in the kitchen, determined to save the flashlight batteries as much as possible. He stacked everything in the dining room to dry. He'd clean them better tomorrow, he told himself. He wanted to make a good impression on Claire, as she may be his only possible source of nutrition for the next week or so.

He blew out the candles in the dining room, and left them there. Using the flashlight, he made sure the front door was locked and climbed slowly up the stairs.

When he reached the small landing, he turned the flashlight off. When his eyes adjusted, he walked through the small bedroom to his waiting bed, his steps heavy and slow from care and exhaustion.

Despite the windows, the master bedroom, like the rest of the house, was now almost pitch dark. The only source of light was a dim, ghostly blur along the window frames. He stepped closer and looked out.

He had never seen so many stars. There was a depth to the scattered pinholes of light, some bright and close, others distant and glimmering in degrees of white and yellow.

But no moon, he thought; that's the difference.

For reasons he only half understood, particularly as he could do nothing about the other window, he closed the working shutters. He would get new hinges tomorrow, he consoled himself, and rehang the broken ones. In the meantime, stubbornly, perversely, he shut the ones that worked, as if in this way he could shut out the night.

He kicked off his shoes, and crawled into his sleeping bag. Of course, sleep did not come right away. He stared numbly up to the shadowed ceiling, the dregs of his adrenaline-filled day giving way only reluctantly to his exhaustion and need for sleep. His head began to hurt from the cold, and there was an unmistakable smell of urine rising from the mattress. He fought off another sneeze and pulled the sleeping bag closer, covering his nose.

All in all, he thought, *not quite what I expected.*

He listened to the absolute stillness and tried not to think of his wife, or what she'd think about the mess he'd made of everything. Again.

He woke with a vague sense of panic, an unconscious dread of something known but not understood. He turned in the unfamiliar closeness of his sleeping bag. Where was he?

A faint stench of urine brought it all back. He reached for the fleeting images and senses of his subconscious, sensing tentatively the memory of his wife.

He felt the chill night air along his forehead and cheeks, but the rest of him was comfortable, the sleeping bag creating a warm cocoon of body heat. He closed his eyes again, willing himself to forget, to sleep again.

He heard the distant creak of floorboards like the sudden crack of breaking ice. He had a brief vision of someone stopped on the stairway, foot half pressed on the creaking step, looking up through the twisting darkness at his room.

He tried to remain perfectly still, as if any movement or sound he might make would draw attention to his location, make him a target, start the stranger up the stairwell again.

His head began to ache with the concentration of listening and remaining still. He slowly opened his eyes, rolling them to the left and the bedroom entrance. But it was too dark to see anything beyond the edge of the bed.

He remembered the flashlight was on the floor by his shoes. But to retrieve the light meant getting out of his bag, and he couldn't do that without making a noise.

The moment seemed to drag on interminably.

Supposing someone was even there, he thought, what the hell was he going to do with a flashlight? IF someone was there. Old houses were known to make noises. He only imagined that it was a creak of floorboards. It might just as easily have been the wind blowing something against the house....

He pulled his arm slowly out of the bag, ignoring his own rationalizations. He rolled just as carefully to his left, but the bag rustled despite his best efforts.

He stopped dead, his ears straining for the sound of renewed footsteps. All was quiet. No, not quiet; still. Still as an empty hole. As if nothing had ever moved in the house, or would ever move again.

He continued his turn, reached carefully to the floor, found the flashlight. He held it tightly to his chest, but couldn't bring himself to turn the light on. When he turned the light on, he would be disturbing the darkness.

No noise, no light; if he remained still and quiet then it would go away.

He felt something constrict in his chest, realized he was holding his breath.

Jesus Christ! What was he four years old; afraid of noises in the dark?

He sat up suddenly and angrily stabbed the flashlight on. He whipped the light all around the room; in the corners, even under the bed. Nothing.

Of course there's nothing, idiot. You're letting your imagination get the better of you.

But then again, he thought a moment later, the sound came from downstairs.

He looked to the bedroom entrance. With a shock he realized the door was open. He was certain he had closed it before he retired.

He climbed from his mattress, standing in his socks on the cold wood floor, and walked swiftly to the open door. He paused briefly in the doorway, then took a quick step in the other room.

Again, nothing.

He padded through the small bedroom, crossed the landing, and started down the twisted stairwell.

There was one bad moment, when the sound of creaking wood broke the stillness again. But it was only his own weight on the loose step. After that, he deliberately took the remaining steps with as much weight and noise as he could manage.

He turned at the final step, and shone the light around the foyer.

Empty. Empty. Empty. The doors all closed. Nothing standing in the kitchen archway. No menacing figures in the shadows.

And I'm a fool.

He felt the cool trickle of relief run down his armpits and between his buttocks. He walked over to the front door. It was still locked. He walked in the kitchen, flashed the light down its long length. It was still empty.

Everything was empty. Everything was still. Still and empty. Slowly he turned to the back room. The doors were still shut. He almost laughed aloud.

Check the room, see that no one is there, then it's back up to bed and a lesson learned.

But as he approached the massive doors his feet faltered.

Despite himself, despite the rational and mocking reproaches racing through his bitter mind, he found himself turning the light away from the entrance.

He stood that way for a moment, forever; his light pointed just away from the doors, his mouth dry, his head aching, the pressing darkness all around him.

He whirled suddenly, waving the light frantically all around. No one. Nothing.

He turned back again, forced himself to shine the light directly on the small handle of the wicket door. He moved step by hesitant step forward. Touching the cool brass of the knob, he held his breath again, and then with a rush opened the door.

The darkness retreated only slightly from his light, like a wary animal girding itself against an enemy. He stepped in, the darkness adjusting to his light, brightening reluctantly where the beam played, growing denser in the spaces left out. He would have to walk the room to check everything. He did. He looked in every corner, under the kitchen table, even in, and up, the fireplace.

Finally he turned to the sealed wall. He played the light slowly up and down its surface, watching the condensation beads glimmer along the blistered line like discharge from an open soar. He reached out and touched a part of the broken line. It was cold as ice. Again, he leaned close, put an ear along the surface. This time he heard, or imagined he heard, a distant echo like the sound of waves in a seashell. Only this was not a sound full of light and air, but dark, like the suck of a deep cave hole.

He stepped back, looked at the ugly scar. He wondered what kind of man would build a house over a mine shaft. He wondered, too, what kind of family could live in such a house even after it was sealed.

He left quickly, shutting the doors carefully behind him, irrationally checking to see if the front door was still locked. He climbed the steps slowly, still listening for any sound of movement or presence. He checked the small bedroom again, and then carefully examined the connecting bedroom door.

The handles upstairs were simple thumb pressed latches, a thin metal bar lifting up the jamb. He pulled the door closed from the small room side. It stayed shut. He reached out and gently pressed the door. It swung open easily. Looking closer, he discovered the latch pin was broken at the tip and unable to find the jamb.

There must be a slight tilt to the house, he thought; or maybe a draft pushed the door open in the night. Simple enough.

He went inside the master bedroom, closed the door behind him, and secured it with one of his shoes as a doorstop. He sat on the bed and removed his now filthy socks, turned the flashlight off and put it on the floor in easy reach. He then crawled back into his sleeping bag. Looking out the exposed window, he guessed there were still hours before dawn.

He closed his eyes, willing himself to sleep, but listening for any noise from below. He lay like that for a long, long time. To distract himself, he tried to think of his plans for tomorrow. Fix the bedroom door; get some wood for the fireplace and stoves; get modern lanterns, oil, and more candles; get curtains, rods, fix the shutter; clean out the meat lockers; get more food, bathroom supplies....

Then, like a physical slap, he remembered: *the other wing!*

He had not checked the other wing. He had looked in the bedrooms, the kitchen, the backroom, but not the wing with the empty bed rails and odd back panel door.

Should I go down again? That he even considered the idea, left a bitter taste of shame in his mouth.

But to not look? To not be sure? It would take but a moment; a quick run down the steps.

He felt the heat rush to his face. *Stop it! There is nothing there.*

He thought, then, of what his wife would make of his sitting in the dark, too frightened to move or stay. An almost overwhelming sense of loss, a sense of despair deep and somehow cruel, took him.

He used this sense of loss to buffer his self-confidence, overwhelm his anxiety, mock his fragile nerves into submission.

He turned his back to the bedroom door.

He then filled himself instead with the memory of all that he lost, all that he would never have again, assuring himself that this pain was far more real than any imagined terrors he felt in a strange house in the dead of night.

But it was a fleeting and false succor and he soon rolled back, stared once more into the darkness.

He did not search the other wing. *Why?*

He had passed the wing a dozen times in his searching of the house, but he had left it alone, perhaps unconsciously.

Perhaps not. He ground his teeth in the dark, wondering if he was he playing some twisted children's game of hide and seek with himself—or someone else?

He spent the rest of the night wrestling with the thought, sleep now a foregone impossibility. Echoes of his wife's gentle chiding pointed out his irrationality and its obvious solution until they became a shrill background to his restless turning.

But he didn't go back down. For all the wrong reasons he didn't, couldn't go back down.

Chapter Five

Dawn came, inevitably, mockingly. But he was grateful just the same. He watched the first rays chase the shadows from the bedroom, his mind reeling with self-disgust and lack of sleep.

Eventually, he climbed from his bag, answering an urgent call of nature. *I didn't check this either,* he thought bitterly, standing at the toilet. *Why didn't I worry about that?*

He rinsed his face and head under the sink faucet, a long goose-neck affair that gave him plenty of space to maneuver. The water, like the kitchen below, was icy cold, clear, and surprisingly fresh. *Well, that's one,* he thought.

He checked his reflection in the piece of hanging mirror. He looked rough. Grain stubble lined his chin, and the eyes that looked back were bloodshot, puffy, exhausted.

He brushed his wet hair back along his head, feeling a cold trickle of water run down his back. His box of belongings contained his kit, but he couldn't bring himself to shave in the cold water. He looked to the tub. In the light of morning it was surprisingly whole and no so depressingly hopeless. A hot bath would set a lot of things right. But how to get the water hot? He needed wood and a big pot. Maybe he could find both in the shed.

Right. First chore after breakfast: explore the wood shed.

He found his basket of food and the thermos just where he left them. The plate and silverware had fallen over some time in the night, but he discovered an overlooked napkin in the bottom of the basket and wiped them off.

The coffee was still hot, and the bread fresh. The jam was obviously homemade, and he piled it on. *Claire,* he thought, *you have yourself a loyal customer.* Between her, and Sol's diner, and what he could scrape up on his own, he thought he could just manage to keep himself fed. The prospect of living in the house looked a little brighter.

Finished, he rinsed the plate and forks as well as he could. *Have to get some dish soap in town.* He left everything to dry again in the dining room, not wanting to use the sink until he gave it a good cleaning.

He poured himself another cup of coffee, and took it out front. (The door was locked, as he knew it would be, and he felt silly for his nighttime fears.) He stood on the steps, sipped his coffee, and took in the view.

Fresh light gave the night's browns and greens a softer radiance, turning the world from cold winter to late fall. Birds, almost absent last night, now poked from under the pines, and occasionally, briefly, touched earth to look for food. A fat, brown squirrel sat comfortably on a bare limb, and ignored him from the corner of his eye.

Frank sipped his coffee, felt a small rush of pleasure at the thought that this was all his. For a brief moment, even the deep ache of loss receded.

He put his cup down on a step. *A porch would do nicely,* he thought. He'd buy an old rocking chair (the older the better) and sit and watch the dawn and setting sun.

He took a deep, bracing breath of the cool fresh air, smiled. He paused briefly as he saw the locked cellar against the house, remembered the sheriff's warning and the unfortunate boy. *What was his name? Thomas?* But he let it go before it took root, deciding not to dwell on the negative in the bright hope of morning.

He walked to the woodshed. Lying against the rustic plank-wood of the door was an old straw broom. The straws were hard and browned by age, the round wood handle snapped in two near the top. He moved the broom and, using the key the sheriff gave him, unlocked the simple padlock covering the ring latch.

The shed was little taller than Frank and had a tin roof, sloped slightly to the back for runoff. The door swung outward with a creak of rusty hinges. It was dim inside, but the morning sun caught the big web across the doorway, like a hanging constellation it glimmered along points and lines. He admired the web for a moment, the stepped hastily backwards as he saw the twitch of the occupant in the center. It was big, very big, with brown, spikey hairs and a black, bloated sac.

Only now did he see a similar web, in the angle of the roof and doorway. Another spider, a slightly smaller version than the first, sat hunched in the middle. Frank wiped a hand across the top of his head. He must have been standing just under the spider.

In his mind he was already planning a trip to Torview for his wood, or if that didn't work, then the hour long journey to the next closest town. *Bought wood; prepackaged and spider free.* He'd fill his trunk and back seat...

His racing thoughts ground to a halting, bitter stop. Was he seriously going to let some spiders stop him from using the shed? If this was how he was going to act with every little challenge of the house, then he didn't deserve it and should take Emil up on his offer right now.

He grabbed the broom near the broken end of the handle and attacked the webs, letting his exhaustion, frustration, and fear spill out in one frantic burst of destruction. First he smashed the roof spider against the underside, then with a downward swing, slammed the doorway spider against the shed floor. In both cases he left the spiders a satisfying mess of twitching brown and black balls.

He stepped back, breathing heavily, his relief and aggression now conflicted with a growing sense of guilt and disgust. He scraped the remains of web and spider from the broom with the edge of the tin roof, then bent slightly and stepped in the shed.

Thin rays of light passed through cracks in the tin roof, helping to illuminate the d a r k interior as his eyes adjusted. He had time to note the pile of wood stacked in the back, and some rusted tools and an old metal tub in the corner. Then he stopped, stared a moment, and then walked out again.

Strewn from every corner and angle of the interior of the shed were more webs, each with a spider of various size, sitting like spots of cancer in a silvery cell. The largest web was across the woodpile. In its center was a spider as big as his fist, its spikey-haired legs tensed, as if ready to spring.

Outside, Frank slammed the door close, slipped the latch over the hook and closed the padlock around it. He'd buy the damn wood.

* * *

He drove to town, bits of napkin on his cuts from the cold water shave, and tried to keep his mind on his growing list of supplies. He stopped first at Claire's. He remembered to pull the napkin pieces from his face just before he got out of the car.

She met him at the front door, where he returned the basket and thermos with many thanks.

"Do you want me to fill it again?" she asked. Her tone was neutral, almost without expression. In the light of day she looked younger, the yellow in her hair softer and hinting at fullness, if it was released from the severe bun. But nothing had changed about the deep worry line running between her arched eyebrows.

"Yes, I would appreciate that very much," said Frank. "But only if you let me pay you."

She named a figure half what he expected, and he quickly agreed. She invited him in to the parlor, and after a time brought back another half of chicken, some sandwiches, a bottle of milk, a container of raw cut carrots, and a piece of apple pie. She also refilled the thermos with hot coffee. He thanked her again, gave her the money.

He watched her pocket the money in her apron. He hesitated, the basket perched awkwardly in his right arm.

"I'm not making much of an impression in town, am I, Mrs. Mundt?" he asked, searching for a way to break through the cold distance.

The worry line deepened. "House belongs to the Mundts," she said softly, but with bitter overtones.

"Yes. But you didn't like it, did you?"

She blinked, caught temporarily off guard.

"My husband inherited that house," she answered finally, as if that explained everything. "He was a Mundt."

This was not the direction Frank wanted the conversation to go, but he took his best shot. "I hope my living there won't come between us, Mrs. Mundt. I didn't know the history when I bought the place."

She looked away, as if she doubted that, or it didn't matter.

He thanked her again, and left, promising to bring the basket back again tomorrow. She nodded civilly at this, and Frank decided it would be a purely business relationship for the foreseeable short term.

That, or she'll take to poising the food.

* * *

He found some more supplies at the local general store, the *Nite Owl*; mostly snacks, and a box of spaghetti he bought to inspire him to clean and use the kitchen stove. He also bought cleaning supplies, including scrub brushes, a new broom and dustbin, some detergent, hand soap, shampoo, a toothbrush, some toothpaste, more candles, matches, a small cooler, and a bottle of aspirin.

The boy at the counter had the look of a Mundt with his full lips and already receding hair, the back of which stood up in the familiar tuft. He watched Frank openly as he shopped, as if he suspected Frank would shoplift. When Frank went to the counter with his goods, he saw the boy couldn't be long out of high school. His face was riddled with acne and still had much of his baby fat. The boy rang him up without a word, and put his goods in an old woven basket.

"You bring that back," he said in a high, squeaky voice. He talked slow as if to a child. "Every time you shop. That's how it is done."

"Name's Frank," he said, extending a hand. The boy looked as if Frank was offering him a turd, but reluctantly took it.

"I know who you are," answered the boy sullenly.

"You have a name?" asked Frank.

"Michalus."

"Nice to meet you, Michalus."

The bell rang over the door, and Emil walked in. The boy quickly pulled his hand from Frank's and mumbled in his squeaky voice. "Bought some stuff, dad. Looks like he's going to stay."

Emil nodded to Frank. "I thought a night in that dump might change your mind," he said. "It couldn't have been all that pleasant."

Frank shrugged. "Just needs some touching-up."

"Then I reckon we need to set you up with some supplies," said Emil. He grinned at Frank, then his boy, bouncing on his heels, all signs of yesterday's animosity gone. "Leastways, for the short term. Why don't you come across the street, and we'll get you sorted out."

Frank hesitated. He knew he needed goods from the hardware store. But he had just about decided to make the long round trip to the next town to get them.

Emil opened his hands in a gesture of peace. "I'm not trying to take advantage of you, Mr. Frank. I figure the sheriff is right: the quicker you get know us the more likely you are to see the value of selling us that house back. We're not bad folks. When you leave the house..."

"If I leave," interrupted Frank.

"When," Emil insisted, with a wink, "we'd welcome you to our town. You ask around, I always take care of my customers. And I never turn down business." He chuckled. "Most of my customers are family anyway, so I can't."

Frank suspected there was more to it than that, but decided he had nothing to lose. He couldn't go around avoiding the Mundts all the time. Maybe he could broach a civil peace. Once they realized he was determined to stay, maybe they'd give up on his moving out of the house.

"Okay," he said.

Emil smiled again, put his hands down his pants and rocked like a little boy told he done well. "That's a good start," he said.

Frank put his groceries in the car which was parked now outside the *Nite Owl*.

"You can leave your car here," said Emil. "I'll have my other boy help you carry your purchases to it."

Frank nodded, and locked the door. Emil chuckled again. "You don't need to do that here, Mr. Frank. There's nothing or no one going to bother your car that wouldn't be known about by Sheriff Kyle. And I guess the sheriff has taken a liking to you. Says we're to work out with you."

Frank didn't answer, but left the door locked. He waved Emil on, and followed him into the hardware store.

Inside, he soon had four new butane lamps, extra butane, a hammer, nails, a crow bar, a big bristle broom, some iron brushes, some industrial stain remover, a garbage pail, a box of heavy garbage bags, three cans of fresh paint, rollers, and brushes. (Frank had no idea what he would use the paint on, but he liked the frown it created on Emil).

He also bought garden and work gloves, a mop, two metal buckets—one industrial size—a new mirror, two metal plates, two rolls of duct tape, a box of utensils, a bowl, a coffee mug, a plastic drinking cup, two curtain rods with curtains, a roll of sheet plastic (for the bed), one bath towel, two dish rags, and a can of *Raid* for the spider infestation in the shed. He eyed a handmade rocking chair sitting among the garden section, but decided to hold off on that one. He did buy a heavy pair of long underwear and a pair of fur-lined moccasins.

He paid at the counter, the Mundts watching him with curious, open-mouthed expressions. Emil rocked on his heels with his hands in his pants again, as the boy counted out his change.

Emil looked like he was waiting for the purchase to be completed before he spoke. Frank beat him to the punch, not wanting to hear what Emil had to say.

"Know where I can get some bed supplies?" he asked.

"Suspect that big bed needs a new mattress," said Emil, with a knowing grin. His other boy, an older twin model of the one in the *Nite Owl*, handed Frank his change with a sneer.

"I can get you one," said Emi. "It will be here in two days. But maybe we can we work something out before then, heh?"

Frank sighed. "I'm going to stay, Emil."

"No doubt. No doubt. That's what the sheriff said. He said: 'he's determined, Emil.' But it's where you stay, isn't it? That's my point today. And you haven't heard my latest offer. I'm willing to pay you half again what you paid, and set you up in a nice little cottage up behind the school to boot."

"That's very generous," said Frank.

"It's more than that," said Emil strongly. "It smooths a lot of waters for you, Mr. Frank. A lot of rough waters."

The stubbornness welled up in Frank as he watched Emil's boy grinning at his father's implications. "I'll think about it."

"You do that," said Emil. "You think about it, in that lonely house tonight. But don't take long thinking."

"You know what," said Frank. "You go ahead and order that mattress."

Emil's expression grew hard, and something slipped in the carefully crafted bearing. A raw, animalistic hatred flickered in his pale eyes, like a candle flame seen briefly in a passing window.

"Fine," he said, his tone suddenly cold. Then, as if aware of the slip, he smiled again, and his voice was full of ironic humor when he added with another sly wink, "Can always use a new mattress up there. Boy, help him with the stuff."

His car packed in every available space, and locked again (*the hell if he would trust Emil's word*), Frank looked across the street at Sol's. It was almost noon and his breakfast was long since used up. The diner looked empty. More importantly, Henrik nowhere to be found.

Sol put down his paper, which looked to be yesterday's, and greeted him warmly.

"Thought I'd get that steak and eggs again," said Frank, sitting close to the register. He wanted a little normal conversation, to rinse the aftertaste of Emil and his knowing winks away.

Sol pored him a cup of coffee and a glass of water without asking. Then he retreated to the kitchen to make Frank's lunch. He served it about fifteen minutes later, and politely hid behind his paper again to let Frank eat.

"Boys in school?" asked Frank, cutting up his steak and eggs. Sol put down the paper, nodded.

"Their mother takes them to Summerset. She's got a part-time job up there as well, so it works out."

Summerset was the next closest town, the one Frank had considered going to for his wood and hardware supplies. It was at least an hour away.

"They don't go to school here?"

Sol shook his head. "I took them out. It's some kind of old traditional school where everybody takes the same classes no matter what age. My boys are smart, and the teachers weren't challenging them enough. And anyway, they do better in Summerset."

If Emil's boys were any indication of the youth in Torview, Frank could understand why.

"How was your first night in the house?" asked Sol curiously.

"It's going to take some getting used to," said Frank with a frown. "Scared myself silly this morning with some spiders in the woodshed."

"Black widows?"

"No, I don't think so. J u s t b ig brown and black bastards."

Sol nodded sympathetically, and they discussed Frank's options until he was done with his breakfast. Sol took his plate to the back, then returned to refill his coffee.

"Your boy learn about the Mundt's history in Summerset?" asked Frank. He wasn't just making conversation now.

"Some. But there's a library in the school here that has some books on the Mundts, as well." Sol met Frank's eye. "If you're curious."

"Is it open to the public?"

"I don't know. No one really uses it, except the students, I guess. Maybe you could go in and ask around. Learning about the Mundts is probably a good thing for a man in your situation. But I don't think you will like what you find out."

Frank sighed. "You're probably right."

Sol tapped the counter idly with a brown finger. "Tell me, Mr. Henning," he asked slowly, "why does a nice man like you want to live alone in a place like that?"

Frank considered his coffee. He liked Sol, and somehow didn't mind answering this time.

"A youthful dream, I guess. I thought at one time it looked...romantic."

"You are a romantic man?"

"A retired Actuary, actually. Does that classify as romantic?"

"You are married?" Sol asked with some surprise.

Frank felt a flutter in his heart. "My wife died of breast cancer recently. We'd been married more than 25 years."

"I'm sorry," said Sol. He refilled Frank's cup in the awkward silence that followed.

"It was sudden," said Frank. "We found out three months ago." He looked to the counter top. "I guess I haven't had a chance to get on my feet since we heard the news. I didn't so much as come here, as run."

"You have no children?"

Frank shook his head.

"Go away, Mr. Henning," said Sol quietly. "You will not find what you are looking for in that house. You will not find healing there, or any place around here. Find some other home, far away."

Frank looked up from the counter top, conflicted and grateful at the same time for the kindness in Sol's expression and words.

"I don't know how to explain it," he said, "but I need the space just now. I need that house. It wasn't what I expected, but it's...what I need." He tried to smile, and settled for a grimace instead. "Who knows, maybe I'll start a trend and bring you some business."

Sol shook his head sadly. "I'm selling this place back to Emil end of the month. Moving my family to Summerset."

Frank was surprised by how much this bothered him.

"Go away, Frank," insisted Sol. "There's nothing here for us."

* * *

Frank spent the rest of the day in a frenzy of cleaning back at the house. The first thing he did was open the woodshed to the sunlight and hold war with the infesting spiders. In the bright afternoon sun, armed with his can of *Raid*, new broom, heavy gloves, and an old ball cap he found in the trunk of his car, he felt almost up to the task.

He set up one of his new lanterns just inside the dim doorway. The lantern light made things clearer and worse—there were far more webs than he imagined.

He turned to the ones around the door first, naturally. The spiders tended to live in the corners and other angles of the frame. They didn't react until he actually touched their webbing. Knowing this he soon worked out a system of hitting them one handed with the broom and then spraying them with the *Raid* to finish them off.

He tried it the other way at first, using the Raid and then whacking them with the broom, and nearly knocked his lantern over when the spider dropped from the web to the floor and began crawling quickly in his direction. He didn't think the spider was actually going to attack him, but it was damn scary just the same. Apparently a shot of *Raid* only confused it at first. After that he took the more direct approach with the broom.

The tricky part was when the webs were close together. He had to make sure he didn't touch the webs he wasn't attacking, or he'd set the spider in motion. He learned to keep his angles close and his swings tight.

The big one he saved for last. By that time he was a spider killing expert. Long gone was his sense of muted guilt. He dragged the broom down the web in a sweeping, almost casual arc, pinning the spider to the ground. He felt a brief struggle briefly under the broom as he pressed down, then nothing. He didn't even bother with the *Raid*.

He spent another fifteen minutes sweeping out spider remains and making sure the shed was well and truly clear. *What the hell did they live on*, he wondered? He swept the surprisingly small pile of spider remains outside the doorway and then out into the yard as a warning to any would be replacements.

When he was finished, he returned to the woodshed and carefully poked the top of the wood pile. This released a horde of flying insects, and the mystery of the spiders' diet was solved. After a time, the bugs returned to their nests and he was able to approach the pile again.

He carefully lifted a log from the top, raising a few fliers and discovering a host of others crawling in the chewed up wood. He set the piece down gently with a frown. All that work and the wood remained unusable. He wasn't about to bring elements of the flying horde into the house.

With sudden inspiration (but little actual hope) he sprayed the pile with the rest of the *Raid*. He had to leave quickly then, as this set up another firestorm of now angry fliers. He dropped his empty can of *Raid*, grabbed his lantern and broom, and shut the door with a slam behind him. Then he locked it again for good measure.

He turned to face the house, filled with a sense of hollow victory. He suspected now his spider pogrom had actually robbed him of an ally. If the flying ants, termites, whatever, got in the house he would have a whole new mess on his hands.

Taking a distracted stroll around his small grounds, he made an unexpected, and ironic, discovery: a pile of cut wood near the back of the house, complete with chopping block and axe.

Who cut the wood and for what purpose he didn't know (certainly not for his use; no one knew he was coming until yesterday). He picked through a few logs. They looked relatively fresh cut, and bug free. He carried two armfuls into the house, setting one pile in the kitchen and one upstairs in the master bedroom.

He was sweating from his efforts by the time he dropped the last pile, and feeling grimy. But he had a long way to go yet if he wanted to sleep in a relatively clean house. He'd reward himself with a hot bath tonight.

As a consequence, he started with the bathroom. He used his gloves to pick up the mirror pieces, then swept the floor with his big, hard-bristled broom. Then he made a small fire in the bedroom stove and heated a small bucket of water.

While the water grew hot, he cleaned out the tub of loose debris and dust, and tossed out the sheet and used condoms. He filled up his first industrial size garbage bag this way.

He poured cleaner in the hot water and attacked the tub, toilet, then the walls, and finally the floor, turning the bucket of water into a dark gray mess that he had to empty three times.

By the time he finished it was late afternoon. He rinsed off the grime and sweat of the day in the cold water of the kitchen sink, then ate a sandwich sitting on the front steps. The sky was a crystalline blue, fading to black, but he could see deep into the woods surrounding the house. A Blue jay, maybe the same one from yesterday, settled on branch nearby to watch him eat. He remembered how quickly and completely it grew dark on the hill, and guessed he had about two, three mores of daylight.

One room a day, he decided. That, combined with a few more trips to town, would see him right by the end of the week. He tossed the few remaining crumbs of his sandwich in the direction of the Blue jay, then grabbed some more firewood from the pile.

He carried this pile to the dining room fireplace. He wondered what effect a roaring fire would have on the room, and decided to build one later for dinner.

He went upstairs, checked on his fire in the wood stove. It was down to embers, but still hot. In fact, it had done a good job of chasing off the chill in the room. He put another log in the stove belly, and this time filled his industrial metal bucket with fresh water. When the water was piping hot, he carefully lifted the heavy bucket from the stove and carried it to the bathroom.

He set the bucket down and stopped up the tub with its plug, which fortunately still worked. He poured all the water from the bucket in the tub, filling it about a third of the way. He filled the bucket again from the bathroom sink, and set it on the stove, this time letting it come to a boil. He emptied this bucket into the tub as well, bringing it to about half full. He decided it was enough.

He tested the water with his hand. It was too hot to sit in at first, so he added some cold water until it was bearable. Then he stirred in some liquid soap, and agitated the mix until the tub was full of frothy bubbles. He shed his clothes and stepped in.

The ache and stress of the day seemed to melt away as his skin turned a rosy red, and the sweat that started down his face was a clean sweat, a sweat of release and accomplishment. For once the stillness was not oppressive, but welcomed.

He closed his eyes, enjoying the contrast of the cool enamel against the back of his neck, and thought: *This at least—and the view—I can hold on to these, maybe make a new life, one simple distraction at a time.*

Distraction. Yes, the afternoon had been that, a time of simple, quiet, busy distraction, spiders and all. He needed that distraction, any distraction. The overwhelming sense of loss, though still present, was temporarily pushed down, repressed under the weight of his immediate everyday problems, and almost he could breathe again, almost he didn't think of her.

Viewed that way, even his running battle with Emil and the other Mundts helped.

He sank deeper in the tub, concentrating on the weariness of his limbs, the balm of the hot, soapy water removing the day from his body and mind. Distraction.

When the water grew cold, he climbed from the tub and put on a fresh set of clothes.

He stood in his socks in his now relatively clean and comfortable bedroom, the wood stove doing a surprisingly good job against the chill. He lit one of his new lanterns in the growing darkness, put it on the floor beside him, and watched the sun set outside the windows.

When it was down, and the darkness began to cover the hills like a slow spill of black ink, he felt the first tremors of memory and loss.

Where's a nest of spiders when I need one? He'd even settle for a visit from Emil. He frowned at his reflection in the now dark window.

Don't call up the devil.

He turned to the room.

He picked up the fallen shutter. The wood holding the hinges was rotted out, and he set it back against the wall, just under the window. He tried instead to mount a curtain rod, but the plaster kept crumbling around the screws. In the end, he settled for taping a curtain across the missing shutter space.

It was ugly as hell, but it would do.

My formula for survival.

* * *

The dining room *was* better with a fire. The general gloom receded, the air was warmer, and the flicker of flames in the hearth made a pleasant distraction. True, the scarred back wall retained its ominous eyesore quality. But he solved that again by putting his back to it.

Claire had not poisoned his dinner yet, or if she had, it was slow acting. He finished off the chicken, the pie, and half the milk, relishing every bite. He saved the rest for the morning, confident the room temperature would keep it chilled.

He rinsed his glasses and dishes, stacked them again against the basket on the dining table. *Kitchen tomorrow*, he thought; *first thing after breakfast; at least space enough to wash and dry the dishes.* He didn't relish tackling the cold lockers.

He adjusted the grill around the fireplace before leaving the dining room. He decided to let his small fire burn down on its own, hoping it would dry out the back room. It certainly helped the odor. He climbed the steps to his bed (*my bed*, he thought), and for the first time he thought of the place as a possible home.

He swept off the mattress again, this time with one of his hard iron brushes. It raised so much dust he had to mop the floor again, and take another cold water rinse. He dried off with his new towel, climbed into his long underwear and moccasins, and then stood a while by the wood stove to warm up.

He rolled the plastic sheet out and covered the mattress. The sheet was too big and touched the floor on both sides, but on second thought that wasn't such a bad thing. He put his sleeping bag on top again, and tonight used a rolled up sweater for a pillow (*another item on the list for tomorrow*). He added another log to the still burning embers of the woodstove, stoked it to life, shut the cast iron door, and opened the vent.

He shed his moccasins, crawled into the sleeping bag, and savored the soft glow of the woodstove against the ceiling. There was still a hint of cold to the air, but nothing like the night before, and the damp smell was replaced by smoky pine. He closed his eyes, exhausted but satisfied.

* * *

In the dream his wife lay naked and crying in the tub. She was staring at a shiny, pulsating bump on the top of her breast. He wanted to comfort her, but remained fixed and silenced in the dream perspective. He watched in sudden horror as the bump broke open, and a brown spider crawled out. It was soon followed by another. And another. His wife began to scream as spiders continued to crawl from the ravaged hole along her breast like living bloody puss. The tub was now full of spiders. Her screams grew louder. The spiders started to bite and crawl frantically along her body. She looked to him in the shadows, and with one final, choked scream the largest spider crawled from her mouth...

* * *

He sat up in bed, the echo of his own screams still in his ears. The house, again, was unnaturally still. He put a hand to his aching chest, the vision of the last spider still vivid in his mind. *And her screams*...he could hear them even now.

He could hear them. With a new pang of terror he realized that the screams were not memories of his nightmare, but actual sounds coming from somewhere in the house.

He grabbed the flashlight by the bed, shoved his feet in the moccasins, and moved quickly down to the first floor.

The sounds took on more definition as he reached the central hall, becoming now a deep throated moan, now a shrill wail. It was as if he were listening outside the confines of an asylum. The cries were coming from the back room.

It's just an odd draft, he told himself, opening the wicket door and thrusting the light around the empty room before he lost his nerve. As he stepped through, the noise grew louder, clearer.

It is the sound of wind in the mine shaft. Nothing human could make that noise.

There were still a few glowing embers in the fireplace, though they cast little light. He didn't bother with the rest of the room, but made directly for the back wall. As he approached, the sounds grew louder.

He played the light up and down the wall's marred surface, which had turned a pasty gray in the darkness. He hesitated, then put his ear next to the wall. As if from a great distance or a deep well, he heard a hopeless cry that rose and rose in intensity, until it was suddenly choked off in what sounded like an angry, almost animalistic snarl.

Wind, he reminded himself, pulling back from the wall with a shudder. *Wind in the tunnel. There must be a hole or crack in the wall somewhere.*

Slowly, he moved his light up and down the scar line—and found it: the thinnest of fracture lines, like a slit in a reed, just about head high. When he put his finger over the line he felt the air pass across it like ice water.

Hesitantly he explored the crack with his finger, felt some of the ancient plaster crumble, and made a small thumb-sized hole. He pulled his hand back, suddenly afraid. The rough aperture reminded him of the dream spider crawling from his wife's mouth.

It was just a dream. And this just a hole in a wall, and that was just stupid wind making noises in the night. The sheriff told you there would be noises.

But when he stepped close again, and put his eye to the crack, he half expected to see a cluster of four, tiny black eyes looking back. Or worse, one blood-red human one.

But if there was something on the other side, it was impossible to see in the tiny stygian recess. He took a deep, shaky breath and stepped away again.

The room had returned to its natural stillness, as if nothing had happened. Feeling foolish, he left the new hole, left the ugly wall, and climbed back upstairs to his lumpy mattress to spend another sleepless night staring at the ceiling.

The morning found him half awake, anxious and irritable and shattered. *Two days now*, he thought. *Two days with maybe three hours sleep between them.* His head hurt, and his stomach roiled with over-active bile. *For god's sake, Frank, get a hold of yourself.*

He glared at the soft light around the curtain across from him, rubbed his tired eyes with the heel of his hand, heard the first twitter of birds. But when he closed his eyes, sleep would not come. He finally gave up and stormed into the bathroom, dousing his head repeatedly with cold water until he was thoroughly awake, and soaked around the collar and cuffs of his long underwear.

He changed quickly, and retreated to the dining room for coffee, glancing angrily at the small hole in the back wall. It looked pathetically unimportant in the morning.

He knew he couldn't go on this way, finding reasons not to sleep. *That* kind of distraction would only lead to serious trouble. He knew, too, that it was his own mind that was his real enemy, not a drafty house and a bad dream.

Sitting in the cold dining room (he didn't bother to make a fire), he ate a perfunctory breakfast, and rethought his plans for the day.

He had no desire to clean anything today. He had no desire to do anything with the house. He had to get out of here.

He would go to Torview again. Maybe see Sol, or explore the rest of the town.

What could it hurt?

Chapter Six

The town of Torview was shaped like two back-to-back brackets, Main Street representing the long space between the brackets. On each end of a bracket were four short side streets, running at slight angles from the main thoroughfare. *Claire's Bed and Breakfast* anchored one end of the northern side street, and a large circular schoolhouse and playground the opposite. The southern ends sported a tavern and open market on one side, and a few forlorn craft shops on the other.

In between the bracket ends, and all along and behind the length of Main Street, sat simple post-war houses with well-trimmed postage stamp front yards. A few office and municipal building ran in the middle of Main, Emil's hardware store being one of the largest.

To change things up, Frank drove past Claire's, down the length of Main and its well-ordered houses, and checked out the opposite end.

The tavern was already open (or never closed), judging from the lit neon signs in the darkened windows. A hanging sign over the doorway advertised it as *Albert's*. It was made of dark pine, with an old West façade and short porch. Frank remembered the sheriff warning him to stay away from it for a time. It was impossible to tell if Henrik or anyone else was inside.

Next to the tavern was an open market. Fruits and vegetables stalls sat under a big canopy tent, a few customers picking through the late season offerings. The women wore thick hose and long dresses under long, plain woolen coats. The few men that were with them wore heavy jeans and flannel jackets.

Across the street, the small craft shops included a handmade furniture store, with rocking chairs on the short porch like the one he'd seen at Emil's. Frank parked on the street outside, but discovered the store was closed when he walked up. Next door was a linen shop, and he remembered he needed a pillow.

He stepped through the door, almost swooned from the smell of potpourri and some kind of cloying, heady mix of body odor, baby powder, and cheap perfume, and knew he's made a mistake.

Before he could escape, a hulking figure in bright purple, and the obvious source of at least two of the pungent shop airs, fixed a strong arm around Frank and anchored him to the floor.

He guessed her to be in her late 40's, big-boned, with a pretty face, now going to fat. The dark red silk scarf tied around her neck did nothing to detract from her heavy shoulders, or the deep cleavage which she wore prominently in an altered lavender muumuu. A row of cheap bracelets clinked continuously on her thick wrists as she moved and she kept her arm on Frank with careless intimacy.

"You must be our new neighbor!" she said breathlessly. Her voice was deep, like a kettle drum, but she kept it at a high, excited pitch, regardless of the topic or tone of conversation.

"I'm Jenny," she said, touching the fingers of her free hand above her cleavage.

Frank nodded, tried to casually disengage from the hand holding his arm, failed. He looked instead to the frilly merchandise, hoping he could make this quick. The store was not large, mostly display bins of various silks and linens, with more merchandise on the shelves along the side walls. A short checkout counter took up half the back wall. A curtained archway beside it led to the backroom.

"You've been the talk of the town," continued Jenny, ignoring his lack of introduction. "We're all wondering what you want with that nasty old house on the hill."

"Just looking for a quiet place to retire," he said. The heavy odors of the shop and his lack of sleep was starting to make him sick. "I was looking for a pillow and some sheets."

"Oh, I'm sure, what with that foul mattress," she breathed. "It must smell of sin."

He didn't bother to ask how she knew about the mattress.

"Well, let's see," she said, releasing him to paw through a box of small, frilly pillows. "I don't really carry bed pillows, but how about something like this?" She showed him a lacy affair designed for a couch, held it up against her chest coyly.

Frank shook his head, pointed to a simple beige throw pillow near the back. She dismissed this with a laugh, then spent ten minutes pointing out and "showcasing" various pink and red and purple selections, touching him occasionally on the arm between displays to keep him close, and giving him ample views of her cleavage.

He finally convinced her that he really did want the beige throw, and strongly hinted that he had another appointment. It still took another five minutes to get her behind the counter so he could pay.

"I'm just certain," she said, ringing him up, "that we're going to get along just fine...I'm sorry, sweetie, I didn't catch your name?"

"Henning," answered Frank, looking pointedly to the register for the total and pulling out his wallet.

"Henning? Now what kind of name is that? Surely your mom didn't call you Henning?"

"She called me Frank."

"There, now that's better!" She giggled, and touched his arm again as she took his money. She counted out his change, but kept it in hand.

"Now, Frank," she said, leaning over the counter with arms crossed under her chest. "I know you didn't get off to the best foot here with everyone. Henrik can be a bit rough, I know *that* better than anyone." She giggled again, winked. "He's my husband. But he's a good sort, all in all."

She leaned a little closer, pushing her bosom up. Frank saw the bills of change poking from under right breast, a world away.

"You know, I told Henrik nobody would want to stay in that old coffin after a night or two. You wait, I said, one night in that silly house and he'll be ready to find a proper home. I can help you with that, Frank." She paused, looked Frank straight in the eye.

"I'm very good at that kind of thing," she added. "Making people comfortable."

"Thank you," said Frank. "I'll keep that in mind. Now, I'm very sorry, but I have to run."

"Of course you do," said Jenny, leaning back and handing him the change with a big smile.

As Frank turned to leave, a figure emerged from the curtained archway. At first he thought it was Henrik, until the boy stepped in the light.

He looked about the age of Michalus, was just as tall, and shared many of the other Mundt traits, including a high hairline and crooked mouth. He was dressed in grease stained purple pants and an old hockey jersey. Despite its size, the jersey strained against the big arms and distended belly. Bits of beard and pimples dotted his puffy cheeks and double chins.

"Walden!" said Jenny with a touch of exasperation rushing over to the hulking boy. "Now what are you doing out here? Momma's working." She put a hand on the boy, turned to Frank. "My boy, Walden."

Walden shrugged the hand off almost before it settled. He stared at Frank, his expression oddly distant, as if remembering Frank from somewhere. Frank nodded at the boy, "Hello."

Walden's deep blue eyes, like his father's, were almost crossed. Despite this, or maybe because of it, they were remarkably striking in the corpulent face. As he watched Frank, something flickered in the back of those eyes.

Like amusement, thought Frank, *but not*. He suspected the joke was at his expense.

A new odor was introduced to the close air of the shop. It threatened to overwhelm even the heavy perfume of Jenny. Frank wondered how long it been since the boy took a bath.

"Well," said Frank. "Goodbye."

"See you soon, Frank!" beamed Jenny. She started to rub Walden's massive shoulder.

The boy casually shrugged this off as well. He watched Frank all the way out the shop, a simple smile starting on one end of his crooked mouth.

Outside, Frank tossed the pillow in the back of the car. He decided to leave his car where it was, take some air to clear his head, and see the rest of the town. He grabbed his basket from Claire's and walked slowly along the west side of Main Street. The thoroughfare wasn't long, and made for a nice walk. There were sidewalks on both sides of the street, and everything was clean and well-maintained.

The air was cold, and the sky was showing signs of weather. Looking at the dark clouds coming from the east, he wondered if should get some chains for his car, like the sheriff suggested. He hoped he wouldn't have to go to Emil's again, but suspected that would be the place to carry chains.

The town was more active this morning. The sheriff car was parked outside the barber shop, talking to a few old men sitting inside, while a truck outside Emil's was being loaded with bags of grain by Emil's boy and a man in a dirty ball cap. *He might be my neighbor, Granger*, thought Frank, judging from the stringy beard and Mundt-like features. A little further down, outside the Municipal Building, an elderly man was talking to a young girl. They both glanced Frank's way at the same moment. The old man stopped talking, while the young girl stared in open curiosity.

Abruptly the old man waved and started walking across the street, heading directly for Frank. As he drew closer Frank could see he was dressed like a banker, with a stylish winter coat, and a felt hat with distended ear flaps and a tiny red feather in the band.

"Mr. Henning, I presume," said the old man brusquely, stepping in front of Frank. He didn't offer a hand but drew himself up as if expecting a challenge. "Judge Delphus Mundt. I stop you sir, because you will be receiving a summons shortly to appear in my court, on the subject of your purchase of the Captain's house."

The crooked mouth was less severe in the judge but when he wasn't speaking Frank saw the familiar wormy lips and suspected there was only a tuft of hair under the hat.

"But perhaps," continued the judge somewhat more cordially, "we can take care of the matter now, if you are free?"

"And what matter is that?" said Frank. His lack of sleep and general frustration with the situation made it sound rougher than he intended. "I bought the house properly. Your own sheriff said as much the other day."

The judge lifted his head as if affronted. He was clearly not used to being addressed so directly or casually. "Sheriff Miller is not the final say in this matter. That would be me."

Like all the Mundts, the judge was tall. He used that height now to look down on Frank with small, intelligent eyes that slowly, imperiously measured and dismissed. Under that glare, Frank became painfully aware that he hadn't shaved that morning, and what with his lack of sleep and rush to leave the house, he must look a wreck. He felt the blood rush to his cheeks, tried to control his rising frustration. Was everyone in this town going to be a Mundt—and his immediate enemy?

"Well," he said, choosing his words carefully. "I think your issue is with the bank. You should contact them. I'm sure they'll be glad to send one of their lawyers down."

"It is you that own the house now, Mr. Henning," answered the judge. "I'm certain that if you contact the bank you will find that they have washed their hands of the situation. Now that they have their money," he added bitterly.

Frank suspected the judge was probably right. *Why should the bank help him now?* But he be damned if he'd just roll over. "Summons, huh? Do I need a lawyer?"

"It is not that kind of summary," said the judge. "Perhaps I used the wrong word. Professional hazard. I'm simply acting in behalf of the community of Torview and would like to talk."

"And if I don't come?" asked Frank.

"Then I will make it an official summons," said the judge flatly.

For a moment, Frank's temper got the better of him. "I don't suppose you see any conflict, what with your last name being Mundt?"

The hard, intelligent eyes were hanging fire now, but the judge did a better job of controlling his ire. That, or he knew he was in a position of power and could afford to be confident.

"I appreciate the bank has put you in a difficult situation," he said. "But you should understand, I am trying to resolve the matter to everyone's best interest. Including yours, Mr. Henning." He lifted his chin. "However, there is a limit to my patience. And it will be resolved, one way or the other."

Frank cast around for some source of support. He saw the sheriff and the other men were openly watching the confrontation from the barber shop window. He frowned at the sheriff, as if to say it was his fault.

"Fine," he said, turning back to the judge. "How long is this going to take?"

The judge nodded in approval. "I think we should finish in time for lunch."

Frank glanced at his watch. At least an hour, if lunch was noon.

"After you...Judge Mundt." Frank was deter- mined to say the full name every chance he got.

The judge frowned, but waved Frank across the street. When they reached the young girl, he stopped and said, "My niece, Elizabeth. Elizabeth, this is Mr. Henning."

Frank nodded.

"Elizabeth will show you to my office," continued the judge. "I will be along shortly. I need to have a very quick word with the sheriff."

Frank almost balked at this further delay, but saw no point in backing out now. He nodded his agreement, and turned to the girl.

Elizabeth didn't look like she belonged in a town like Torview. A prominent nose ring glittered from one nostril, and her eyes were drowned in dark eyeliner. A red and blue butterfly tattoo poked from the collar around her neck, and she was dressed in torn jeans and a skimpy leather jacket despite the weather. She returned his stare with suspicious caution.

She might be pretty, he thought, *but for the scowl.*

"C'mon," she said, feigning boredom, and headed for the Municipal Building.

The brick façade entrance sported two enormous glass doors with corrugated metal frames and, *Torview Municipal*, painted in gold on both panes. Inside, the first floor was a large open room divided up in sections of gray board clerk cubicles. Each section had a sign post on a metal stand in front of it: *License Bureau; Marriage Licenses; Clerk of Courts; Records.*

There were only two people in the room, standing by the water cooler as if they owned it. They looked up at Elizabeth's entrance, then stared as Frank stepped in behind her. One started to move in their direction, but stopped as Elizabeth ignored them and walked directly to a broad, carpeted stairwell along the right hand wall. Frank followed, sensing the eyes at the water cooler watching him the entire way.

The plush, dark green carpet muffled their steps as they climbed. Elizabeth was moving fast now, but he had time to note the ornate frosted fixtures with soft yellow bulbs in the ceiling, and the framed portraits of old men in dated suits along the walls. From their appearance, he guessed them to be Mundts. It all reminded him of an old bank...or a museum.

They quickly passed a frosted door on the second floor landing marked, *Library*, and kept climbing. A similar door sat at the top of the third floor. On its square frosted pane, stenciled in black simple letters, read the legend: *Torview Court, Judge Delphus Mundt.* And underneath, in smaller letters, *Mundt Archives*.

"In here," mumbled Elizabeth, opening and sliding through the door without looking back. Frank stepped in quickly behind her before the door could close again.

He stood a moment, taking in the rich woodwork trim along the baseboard and ceiling, the wall to wall shelves of law review books, the large, rectangular oak desk sitting in front of the oriel bay window in the back wall. Everything had an air of propriety and class, the kind of class that enjoyed its distinction from the mundane or common.

The desk held a traditional blotter, gold pen set, and a banker's green desk lamp. A framed photo sat in one corner, facing away from Frank. The lamp was on, despite the time of day and the high, uncovered panes of the bay. Outside that window, the promised storm clouds were now over Torview, darkening the skies and making the green of the lamp shade and the room's other light fixtures pop with ghostly luminescence.

Two straight back chairs sat across from the oak, but apparently the judge preferred a more opulent leather seat variety. Elizabeth was now plopped in that chair, rocking back and forth on the swivel. She had pulled off her wool cap, revealing a tangle of red streaked black hair. She watched Frank from under the heavy black of her mascara.

Across from the entrance from where he stood was a thin door, made to look like a continuation of the bookshelves with realistic wallpaper book spines. It was slightly open, spoiling the effect, and revealing a small back room.

"What's in there?" he asked, nodding to the open door.

Elizabeth turned to the door, dismissed it with a shrug. "That's all the old records. They've been going through them like mad ever since you arrived."

"Is that so?"

She snorted. "Oh, yeah. You made a big impression."

"So, you heard about that?"

"Uncle told me."

"The judge is your uncle?"

"Not really, but he likes me to call him that. My mom was married to his nephew." She made a face. "But he's not my father."

"So, it's not Elizabeth *Mundt*?"

Her nose wrinkled. "Liz. But yeah, it's Mundt. Mom kept the name."

"If it's Liz, then you call me Frank."

"Okay. They talk about you a lot."

"Who does?"

"Uncle, the sheriff, everyone. And thank you, by the way," she added with a smirk.

"Why is that?"

"Now they don't talk about me."

He grinned. "I get it. I'm the new pariah on the block. So, I guess you're the one person who won't tell me to get out of town?"

"No way," she laughed. "But why would anyone want to stay?"

"You don't like it here?"

She shrugged again, picked at a spot on her chin. "It's all right. Better than where I was."

"And where was that?"

Some of the mirth went out of her expression. "With a creep my mom hooked up with."

"You mean the judge's nephew?"

"No. He took off a while back."

"Your father?"

She shook her head, looked away.

"Sorry," he said. "None of my business." He turned to the open back room again.

"Can I take a look?"

She hesitated, still staring out the window. "I guess so." Her voice as distant as her thoughts.

He stepped through the small opening, happy to give Liz a chance to recover from his inadvertent faux pas.

Like its neighbor, the back room was covered in wall to wall shelves lined with texts. But instead of similarly bound and stylized reviews, the shelves held a mishmash of texts and material. Three-ringed binders, hard cover journals, and rolled parchments sat alongside traditional books and stacks of loose leaf paper. *A utility room*, he thought. *A closet of memories and records.*

A rickety card table sat in the center of the room, covered with papers and what looked to be a record book of some kind. A quick glance at the last revealed a listing of deeds and last will and testaments. He had a good idea why this was out on the table when he spotted the family name on most of the listings: Mundt. The judge was obviously trying to find a loophole to retrieve the house.

He turned to the shelves, drawn to a sliding glass door section, presumably protecting important archives, but now unlocked and opened.

He picked through a few of the journals and looser papers, noting the titles and dates. Many were records of the town of Torview, including an early census around 1850. One was an article cut from the town paper detailing the 75th anniversary of the Pinecone Festival.

It was while he was idly flipping through a heavy binder of best farming practices, (and thinking that he should return soon to the office before the judge caught him snooping in the closet), that he discovered a small journal, stuck to the inside of the back cover of the binder by time and condensation. He pulled the journal carefully from the binder, trying not to rip or peel the leather cover in the process.

When he opened the journal, and read the title on the first page, he felt a tingle of apprehension and excitement, not unlike finding a stranger's wallet in a public bathroom. There on the yellowed paper, in faded black ink, though still clear, was written: *The Personal Recollections of Captain*

Able Mundt: An Account of my finding and establishing Torview.

He looked to the open door. No one was in sight, no one could see him. He carefully opened the brittle, yellowed pages. The black ink was faded in places, but most of what he read was still legible.

> *I discovered signs of minerals in the hill today, and mean to claim the land for my own. Will seek the land rights in the name of Mundt, which is mine.*

The unusual stress about the name reminded Frank of the Captain's dubious origins. He wondered if this was the Captain's way of setting the record straight.

He was about to flip to another page, when he heard the sound of movement behind him. Without thinking, he put the journal inside his coat pocket, and, almost in the same motion, reached out to touch one of the books in front of him, as if he were putting something back.

He turned to see Liz in the doorway.

"I think you probably shouldn't stay in there," she said, digging a toe in the carpet. "Uncle could be back any moment."

"Of course," he said, and walked directly out of the room. He watched her out of the corner of his eye, but if Liz had seen him take the book, she didn't indicate it by expression or word.

He took one of the wooden chairs across from the desk, feeling flush with guilt and excitement. *Why on earth had he taken the journal?* He had never stolen anything in his life. *I'm not stealing, just borrowing. I'll bring it back. It is a library of sorts, after all.*

But he knew this for the rationalization it was. *Exhaustion*, he decided; *that and a small measure of retaliation against the Mundts.* But in truth, he just didn't care.

This time, Liz sat across from him in the other hardback chair.

"Mom's not much of a mom," she said, apparently deciding to pick up their conversation where they left off.

He tried to look sympathetic. He had no idea what to say. His thoughts kept wandering to the journal in his pocket.

"Uncle Del wants me to stay here," she said, dropping her eyes and discovering a piece of skin to worry by one of her nails.

"Do you want to live here?" he asked.

"I don't know," she said miserably. "That guy— mom's last—he was definitely a creep." She pulled hard on the skin. "But he wasn't the first."

He felt very uncomfortable now. Elizabeth's face was full of contempt and bitterness. *Where was the judge?*

"Anyway, when we got here, Mom took me to Uncle. They argued all night, mostly about money and me. The next day she was gone. That was about a month ago. Uncle said she wasn't coming back, ever, and that I was to live with him now. Says he's going to make me his ward. Made some papers up for me to sign."

"Why aren't you in school?" he asked, curious despite himself.

She scoffed. "I'm way beyond that place. First week in, I told Uncle it was a no-go. I said I'd be better off home schooling if I wanted a chance for a decent college. He was surprised to hear I wanted to go to college. But he supported me. He's letting me work with him, and is getting me ready for the G.R.E." She started picking her nail again. "I don't know if I do, really. Want to go to college, that is. But I like having the option." She looked out the window. "Can't really see myself staying here long time, you know."

"But you may change your mind," said a voice from the doorway.

Frank turned to find the judge shedding his hat and coat.

"The place will grow on you."

The judge hung the coat and hat on a rack of wall hooks near the entrance door. Frank could now see he was clearly a Mundt. A white patch of hair, a standing tuft the size and shape of a shoehorn and every bit the family trademark, rose from his otherwise bald head at the back.

"Elizabeth," said the judge, taking his seat in the big leather chair. "Would you be so kind and bring us some coffee. Mr. Henning?"

"Coffee would be great," said Frank, thinking he would need it for the confrontation ahead. "If it's no trouble."

"No trouble," answered the judge, apparently speaking for Liz as well.

She stood. "How do you take it?"

"Black is fine," said Frank.

The judge leaned back in his chair as she left to get the coffee. He fiddled with his watch chain for a time, obviously in no hurry to get started. Frank wondered if the whole thing was a ploy.

"We'll wait until we have our coffee," said the judge, as if guessing the direction of Frank's thought. "I find it helps calm my nerves."

The waiting did nothing for Frank's. The journal felt like a lodestone in his pocket. He couldn't meet the judge's eye, fearing he'd give himself a way. To distract himself, he studied the photo on the desk, now visible to from the chair.

The photo was of two college students, taken some time ago, judging by their dated uniforms. They were standing in front of a library bookcase, smiling, each with an arm over the other's shoulder. One was obviously a young Judge Delphus Mundt, already balding but with a full, dark tuft rising like a scrub brush above his pate. The other was small, with curly blonde hair and soft, almost feminine features. His uniform hung loosely on his frame.

Frank nodded to the picture. "Friend of yours?"

The judge looked to the picture, blinked around a memory, then said dismissively, "The past."

Liz brought the coffee in at that point.

The judge thanked her and asked her to wait downstairs. "Close the door, please."

"She's a good girl," he said, when the door was closed. "The mother on the other hand...." He sighed, shook his head, then sipped his coffee.

"It's kind of you to take her in," said Frank.

"But it surprises you." A cool, mirthless smile warped the crooked mouth. "I imagine at this point, you do not have a very good impression of my family, Mr. Henning."

"I've had better welcomes."

The judge nodded, as if conceding a point. "I apologize for my nephews," he said, tapping one long, hoary finger on the desk. "The sap is running thin in that branch of the tree. All of this could have been, should have been, handled better."

"I'm willing to live and let live," said Frank. Then, to make it clear, he added, "In the house I bought. That shouldn't be so hard."

The judge pulled a face. "I'm afraid I'm not about to make it any easier." He toyed with his watch chain again, lost in thought.

"Philo," he said finally, abruptly, "was an idiot. In hindsight, we should have taken the house from him a long time ago. But we are slaves to our tradition here, Mr. Henning, and the oldest direct son inherits the Captain's house, always."

"Always? What if there is no male heir?"

"That's never happened." The judge leaned back in the chair. "Apart from me, we are a very prolific family."

"You never married?" Frank had no problem asking the judge potentially awkward questions. He suspected that this 'summary' was little more than a judicially veiled threat. In fact, he welcomed a faux pas or two. He glanced quickly at the photo, then back to the judge.

The judge didn't answer right away, his eyes temporarily swallowed up in the wrinkles of loose skin around them.

Is he thinking, or angry, or both? It was impossible for Frank to say.

"No, I never married," he said finally. "It was not necessary, as I am from the sister's branch of the family and we are not responsible for the house. I serve of course in other ways."

Frank didn't know what to make of that, but before he could ask a question, the judge carried on.

"But that is neither here or there. My point is, the only reason you have the house is that Philo, the idiot, was in some ways very clever. He managed to hide the extent of his...problem." The crooked, fat lips compressed as far they were able, and the eyes were lost again in the folds of fat. "Until it was too late for us to do anything about it. Of course, he never intended to lose the house. But a gambler's plan of retreat is always more risk, in the vain belief there will be more reward."

Frank was distracted by the fall of snow in the oriel window behind the judge. Small, swirling drifts framed the big chair and the judge. *Like a Rockwell painting*, he thought, *minus the good cheer*. The room was well-heated. That, combined with his sleepless nights, the judge's droning, and picturesque snowfall, set him to yawning.

After the third one, the judge scowled. "Am I boring you, Mr. Henning?"

"Sorry. I haven't been getting enough sleep." He took a quick sip of coffee and sat up straight in his chair. "So, Philo mortgaged the house to the hilt and couldn't get up from under, and he lost it to the bank. Is that about right?"

"If it was just a matter of paying off a mortgage loan or bad debt," answered the judge, slightly mollified, "I assure you we would not be having this conversation. But Philo actually sold the house to the bank, without telling anyone. You are right, he was in dire straits, and for various reasons, believed he could not approach the family for money. In this he was partially correct." The judge's eyes hung fire now. "We would have taken everything from him."

A moment later, he sighed, put his hands together as if in prayer, and looked over the tips of his fingers to Frank, who was trying to stifle another yawn. For just a moment it looked to Frank like the judge would lose his temper. But then, he lowered his hands and waved the matter away.

"But my nephew," he continued, "the idiot, sold the house and, and everything else he owned. I understand you have met our other new resident, Mr. Sol Rodriquez. He, too, profited from my family's misfortune."

Frank left that alone. "What happened to Philo?"

"He left town."

"You can't find him?"

The Judge's eyes grew hard again. "No. But at this point, that's probably for the best."

Frank let that one alone as well, for different reasons. He suspected there was only so far he could push the judge on some subjects. "All right," he said. "But I don't understand why you didn't just buy the house back from the bank?"

The judge shifted uncomfortably in his chair, waved his hands in exasperation. "Because my other nephew, who thinks himself clever but is turning out to be little better than his brother, made a hash of that opportunity as well."

"Emil?" asked Frank.

"Yes, Emil." The bitterness with which the judge said the name caught Frank by surprise. "Yes," continued the judge, noting his expression. "You see, I'm sharing some of my personal secrets with you. I hope in this way to convince you of my sincerity."

He crossed one leg over the other, leaned back in the chair. "Let me share some more, so you understand how you got the house, and why it so important that you give it back."

He measured Frank behind his folded hands again, then lowered them and continued. "Because of that tradition I mentioned earlier, it is difficult for me to involve myself too far in the other's affairs. I foolishly believed Emil was worldly enough to handle the situation. Instead, he seriously under bid the bank's asking price, and when it was naturally refused, he called the bank and behaved quite badly." He shook his head in chagrin, looking to his desk as if reliving the lost opportunity. "The Mundts are not without certain pull in the little town of Torview," he muttered, not looking at Frank. " My nephew was under the mistaken impression that this extended to other places."

He suddenly looked up again, spoke with heat. "Oh, I can understand his frustration. Having to buy back what was in the family for so long is galling, most galling, Mr. Henning. But it could have been done. God knows Emil has the money. It should have been done. All to save a few pennies."

The judge glanced quickly at Frank.

Is he regretting the last statement, thought Frank, *or checking to see I can be bought?*

"Emil left a standing offer," continued the judge eventually and settling down again. "He believed the bank would eventually come around, and he had time. After all, who would want such an old house so far in the hills, and on an unused mine? Greed, Mr. Henning; my nephew's sole motivation in almost all matters."

The judge chewed his lips in bitter reflection. "And what happens? You came along with your more than reasonable offer, and buy the house, regardless of its condition or the actual value of the property it sits on." The judge measured Frank again with those hard, intelligent eyes. "You know of course that the land you bought is considered junk. The mine is long since played out, and you cannot farm it for profit."

Frank shrugged. "That's not why I bought the house."

"Yes," said the judge slowly. "I thought as much." He shifted in his seat again, grew coy. "In fact, the sheriff told me of your real motivations."

He smiled, obviously pleased at finally getting a reaction from Frank. "But we'll return to that later."

He took a sip of coffee, nodded his approval. When he continued again, it was with an air of assurance, as if he now had Frank's number and it was only a matter of details.

"Of course the bank was only too happy to take your bid," he said. "You even had the grace to be professional about it, or at least your agent was. A welcome difference, I am sure, from my nephew's behavior."

He took another slow sip of coffee, put the cup carefully down on the blotter, touched the edge of the desk.

"Now," he said, casually leaning forward. "You might be wondering why I am telling you this feeble account of my family's behavior, instead of getting directly to the solutions."

"I imagine you are trying to make yourself more sympathetic," interrupted Frank. "The hard line approach of Emil and Henrik having obviously failed."

The judge swelled slightly at this, then forced a smile. "You are right. In part, that is my motivation. But I also want you to know just how you came by the property, and how dear it is to us. I appeal first to your good will. You have something that is precious to us and does not really belong to you." The judge waved a hand in the air, as if shooing a fly. "Oh, I know. You insist you bought the property legally. Free and clear, I think is how you put it to the sheriff. But should common decency not move you, then know, the law is a very complicated proposition, Mr. Henning. In all matters, but particularly property rights. I tell you this not as a threat, nor do I mean anything personally against you, but so you can extricate yourself from a situation before it grows too painful and expensive. I assure you *I* know the law. It was a mistake that you were allowed to buy the house in the first place. I will see that it is rectified."

It was snowing heavily outside the window now. Frank felt the weight of his exhaustion like a lead blanket. Almost he touched the journal in his pocket, but in the last moment moved his hand to his chin, as if in thought.

"Your Honor," he said slowly. "I've heard you out. Now let me save us both some time. I intend to stay in that house. There's no appeal to my good will, or money you can offer, or threat you can make..." He shook his head at the judge's start. "You can color it however you like, we both know you have that card in your hand. And you just made a point of showing it."

"I believe you when you say that you know what you are about, never doubt it. But that house has been a dream in my head for over twenty-five years, and now I have it, and I want to see the dream through. And yes you are right it is not what I thought it would be, but it is mine and I'm keeping it. I'd like to hope you can accept that and we can get along, maybe even be friends. But if you can't, then I'll get a lawyer and we'll see just how complicated that law can be."

The judge drew a breath as if to respond, but then checked himself. The silence that followed was only broken by the whirl of a heater kicking in somewhere in the bowels of the building, and the light tap, tap of the heavy wet flakes against the window.

Finally, the judge looked at his watch.

"I promised you time for lunch," he said, his tone and posture now formal, official. "Let me just a cover a few legal details and then we'll call it a day."

He then proceeded to make his legal case. He spoke officiously, but calmly, on Property Zoning Laws, Historical Landmark Oversight Committees, and other erudite technicalities, sighting case histories, precedents, and rulings that Frank neither recognized nor cared about. All in, it was about fifteen minutes, the background of falling snow growing heavier outside the window, and the drone of the judge's voice making it hard for Frank to keep his eyes open.

"Simply put," said the judge finally, "I can see to it that the house status is changed, probably to Historical Landmark status, and you will be forced to accept the township's bid and move out, or reject it and be forced to move out anyway."

Finished with the official argument, the judge leaned back in his chair again, the swivel creaking slightly as he rocked slowly back and forth. He looked perfectly comfortable.

"You could get a lawyer and fight it," he said casually. "I will see to it that the case is fast-tracked. You will lose."

"Here maybe," said Frank, struggling to meet the judge's surety. "They might have a different opinion at the State level."

"You have that kind of money, Mr. Henning?" asked the judge, curling his fat lip. "Well, it doesn't matter. *I* don't think they will have different opinion, and I know them a lot better than you. Besides, the State and Federal courts don't like to involve themselves too much in these matters."

"But it could go on for years," countered Frank.

"Possibly," admitted the Judge. "But are you sure you will be allowed to stay in the house during that time? An injunction of occupancy will be my first order of business."

Frank wasn't sure of anything where the law was concerned, and he wasn't about to try and bluff the judge.

"You can't fight City Hall," quoted the judge with a smile. "It applies equally well here—maybe better."

Frank stood. "If that's all then?"

The judge dropped his smile, looked again at his watch. "Sit, sit, Mr. Henning. I do not want you to leave angry."

Frank remained standing, but stayed. He was tired, tired of the threats and implications, tired of his anxiety, just plain tired.

The judge sighed. "I was hoping to avoid this, Mr. Henning. Truly." He looked to the standing Frank, shook his head. "I am not unsympathetic to your plight. Won't you sit down?" he pleaded. "No? Fine. Then I will be direct.   The sheriff told me of your wife's passing. I may never have married, but I know the loss of love. It is because of that that I am trying to broker an agreement that will cause you the least distress."

"Let me be," said Frank. "That would be the kindest thing you could do for me."

"I'm not certain of that," said the judge, the intelligent eyes dancing now with unexpressed implications. "If Torview is so important to you, then tell me, why don't you simply take Emil up on his offer? I assure you I will personally make sure you come ahead in the deal, and whatever house you build or chose will be much better than the one you are in now. Emil did make you an offer?"

"Of sorts."

"Then let me make it clear..." started the Judge.

"No need. I know you will do anything to get me out of that house, including setting me up in a new place."

"For your benefit as well as our own," argued the judge. "In your present situation I do not believe that house will serve you well. Your loss..."

"Is my loss," interrupted Frank, this time brusquely.

The judge nodded. "So it is. I apologize. Then there is nothing I can say or do at this point to change your mind? You choose a bitter battle over a peaceful solution?"

Frank chuckled. It was all too much. "Judge Mundt, can I go?"

"Very well, Mr. Henning, but remember you had another choice."

* * *

He found Liz sitting alone at an empty desk on the first floor.

"Are you staying?" she asked; "in the house?"

"I think so. For now. And you?"

She shrugged, looking down at the floor. "I think so. I'm glad you are staying. They shouldn't get everything they want."

"Does that mean I actually have a Mundt friend in Torview?"

She looked up and smiled. "I guess. But its Liz, remember?"

Chapter Seven

He finished his walk down Main, picking up another basket from Claire. Maybe in another week he wouldn't need her services. He skipped the chains for the tires, deciding one Mundt encounter a day sufficient. Somehow, Liz didn't count.

The snow stopped by the time he returned to his car. The roads were still clear, though the house lawns and roofing had a white dusting. He drove through town and back to his house, deciding to follow the sheriff's advice and park at the car port.

When he finally reached the top, he found the sheriff waiting for him. For a brief, panicky second he felt the weight of the liberated journal, still in his coat pocket.

He climbed out of the car, shifted the grocery bag over his coat where the journal was, and balanced the basket and pillow in his other arm. The sheriff nodded as he drew near.

Before he could speak, Frank saw the back of another man walking away down the hill. He turned back to the sheriff, a question on his face.

"Your neighbor, Granger," said the sheriff. "Wanted to make sure I told you where his property begins, and yours ends."

"Isn't he on my property now?" asked Frank, trying to sound calm.

The sheriff looked to the retreating figure, as if considering the idea. "Yeah, I guess so." He didn't elaborate, but turned back, calm, unruffled and unhurried, as always. "I wanted to make sure you were all right."

"Well, I met with the judge. I can't say I'm all right, but I'm still here."

The sheriff nodded, looked again to where Granger had retreated.

Frank had a sudden, unwanted vision of the judge looking repeatedly at his watch. He assumed at the time it was all about lunch and control. But now, exhausted and full of conflicting emotions of suspicion and guilt (the journal pressed like a weight against his chest), he wondered.

What was the sheriff doing here? And Granger, his neighbor? Was the meeting with the judge also a means to keep an eye on him, while someone else checked on the house?

"We got a little snow while you were in town," said the sheriff, "so I came up here to check the roads. I often do. Part of my patrol."

Well, that's convenient, thought Frank, his mind working overtime on conspiracy theories.

"I also wanted to give you these." The sheriff nodded to a pile of chains by the gate. "I figured you might not have time to get a set yourself." He picked up the chains and started to Frank's car.

Frank looked for somewhere to put his bags down and help.

"Won't be a minute," said the sheriff, glancing over his shoulder and seeing his struggle. "And quicker if I do it myself. I'll show you how later."

"Thanks." He watched the sheriff work, wrestling with conflicting emotions of gratitude and suspicion.

Finished, the sheriff offered to hold every-thing while Frank opened the gate.

He hesitated, then handed the groceries over, hoping the journal remained hidden, or that he didn't look guilty. The gate open, he quickly took the bag of groceries and pillow back. "This is very decent of you, Sheriff," he said, to hide his anxiety. "And I'm sorry if I don't sound more grateful. I didn't get a lot of sleep last night."

"I imagine the meeting with the judge didn't help matters, either," answered the other, with a knowing wink. "C'mon. I'll give you a ride up. I'd leave your car here, even with the chains."

Frank didn't see how he could refuse.

They put the groceries, basket, and pillow in the sheriff's car and he drove them up to the house. Frank explained he hadn't cleaned the kitchen yet, so they carried the stuff into the dining room.

"Look," said the sheriff, walking back with Frank to the front room. "I know that bothered you, seeing Granger. And I don't want to add to your anxiety, but I think it a good idea to stay close at home until you know your property line. Granger is not as bad as Henrik, but he is particular about his place. He's a little jumpy right now, and I wouldn't be surprised if he took a pot shot at you if you got on his land, or even near it." The sheriff sighed around a frown at this last part.

"Fair warning. I assume the reverse is true?"

"Come again?" asked the sheriff.

"I mean," he said, feeling his gourd rise, "if Granger strays near *my* house I can take a shot at him."

The sheriff pushed his hat back, cocked his head, and gave him a curious look. "You got that gun?"

"No," he said stubbornly.

After a moment, both men chuckled.

"Probably for the best," said the sheriff.

"I suppose you're right. I couldn't hit the broad side of a barn anyway."

The sheriff pushed his hat back down and turned to leave. He stopped, hand on the handle, and said over his shoulder. "Oh, and I put some extra wood on the pile by the house. Might get a little cold tonight."

He felt his suspicions melt to a small, warm lump in his throat. "Let me give you some money for the wood."

The sheriff shook his head. "It's just a couple of logs I had in the back of the trunk."

"About earlier..."

"Forget it," said the sheriff. "You've got some cause to be a little irritated just now."

"Yeah, but you seem to be one of the few people on my side. I don't want you to think I'm ungrateful."

The sheriff grimaced slightly, turned from the door to look him in the eye. "Mr. Henning…"

"Frank."

"Frank, I'm not really on your side. I'm still hoping you'll change your mind and quit this place, and soon. I just don't see any end in being difficult in the meantime."

"You want something to drink?" he asked, trying to hide his disappointment. "I have water, coffee, and milk? I even picked up some beer in town if it's not too early."

"Next time," said the sheriff. "I have to get going. Keep a fire tonight."

He watched him leave from the doorway, thinking, *if I stay here, I'll sell the sedan and get a SUV like the sheriff's.*

If I stay? Where had that come from?

The sheriff had been humble; the fresh wood nearly replaced all that he had burned before. He refilled his supplies in the dining and bed rooms, then put the rest of the groceries away downstairs.

Finally, he climbed back up the steps, tossed the pillow on his bed and, with another pang of guilt, pulled the journal out of his coat.

A bedside table, he thought, would come in handy. He looked to his personal boxes. One held some paperbacks he brought from home, mostly his wife's. He took the books out, turned the box upside down and made a temporary table. He set the journal on it, lined the other books against the wall. He stood back, looking at his work. It would do for now.

There was a chill in the room, the embers of his earlier fire long since grown cold. He made another fire, took off his coat and shoes, and sat on the bed. He decided to skip lunch, and crawled into the sleeping bag.

* * *

He woke hours later, the sun going down outside the curtained window like a spilled mustard jar. He was grubby and disheveled and hungry. But he was better for the rest.

He shuffled downstairs in his socks, wolfed down a sandwich and some milk, and then climbed back upstairs to bed.

His woodstove was still breathing, though it was down to its last embers. He added another split log, poked around the embers with a stick of kindling until the log caught, and then tossed in the kindling after it. He squatted by the open grill, listened to the crackling pop of the wood. It was a welcome change from the otherwise pregnant silence of the house. The smell of urine and stale air was gone now, too. Well, mostly.

He stood, stretched, used the bathroom, including a quick cold rinse over the sink, and put a pot of water and on the stove. He felt almost human again.

Standing by the window, he moved the curtain to get a better look outside. More snow had fallen while he slept. The tree tops and ground were now covered in a thin white blanket, bringing out the dark colors of exposed bark and the occasional bare rock. He watched the last rays of sun fall along the horizon, coloring the sky in soft reds and purples, blurring the hill line into dark shades of green.

Something moved in between the trees, heading toward the house. An animal of some kind, judging from its low position and movement.

As it drew closer he could see it was a dog. It moved confidently through the front yard at first, but soon stopped to test the air, listen. It was big. He guessed part Labrador, part something else, maybe German shepherd. It lifted its head and looked up to the window. He lifted a hand slowly, not sure the dog could even see him. With a sudden start, the dog turned and ran back down the path, disappearing into the thick of the trees.

He dropped the curtain, used his now hot water to wash his face and shoulders in the bathroom sink, climbed into a clean pair of underwear and t-shirt, jeans, and moccasins, and went downstairs for a beer.

The beer, cold at room temperature, had an almost immediate effect. He made an inspired decision to have another with a hot bath before bed.

But for that he would need more wood. He put on his coat and work gloves and went for the wood before it grew too dark or he grew too tired.

As he collected the wood from the fresh pile, he saw the gold painted lock sticking from the snow on the cellar door. He had the key on his chain, which was in his coat pocket. He could take a quick look; he didn't actually have to go down the cellar. *But why look for more trouble?* He loaded up on more wood, and headed back to the house.

He turned the corner, and almost dropped the wood. The dog was standing in the middle of the yard. It was even bigger up close, with heavy tangled black fur, and just a touch of light brown under the heavy throat. Neither moved for a moment, each watching the other carefully.

"Hello," he said.

The dog didn't move. *If he rushes me,* thought Frank, *I could toss the wood at it, try for the door in the confusion.*

But a moment later the dog lowered its massive head and took a few hesitant steps to the right and toward the tree line. It looked back at Frank, waiting. He tried to recall everything he'd seen or heard about dealing with strange animals. It was a short list.

Don't show fear.

The dog took a few more tentative steps in direction of the trees, its tail low and eyes watching him the whole while. It stopped just outside the tree line, made a sound deep in its throat, not so much growl as whine.

Frank took a slow step toward the door, then another. Soon he was at the front and, watching the dog out of the corner of his eye, carefully, slowly opening the door. Inside, he looked back.

The dog was watching him again, its ears forward and head raised, the big tail wagging slowly from side to side. Maybe it was his exhaustion, or the beer, or his own sense of loneliness talking, but Frank thought the dog looked expectant, almost eager.

He put the wood on the floor, and pushed the door open wider. He then walked back to the dining room, listening all the while for sounds behind him. He grabbed a piece of chicken from the basket and returned to the front.

The dog was still there, maybe a few steps closer to the door. Frank tossed the chicken at its feet, watched it disappear in quick, bone cracking snaps. Finished, the dog looked up for more, took a few steps in Frank's direction.

Frank turned, the door still open. He repeated the process with another small piece of chicken which was engulfed almost before it hit the ground. Now the dog was just outside the door, and he could see it was clearly malnourished, the bones poking up from under the heavy fur despite its size.

He pulled another piece of chicken, but this time set it on top of the steps, just in front of the door. He retreated a few steps inside the house and dropped another, bigger piece.

The dog climbed the steps slowly, head and tail down, snapped up the first piece, chewed it down. It then looked to Frank and the other piece inside, bobbed its head up and then down with indecision.

Frank took another step back, gestured to the meat. "It's all right," he said quietly. "I'm getting tired of chicken anyway."

The dog made a small, muffled bark and leapt for the chicken, pulling it back outside the door to eat.

He left the front door open and walked back to the dining room, set about making his own dinner and a fire. After a time, the dog stepped through, head almost near the floor.

Frank slowly took a chair, giving the dog plenty of space.

"Well," he said, tossing the last of the chicken and some bread to the dog. "I'm guessing you ran from home. Are you Granger's, by chance?"

The dog didn't react to the name, but then he didn't expect it to. He recalled the Gary Larson cartoon, about what we say, and what dogs actually hear, and chuckled. The dog lifted its head curiously at the sound, then went back to the chicken.

They ate in silence for a time, the dog finishing first but apparently in no hurry to leave. It did sit close to the open wicket door, however.

He popped another beer. "I'm guessing you're thirsty too." He looked to the wicket door. "Now, don't panic. I'm just getting you something to drink."

The dog rolled its pointed ears forward, breathing heavily, and sprawled out on the floor. Frank stood slowly— and so did the dog. He moved to the wicket door, and the dog preceded him. There was nothing menacing or frightened in the dog's demeanor now, but it managed to keep its distance.

It stood in the foyer, glancing occasionally to the open front door as Frank went to the kitchen in search of a bowl and some water. He carried a cereal bowl of water back to the dining room, the dog watching him hungrily now, and set it next to the fireplace, away from the wicket door.

When he back, the dog shuffled forward, investigated the bowl briefly, then started to lap up the water.

"You're welcome to stay," said Frank. "To tell the truth, I wouldn't mind some company." He looked to the open wicket door. "I'm not sure how this going to work, though. I imagine you're going to want outside soon, but I can't keep these doors open all night."

He looked to the fireplace. "It's going to get cold tonight, according to the sheriff. Here's what you get if you stay." He built up the fire. *I guess I am lonely*, he thought, *trying to court a dog with a fire.*

The dog, obviously satiated, lay on the ground and watched him, its long black tongue lolled out to one side.

Finished with the fire, Frank stood up, looked down at the dog now resting its head comfortably on its paws. "You look like you've been here before. I bet of those trespassing teenagers the sheriff spoke of let you in and feed you from time to time."

He sat down and sipped his beer, watching the dog watching him, taking pleasure in the company and warmth of the fire.

He finished the beer with a sigh and stood up again, the dog lifting its head to watch him.

"Okay, decision time. Here's what I suggest. I'm going to clean some dishes in the kitchen. While I'm doing that, you make up your mind about staying. I'll leave the front door open until I'm finished. Then it gets shut. Okay?"

The dog barked softly, wagged its tail on the floor, and looked expectantly to the basket on the table.

"Sorry, pal. Diner's closed."

He walked to the kitchen, listening for sounds of the dog behind him. He heard the click of hard nails against the wood floor, then nothing. He turned. Outside the open front door, night had fallen. The house was already growing colder, and the icy cold draft from the open door was not helping matters. He stood a moment in the doorway, looking around in the dark yard for a time. The dog was nowhere to be found. He closed the door and locked it.

He finished the dishes in the kitchen, then took them back to the suddenly very lonely dining room to dry. He checked the fireplace grille, then closed everything up behind him. He used a candle to negotiate the shadowy foyer and stairwell. He hesitated only once, on the first step on the stairs, listening for a scratch at the front door, knowing it wouldn't come, but hoping just the same.

* * *

He used a lantern for light, setting it on the bedroom floor and adding wall hooks to his list of upcoming purchases. He lit another lantern in the bathroom to chase away some of the gloom. He then stuffed as many logs as he could in the woodstove, which still had a little fire going. Finally, he raced back downstairs in his stocking feet to grab the forgotten beers for his promised reward.

He put his long underwear on the bed. *Have to do laundry soon*, he reminded himself. He then made his bath, like the night before, one hot bucket of water a time.

When it was ready, he shed his clothes. He put the beers on the floor by the tub, set the lantern on the closed lid of the toilet to get it as close to the bath as possible. Then he went back for the journal.

Putting the journal carefully on the floor beside the tub, he eased into the hot water, opened a beer, and soaked for a time, letting the hot water relax his limbs. He thought for a time of the dog. Tara would have laughed to see him, talking as if it could understand him.

Tara. He had not said her name, not even to himself in so long; certainly not since the funeral.

He took a long shaky breath, and finished his first beer in one long swallow. He crushed the can down the middle and put it down by the others. Then he washed his face with the hot soapy water until the reaction passed. And then, almost gratefully, he reached for the journal.

He read to the soft hiss of the lantern, and the faint echo of a winter wind outside the walls. He held the book well above the steamy water, and with both hands when he didn't sip his beer. In this way he left his own fragile reality and willed himself into the Captain's world, a necessary, and at first welcome distraction.

The first few pages were little more than simple one line entries with no dates or even a signature.

> *Schroeder tells me the name Mundt means guardian. It is fitting.*
> *Arrived at the site. Believe things will prove out. Pretty country, though lonely and difficult to navigate.*
> *Schroeder is proving to be valuable in making camp, and his knowledge of the area is sound. But I cannot abide his habits or the way he looks at Sister. Thankfully, this is open country, and there is plenty of room for all. We sleep well apart.*

Frank noticed a few of the pages were torn out at this point. When it picked up again, Schroeder had apparently disappeared, never to be mentioned again.

> *There is wealth in the hills, one in particular. I leave tomorrow to secure it for my own.*

The next few pages were little more than blatant attempts to authenticate the Mundt name as the Captain's own, including sketchy references to 'the old country' as his birthplace. Indeed, a more recent note, penned and signed by some official in the State registry, marked it as *Item 1 v. Mundt*.

But if the journal were offered as some kind of proof of identity, it left a lot to be desired. For one thing, Mundt offered no actual family history, nor did he indicate what part of "the old country" he was from. For another, it was clear that some of the language was contrived, with blatant and purposeless German articles thrown in for effect. Some of the latter were scratched out and corrected as if someone told the Captain he used the wrong form.

There followed another set of torn out pages before the journal picked up again. Frank wondered briefly what the removed sections entailed, and who removed them.

Now the Captain settled into longer and more intimate reflections, the language more consistent and without obvious editing. The journal became less a document of record, and more of a true diary.

Frank sat in his cooling tub of water and learned how the Captain secured the rights to the hill, then borrowed money to start mining. The mine did prove profitable, offering copper and smaller pockets of other valuable minerals. The Captain guarded his new found source of wealth jealously, but it was clear that 'the Hill,' as he called it, was more to him than just a source of revenue.

> *I live now most often in the mine. I find a certain peace in the depths under the Hill that oddly fits my nature. I'm tired of the open world, and*

particularly the small minds and small judgments of men who inhabit it. I want to find a quiet place of my own, away from busy eyes and the noise of inanity. In this capacity, the mine is ideal. In fact, it seems almost made for me. I hardly need to excavate, as natural shafts and fissures allow me to descend to great depths with little effort. I gladly spend my time below, securing the ore, and searching out the many secrets of the natural shafts. As Sister seems content to live on top, I often do so, sometimes for days on end. Our reunions are happy times. But we have rigged a bell rope, so she can call me up if she needs me.

There appeared to be another jump in time on the next page, but again the Captain's failure to mark the date made it difficult to be sure just how long it was between entries.

The operation is too large for me to run alone now. As I have no family in the country, I must secure professional men. I will choose them carefully, and turn them over frequently should I find them unfit.

Then, a little further down:

I have created a band of loyal men, bonded to me both financially, and in a manner of a Captain to his crew. I list them...

But the list was gone now, torn out.

When the journal picked up again, the Captain was now a powerful as well as wealthy figure in the small burgeoning community around his "Hill." He had built a house over the mine, and married. He did not record his new wife's name, but said this about her.

Some say she is fair, but this matters little to me. It is enough that she comes from good stock, with wide birthing hips and a strong constitution. I intend to have many children.

Though it was at Sister's encouragement I made the marriage, I suspect that she is not completely happy at my choice, or the time I must spend with my new spouse. I must see her to her own needs soon.

Apparently, the Captain was wrong about his new wife's constitution. She died giving birth to their first child, Helmut, who followed his mother to the grave in his six month.

The Captain wasted little time remarrying (something he did more than once, though it was difficult to determine when and how often, as there were little more notice than "Sister's" approval). This time his luck was better, or the girl of stronger constitution, because he soon began listing his progeny.

There followed a number of pages that detailed the births by name and gender. Judging by the sheer number of entries the Captain accomplished his goal, siring at first at least fourteen children on his own, nine of which lived, two of which were girls. The list was later enhanced by at two dozen grandsons.

It was clear the Captain preferred, or at least was more interested in the male offspring. Not only did he not record female grandchildren, he barely noted the birth of his own daughters. The males, however, had a series of running short notes by their names, sometimes running to half a page (if they pleased the Captain in some way, and they lived long enough). The notes recorded odd details regarding their health and dispositions to the mine.

Theodore. Small at birth.

Shows early promise of intelligence.

Too meek; wails incessantly every time I take him down the shaft.

Married him off to town girl, daughter of one of my former men.

Nina. Girl.
Arranged marriage with foreman Bennington when she came of age.

Fredrick. Large at birth, good lungs.
Loyal, but slow.
Will accompany me down the mine at times, but prefers to remain above.
Married to cousin late in life.

Frank looked, but found no mention of the sister's marriage. He wondered what the Captain meant by "cousin."

Han. Born deformed.
Has taken to accompanying me to the mine. His deformity does not prevent his climbing through the fissures and caves, which he does very well. I have great hopes!
Han fell yesterday on the sluice. I buried him by myself in one of his favorite hiding places down below.
Had new fencing put around the sluice.

With Sister's approval I have married again.
Procured from the orphanage in another town when she came of age. We hope her youth will prove out.

Thaddeus.
Sister is pleased, as am I. There is something about the boy's pallor that suggests potential. I took him down to the deeps just from his mother's womb, wrapped against the cold. He made no complaint.
The mother died at birth. Sister said it is a blessing and will see to the boy herself.

Frank skipped through the rest of the offspring listings, and turned to the next long entry on the mine.

The mine is tapped out. It is no matter as it has made me a relatively rich man. In fact, I am happy that there is no need to keep the mining crew around. I have dismissed all but a few of the most loyal, potential spouses for my children and necessary craftsman for the next project.

With my money, I secured most of the land around the mine and mean to establish a town below my Hill, made up of my family and those who understand our ways, thus securing a space for me and the outside world. Sister will, of course, continue to live on the Hill as long as she wishes.

Each son will be provided for in proportion to my estimation of his worth, with one being designated the heir to the Hill and my fortune. I do not intend to be bound by tradition in this matter. In fact, at this time I am leaning to Fredrick over Theodore, though neither in truth is my equal.

This last fact is a telling blow to me. Somehow my essence is diluted in the mingling of blood and humors with my wives. I have no confidence that Theodore can face the challenges ahead, if we are to remain independent and strong. Fredrick, though strong enough, lacks the intelligence. The other boys are too young yet to know what will come of them.

How I wish my Han had lived! Maybe one of the later issues will take after him and emerge as my natural heir.

I take some consolation in the fact that there is Thaddeus. But for him I have chosen another path.

At this point Frank felt a crick in his neck, the water in the tub having grown tepid and the night air cooling the chipped enamel under his head and shoulders. He set the journal carefully on the sink, and climbed from the tub, wobbling a little from the long soak and beer. He dried off, took the journal with him to the bedroom, and climbed into his long underwear and moccasins.

It was snowing heavily outside the window. He held the curtain back and watched the rush of racing white flakes strike the window in futile, temporary dashes that saw them disappear a moment later against the pane. He could just make out the gate...

He almost dropped the curtain, then felt it bind in his tightening hand. There, standing by the gate, was a man looking back up the house.

He was not the sheriff, though he was tall. It looked at first like he was wearing a loose scarf, but it might be a beard.

Granger has a beard, he thought. *But so does Henrik.*

Either way, what were they doing down there? Could they see him? Was he framed in the light of the window? He remembered suddenly that his car was still at the bottom of the incline, out of sight. Was the man a lookout while someone had at his car? And to do what?

The figure did not move, but continued to look up. Frank was caught between emotions, wanting to brazenly meet the man's gaze, show his unconcern, or better yet, rush outside and confront him. But another part of him wanted to drop the curtain and retreat to the safety of the shadows. Before he could do either, the man turned slowly and headed back down the hill, disappearing in the snowfall.

Should he go out and make sure he was gone? Should he call out? Should he go check on his car? And what good would it do? And what would he do if the man were still there?

He stood there for five minutes searching through the broken curtain of falling snow, his eyes and head starting to ache from the effort. Finally, he let the curtain drop and returned to sit back on his bed.

As he did so he heard the distant moan from below, similar but different to the strange cries he'd heard before. Tonight they were full of hunger, pain, and anger.

Drafts in the walls, he told himself.

And a man out on a midnight walk; maybe Granger, maybe looking for his dog.

The reasonable explanations tripped through his mind like mantras. But somehow they were little comfort. He spent another sleepless night staring up at the ceiling, listening to the occasional moans, expecting any moment to hear the creak of his front door or the flooring.

Chapter Eight

He woke late in the morning, not remembering when he fell asleep, but it couldn't be more than a few hours ago. The house was still again, the crack and pop of his woodstove fire long reduced to silent embers. He got up, went to the window, hesitated a moment, then pushed back the curtain.

Overnight, the world outside his window had shed its last remnants of fall and was now fully clothed in winter. Everything from the pines to the grass to the standing rocks was now covered in a thick layer of sparkling white powder. His windows were frosted around the edges, adding to the illusion of being inside a living snow globe. He watched his breath fogged the glass, and numbly rubbed his hand across the surface to clear it again.

The stove had kept the room reasonably warm and comfortable for most of the night. Only now was a chill starting to creep through his moccasins and underwear. He tossed the last of his wood in the stove, dressed, and went downstairs.

He found the front door closed and locked, a muted comfort to the hangover of his last night worries. He opened the door to a bracing cold draught, saw the pristine snow piles on his front lawn were untouched by human prints. There was not a sound to be heard now, not even his grumpy Blue jay neighbor.

The snow was a good four inches deep. He walked to the gate, which remained locked. He climbed it, not bothering with the keys, and, carefully avoiding where he saw the man the night before, went to the edge of the of the gravel turnabout.

There was his car, seemingly untouched but for a blanket of crusted snow along its top. He turned around and explored the area where the man had stood. He thought the small indentations by the gate might indicate footprints, but the snow fall had covered any tracks.

He climbed back over the gate and followed his own footprints home. The fact that his were the only footprints around made him feel slightly better. It started to snow again.

When he got to the front door, the dog was waiting for him.

He smiled. "Come for another free meal?" He opened the front door and waited. The dog watched him but made no move to go inside.

"Nope. I'm done doing room service."

He stepped in, leaving the door open. The dog snorted, then followed him in.

* * *

Later, sitting at the dining table, sipping coffee from the thermos and watching the dog doze by the fire, he took stock.

"Here's how I see it," he said, sitting forward and looking to the dog, who, now fed, merely rolled a big brown eye briefly in his direction before returning to its contemplation of the fire.

"I'm working on three nights of no real sleep," he continued, grateful for the audience, however jaded. "Naps and morning lays-ins notwithstanding. This is my fault. Yes, there is an element in town that has made threats and would like to see me go, but it is my overactive imagination that's my true enemy. You see where I am going?"

The fire popped, drawing a wary glance from the dog.

"However much this has benefited me in other ways..." Here he paused, a brief, painful image of Tara in the hospital bed passing like a cut across his eyes, followed by another, more complicated memory of her ironic, muted smiles.

"I can't go on this way," he said, staring at the fire.

He took a deep breath, pointed with his cup to the dog. "This is where you can help."

The dog, seeing the movement, turned in his direction, his big eyes rising and falling in expectation, moving from Frank's hand to the basket on the table.

"For my part, I offer free room and board. As you are obviously house-broken," (demonstrated shortly after the meal) "you have free reign to the house, short of the bed, which is mine. I'm afraid at this point that's non-negotiable, as one of us is in serious need of a bath."

The dog continued to stare expectantly. Frank thought of Tara again, wondering if she'd appreciate the irony of his talking to the dog.

"I won't have you sign anything. But I hope you'll agree to terms."

In the silence that followed, the dog sat up a little higher, eyes darting again from the basket to Frank. It shuffled a little in his direction, barked softly.

"I'll take that as a yes."

He stood up. The dog followed suit. Almost Frank reached out a hand to pet it, but at the last moment decided against it.

"I'm skipping a trip to town today. That may mean getting in trouble with Claire. She's your source of chicken by the way, so there's some risk for you too. But I just can't see me driving that road, chains or no chains."

The dog wagged its tail, stepped in the direction of the open wicket door.

"Now as for today, I intend to clean the kitchen, particularly those meat lockers. I think it is very important to make an effort, don't you? This house needs to become a home if I stand any chance of outlasting the judge and his nephews. You are welcome to help."

The dog barked again, then sprawled out in front of the fire.

He took that as a no.

Despite the dog, his resolve died almost the moment he stepped into the kitchen. The weak light from the windows barely penetrated the gloom, and any romantic sense the frost along the sills offered was soon lost to the damp, smelly cold stink of the close air.

He half-heartedly opened the first foul locker, thinking to conquer the tough parts first and then finish with the rest. The heavy stench of stale air hit like a bout of nausea. He closed the locker again quickly.

I could boil some water, soap it down...

No. He couldn't do it. It wasn't just that he was overwhelmed with the task. He simply couldn't see putting anything in the locker that he would eat afterward, ever; no matter how clean he made it.

For a moment the futility of his situation sat like a bucket of ice in his belly, and he was close to just giving up, walking away. But the thought of Emil's smug face made him rally, and he had another thought. He could toss the lockers. Replace them with new, more modern models. Why did he have to keep them to make his stand? He had enough money to refurnish the house from top to bottom if he wanted. Hell, he could even make improvements.

He visualized a team of carpenters and home improvement experts swarming over the red house. The thought of what that would do to Emil's expression made his heart swell to the point he wanted to cry. His emotional reactions were swinging to extremes, without rhyme or reason.

"I'm tired," he said aloud, recognizing in the same instant that he was now officially talking to himself. The dog was still in the other room.

He looked to the dirty stove, and then the floor which badly needed sweeping, and felt again a wave of despair.

But he couldn't just go back to bed or sit in front of the fire. He spoke the truth earlier, however flippant; he needed to make an effort.

He picked up the broom and started in on the floor. Then made a bucket of hot water and floor cleaner and mopped or scrubbed the entire kitchen surface, including the shelves and the top of the lockers. Then he made another bucket and scrubbed the stove and cutting board. Finally, he poured what was left of his undiluted cleaner inside both lockers, quickly shutting them again afterward.

When he was finished he looked around, exhausted but with another exaggerated emotion, this time of satisfaction and renewed determination.

The smell of rot was almost gone now, masked by the pine scent of the detergent. The clutter of garbage and years of grime had been removed, exposing stained and worn but now relatively clean surfaces. Better Homes and Garden it was not, but it was a start, and he could walk in tomorrow morning and not be revolted by the thought of making breakfast here.

The dog had come to check on him from time to time, but generally left him alone. When he finished, the dog made a quick patrol of the kitchen, snorting at the heavy scent of liquid detergent coming out of the lockers and sniffing long and curiously at the back trapdoor.

Frank had ignored that chore. He didn't see any point in poring soap down it either.

The dog barked once at the trap, then walked away to stand by Frank

Despite the pine scent in the air, Frank knew he needed a bath, almost as much as the dog. He considered his new roommate curiously, wondering if he had the reserves to tackle that project.

He grabbed the big industrial bucket and made some more warm water, poured a little soap in, and brought the slopping bucket to the dining room fire. He was happy to see the dog followed him.

He tapped the bucket with a hand. "How about it? Who's first?"

The dog, standing in front of the fire, refused to look at Frank or his bucket.

Frank sighed, stripped and then stepped in the bucket. He soaked his head and neck, then squatted to rub and rinse his back, front, and undersides. Water was now everywhere on the dining room floor, but he had a plan for that.

He quickly toweled off in front of the fire and looked around with a hopeful expression. But the dog was long since gone.

He went upstairs, where he found the dog, put on a clean shirt and a sweater. Then it was back downstairs, first to the kitchen to grab the mop, and then to the dining room, where the dog (who had followed him cautiously) stopped and watched him carefully from the wicket door, its eye on the big bucket of soapy water.

"You get a pass for now," said Frank to the dog, and started mopping the floor with the water from the bucket. When he was done the metal tub was filthy, but the dining room floor looked almost passable.

And with that, Frank finally and truly felt like he could stop.

A little effort like this every day, he reasoned, leaning heavily against the mop handle, *plus some small investment in furniture and other modern amenities, and I'll soon have myself a livable home.*

But he did not look at the blistered wall as he thought this. He set his mop and bucket against the wall for the next round tomorrow.

Maybe he could read a little more on the Captain before lunch and a nap.

* * *

But the Captain proved difficult reading at first. Tired, physically and emotionally, he couldn't concentrate on the words. After a time, he gave it up and put the book aside.

The dog, which remained nameless, was lying in front of the bed stove, head on his paws. Occasionally it snorted on the wood floor, bored or content it was impossible to tell.

Frank lay against the headboard, staring at the curtained window, picking over his problems like a man with a scab.

"I can't make the sheriff out," he said. "I want to like him—I do like him—but is this Gary Cooper act for real, or just a ploy?"

He looked to the dog, but found no answers in that direction.

"It occurs to me those chains might have been a clever excuse. Maybe he carries them around in his trunk. Maybe he saw me coming, had his friend, Mr. Granger, scoot and pulled the chains out to distract me."

The dog sighed, rolled a filmy black eye in his direction, and then turned back to the floor.

Okay," said Frank, as if agreeing to a point. "He's a complicated read, and maybe I'm being unfair. The judge is another complicated man, though his position was clear enough."

He felt fresh flush of indignation as he remembered the judge's heavy-handed legal threats. *That someone in this day and age had to put up with small town politics, could literally be run out of his home.* It galled him to no end.

Yet he suspected the judge, like the sheriff, bore him no personal animosity. The same could not be said of the Mundt brothers. However much Emil masked his intentions, Frank could not forget the raw hatred in his eyes their last meeting. And Henrik.... *Henrik was the kind of guy who would stand by a gate and stare up at fellow's bedroom in the dark of night.*

He spent some time staring at the ceiling, rehearsing words and steps he should have taken, would take, to stand up to the injustice of the Mundts. He would get a lawyer, and a gun. Let Granger or Henrik walk across his property one more time and see who took a pot shot at who. Didn't Tara have a distant cousin in the F.B.I.? He imagined the scene in the judge's chambers, curious as to who was standing by Frank, and Frank calmly introducing Agent Such-n-Such, friend of the family, who's got some questions regarding blah, blah, blah...

But the fantasy of confrontation soon faded, and he was left with nothing but a cold room and his ever-increasing doubt. Who was he kidding? What the hell was he doing here? Everybody was telling him to leave, or at least move to another location. He had no doubt that they would even make it easy for him. Why was it so important that he stay in this house? He didn't even really like the house to tell the truth. It was damp and cold and kept him up at night with strange noises. He was a city boy, for Christ's sake. The nearest he got to this life before was a weekend in the Poconos with Tara, and that had a hot tub on the front porch. And now that he thought about it, Tara didn't have a cousin in the F.B.I. Why was he being so obstinate?

He looked to the dog, apparently asleep. Would that he could so easily drop his cares. But his mind raced again, jumping from one emotionally-charged image to the next, like bits of bacon popping on a hot pan: the judge's measuring eyes; the sheriff's maddening passivity; and Henrik's tobacco-stained teeth beneath a crooked mouth...

"Stop it," he said aloud, causing the dog to raise his head.

"Sorry," he mumbled. He picked up the journal, for lack of something better to do. "Go back to sleep," he told the dog. "You've got the late watch tonight. I plan to be dead to everything." The words were hardly out of his mouth when a chill of superstition made him clarify, "I mean asleep of course."

He opened the journal and found the place where he'd left off. The Captain kept his habit of not dating the entries, and the pages were too brittle to dog-ear, so Frank used a piece of napkin to keep his place.

It came slow, but eventually it came:

***

After shutting down the mine, securing much of the surrounding property, and establishing the town of Torview, the Captain turned his attention back to domestic matters. Specifically he began making changes to the house and its residence. The upstairs were now the adult bedrooms, and the mine was now officially closed off by a new curtain wall.

The curtain wall was described in detail and it became clear that this was not at first the ugly blistered plaster fortification that now spanned the back end of the dining area. Instead, an elegant screen of scrolled pine and woodwork cut off the open mine, but with doors on either end for continued access. There were certainly no doors in the ugly plaster wall.

Nor were these the only changes the Captain made.

> *I have completed my refinement of the house, and in doing so reached its final destiny. What started off as a simple work shack is now a true extension of the Hill and my personality. One merges into the next, like a nail in a finger. And like its subterranean host, the house has its secrets and purposeful design.*

What those secrets were the Captain did not say. He was, however, more forthcoming on the matter of *purposeful design*, including his stance on new amenities. There would be none. No electricity, no lighting, not even a boiler. The severe conditions this created for himself and his family were *"in keeping with my general philosophy and aesthetic disposition and, will be a fitting and necessary heirloom for future generations."*

So important was this Spartan existence that the Captain made it a condition of the house's inheritance:

> *No heir in name or possession shall alter my house or its design in any form, save small repairs to the original structure. It is my will that the house stand in perpetuity as it is now, and should any of my kin who inherit it try to change it then the others should immediately remove this person from the house, and all their claims to it are null and void, including any monetary compensation they should feel entitled to. This is only proper, as the heir is a privileged keeper of my name and legacy, a legacy*

*that is embodied in my house on the Hill. To change
one corner of that house is to change the very
foundation of the name I give you.*

That the Captain's decree remained inviolable over
the years, at least as far as the Mundts were concerned, was
evident by the house's still austere condition.

It wasn't hard for Frank to see why Philo or Claire
had preferred to live in town—or why Philo might be
willing to part without the others knowing, particularly as
he would lose not only the house, but any money he could
garner from its sale.

Frank did not believe himself bound to the
Captain's edict. Nothing about the condition had come up in
the point of sale, and he was pretty sure the judge
would have mentioned it already if he could enforce it. Was
this the real motivation behind the Mundt anger? Were
they afraid Frank would make changes to the Captain's
precious legacy, a legacy that every Mundt who inherited
the house had apparently accepted and maintained
through the generations?

He thought about his plan to remove the meat
lockers, and about having hot water from a tap, about
central air, and a new, better back wall over the mine. It
would make the Captain roll over in his grave, and probably
drive the Mundts to distraction.

*But I won't come to love this grim monument to the
Captain as is, no matter how long I stay here.*

No, if change was the big worry for the Mundts, they
were right to fear it from Frank. The meat lockers would
be the first thing to go, but a generator and boiler would
soon follow. And to hell with Henrik, Emil, and the judge.

But it was strange, just the same, he thought a
moment later, *that they should remain faithful to such an
obscure and obviously personal obsession all these years.*

He turned back to the journal.

* * *

Apparently the right hand wing with the bed stands was once the former workers' quarters. With the close of the mine, the Captain converted this to a children's room. He insisted that all his progeny, including his grandchildren, spend a period of their youth in the house, so that he could "*measure their potential.*"

The children were given a rigorously maintained schedule, overseen by Sister and the Captain. One of the more disturbing things about this schedule, was the time required to be in the wing, and sometimes the mine itself.

The children were tested for their "*suitability to the enlightening darkness,*" going sometimes days without being let out of the wing. Their meals were brought to them, along with their washing, and most of the day was spent in "*lessons.*" That the children did not take to this confinement well, was a frustration for the Captain:

> *They seem to have no understanding of the purpose to which we do this. I can hardly believe that any of them are from my loins or blood, they act so contrary to my nature.*

There followed a number of bitter short listings, boys found to be "*unsuitable,*" "*recalcitrant,*" or simply, "*failures.*" Frank cross-referenced the names with the original offspring lists, but many were appearing for the first time. Where did they come from? Were they more "cousins," or children from town? The Captain didn't say.

The Captain took to spending more and more time down in the mine with individual children who showed "*early promise.*" There he could oversee their education personally. But he worried that the others were being spoiled in his absence.

> "*Malcontents will naturally infect the others while I am away, including potential heirs. I am daily more disappointed with the lot. They whine and complain endlessly when I return. I'm at my wits end.*"

There followed another section of torn pages. Then,

Again, Sister has come to my aid.

Seeing the problem more clearly than I, she personally took a hand in the matter. It is a credit to her that she procured many of the tools before we even saw the need. She is possessed of endless talents and wisdom.

Sister assures me that these measures are commonly used in official medical houses to great effect. To insure that there are no complications, I have installed and tested many of the elements personally. We begin the practice tomorrow.

I am pleased to record we have seen a notable drop in willfulness over the last week. The boys are much more subdued and I feel—and Sister feels— this can only help us in our quest.

What would I do without Sister? I confess that I was losing hope. But daily she carries on the struggle without showing complaint or frustration—and with results! She has a keen knack for bringing out the best in even the most unlikely candidate. Certainly she has made the wing's atmosphere more conducive to our needs.

There was another page ripped from the journal at this point.

The scion has arrived! Thaddeus is quite suitable. When I think that we almost missed it...!

The father, Fredrick, called him a freak, wanted, I believe, to dispose of him. Even I did not see his full potential all those years ago.

But Sister saw the markings for what they were, and took the boy under her own care. She has kept his potential a secret, even from me, lest it should prove another bitter disappointment. It was no easy task, alone with the boy, keeping him isolated from the others. I confess I was upset at first that she should have kept the boy from me, but she said it was the only way to reach his potential.

She presented him to me yesterday, and I saw the truth in it.

Frank skimmed the next few pages, looking for more about Sister's "methods," or what happened to the other children the "unsuitable."

But the Captain had only eyes and time for the scion now.

Today Thaddeus discovered a small cave all by himself. I could not find him for hours. I worried, but I should have trusted his natural quintessence. He takes to the mine like my true blood. It is becoming more and more difficult for both of us to return from its protective arms. If not for Sister, I would gladly remain below with the boy, until I passed into the natural final resting place of all men.

I am nearing my end but now it is with peace of mind.

It is clear to me the arrangement I must leave behind. Fredrick will inherit the house after Sister, with the conditions I have laid down clearly before him and the rest.

Thaddeus will be my scion, and inherit all that goes with it. Fredrick will be my natural heir. Each understands the roles they must play.

So correct, so fitting is this dual legacy that I have made it clear I wish it to continue long after the first generation. An oath was made, in blood, by all my children and children's children. Sister and I believe their time in the wing will prove helpful in holding them to this bond. The training makes them strong in this way, regardless of their varying natures.

He set the journal aside, his mind racing with implications and horror. He sat for a time, staring at the door to the next room, trying to remember what he'd seen in the wing. Finally, his morbid curiosity grew too great, and he grabbed a lantern and went downstairs.

The dog followed him down the steps and into the entry hall, but stopped just short of the wing when Frank approached it. It stepped back hesitantly, the hairs along the back of its neck bristling, its massive head low to the ground and growling at the wing door.

He looked from the dog to the door. The dog's reaction bothered him more than anything he experienced in the house so far. But he didn't see a choice in the matter.

He opened the door, releasing the trapped smells of time and corruption like a foul cloud. He had not entered the wing, or even opened the door, since his first exploration of the house, not even the day after he thought someone was in the house.

He hesitated briefly in the open doorway, but no sounds disturbed the dark interior, no menaces rushed from its cold depths. He turned the lantern as bright as he could make it and stepped in, raising the light above his head to chase as many shadows away as possible.

The wing was longer than he remembered, the sloping back end disappearing in shadows despite his lantern, a darker shadow running across the back indicating the panel door. The rusted bed frames were still stacked against the wall, the planking still piled beside them. He guessed there to be at least two, maybe three dozen beds. He stepped closer to the nearest frame, and felt his stomach turn.

Somehow he missed it the first time, or maybe he just didn't want to see it. Secured to the floor near the wall where iron hooks, a few with broken and rusty bits of chains still attached. Hanging from the bed frames were similar chains, some with rotted bits of leather cuffs on the end.

He lifted the lantern and looked down to the dark shadow of the panel door, remembered the hospital bed with the rolled up stained sheet atop it. He looked back to the open door. The dog was watching him from just outside, but refused to follow. Slowly he walked to the back.

He opened the panel door and set the lantern down, moving the rusty hospital bed to one side. He found it there, halfway down the wall. He found it because he knew it had to be there, because Sister took *a personal hand.* A square cabinet door built flush to the wall and almost hidden by dirt and cobwebs. There was a small key hole in the right hand side. He pulled at the little wooden knob handle just above the hole. It was locked.

He went back for a loose bed rail, then attacked the small paneling until it was a mess of broken pieces, the dog barking furiously all the while.

Inside he found the tools. They were of varying designs, and some of their purposes unclear. But the short club and the small pincers were plain enough...and the scalpel. The instruments were obviously old. The metal showed spots of age, and the leather handles were dried out and retreating from their edges.

He picked the lantern up, looked to what he had thought was a latrine in the floor, looked to the stained bed-sheet. He took a sharp, shuddering breath and heard the frightened, confused, agonized cries of the Captain's testing room.

But the cries were only his own imagination, and when the nightmare passed, he was left alone in the silence of a forgotten, twisted room.

He looked again to the tools, disturbed by their muted presence, the pristine quality of their layout. Each was held in place by tiny wood pegs mounted to the backboard.

Pristine? He picked the scalpel up, held it to the light of his lantern. It was free from dust, and the edge glinted with razor sharpness. Either the natural air of the wing and the quality of the cabinet had preserved the tools...or someone was still looking after them. He put the scalpel back with another shudder.

When he left, he slammed the heavy door behind him, vowing to have the wing torn apart from one end to the other.

Damn the Captain. Damn his sister. Damn the Mundts.

***

He spent the rest of the day sitting in bed, trying to get the images of the wing out of his mind. The journal lay on his ad-hoc table, next to the bed. He couldn't look at it, but felt it there just the same.

He still needed sleep, but of course sleep didn't come. Even in the relative safety of the day and with his new found companion the dog, it didn't come. It wasn't anxiety or fear that kept him up now, but anger. Hot white, revolted anger.

His eyes strayed in the direction of the journal. But he couldn't bring himself to take it up again, not yet. Instead he stared out the windows, watching the light of day gradually fade against the winter panorama, as if there had never been any Sister, or Captain, or testing.

He ate upstairs, as far from the wing as possible. He didn't think he could get anything down, but he managed half a sandwich. The dog had no such inhibitions, and devoured most of Frank's food as well.

There had been a brief moment when he thought he lost the dog. Just after eating, he let the dog out to relieve itself, only to see it dash off in the woods out of sight. He stood for fifteen minutes in the doorway, shivering in the cold, refusing to accept that his new companion might not come back. It had stopped snowing and some of what was on the ground was already beginning to melt. Somehow, it made the loss of the dog worse.

Then, just as he was closing the door, he heard a bark and the dog was suddenly climbing over the hillside, rushing past him and into the house. He found the dog upstairs, sitting in the same place by the stove, looking as if it had always been there.

Now, twilight filling his windows, he sat with his dog (I'm already thinking of him as mine), and searched for some way to wash away the stains of what he read that morning. The thought of stains made him sniff the pungent air and look to the dog.

"One way or the other," he said, trying to find a spot of normalcy, "you're getting a bath tomorrow."

The dog did not reply, but for a shift of its heavy shoulders—and Frank knew doubt.

They sat for a long time in silence then, the dark implications of the morning's read rising like bile in his throat over and over again, no matter how he chased them away with thoughts of tomorrow's tasks, the day's successes.

Then, "We didn't have children."

There was a once-removed quality to the words, as if they were intended for another time and place. He didn't bother pretending he was talking to the dog. He watched the softening sundown framed in the frosted window pane and said the words, but didn't hear them.

"Maybe we both wanted them for a time, but it didn't work out. And then later, it was okay. But she would have been a good mother, a great mother."

He glanced at the dog then, as if expecting an argument.

"We met at a college," he continued, nodding slowly to himself. "I was a TA for the Math Department, and she was a graduate student. It sounds like one of those meetings you read about in romance books or see in a silly movie, but it really happened that way.

"She walked in the Professor's office where I was working. It just a coincidence that I was there and not him. She wanted to know about a class for registration. I don't even remember asking her out, or any of the details of the next year. But then, there we were, walking down the aisle. I was never happier in all my life. It was perfect."

He sighed, looked back to the window. "Anyway, that's the story we would tell people when they asked how we met. Or, at least, that's the story I would tell." He paused. "She'd just roll her eyes, and said she did it for the money. Then she'd look around our apartment, if we happened to be there. It wasn't much. She could really sell the irony."

He winced softly, moved his lower jaw slowly from side to side.

"And nobody ever doubted we were in love. Just one look at us and it was obvious. Storybook. All the way...until it wasn't. And she died."

Until it wasn't. He licked his lips, pushing down that memory, reaching for something else, something real, something life-giving, life-affirming.

Irony...

She would always fall to irony, even in the bad times. Calling up with a grin or raised eyebrow the other answers, those not immediately apparent or even wanted by the analytical mind. And in truth, he was never her equal for the subtle, deeper expressions of meaning. His was a world of ordered formula and rational logic.

Except when it came to her, he thought. *Then I was an open sieve to every whim and mood of pure, unfiltered emotion.*

"Here's the real story of us," he said, almost in a whisper, his eyes losing their focus. "The story I never told anyone."

"I guess it was about two years into our marriage. I came home early from work. It was a crummy job. I always had crummy jobs for the longest time. But somehow she made that okay. And later, when we got money, we just saved it. Because that was okay, too."

He closed his eyes, remembering. And it was so clear, the memory, it hurt.

"And I came home that day, and there she was in the backyard, hanging up laundry from a basket, standing in one of my t-shirts, jeans, and a ball cap. I remember her feet were bare, and the way they stood out in the grass. It was summer, and she was a dark brown from the sun, and her hair was in a ponytail. I always liked that. The ponytail. Maybe she knew that, because she rarely wore that way. It was her, to tease me.

"She saw me. She started talking. She was always talking back then. But I couldn't tell you what she said. I just walked up behind her as she hung another piece of laundry. Her shirt was tied in a knot up front, and the jeans were hanging off her hip. I couldn't take my eyes off the brown curve of her backside. It was like something arcane, a mystery of small, almost hidden, impossibly perfect, shadows and lines, just there, just above the top of her jeans."

He swallowed, the memory going down in a wet lump in his throat.

"She had a beautiful body."

When he could speak again, he opened his eyes, saw the last of the day outside his window extinguish like one of his lanterns being slowly turned off.

"I stood close to her, kissed her on the neck. I can still remember the taste of sweat and oil on her. It was like tasting the sun. And I just kept thinking how much I wanted her. I took her to bed and we spent the afternoon there. I remember laughing as it started to rain, and we remembered too late the laundry on the line, and the forgotten basket."

He closed his eyes again, as if to preserve the image forever in his mind.

"And that was the story I never told, should of told, though of course I could never tell. That was us. That was my Tara."

His voice fell off. His heart felt pressed, as if in a vice. It grew difficult to breathe, and he felt the sudden hot flush of tears along his cheeks.

And then something touched his hand. A warm, soft, and wet weight.

He looked down to find the dog with its head on his hand, looking up at him. The simple brown eyes were full of concern, or maybe it was just the beautiful, artless empathy of an animal extending trust. Whatever its purpose, it gave Frank the release he needed, restored in some measure his faith in life. He took a deep, grateful breath, reached out carefully with his other hand, and gently stroked the long ridge of the brown nose.

And eventually, in this way, he finally fell asleep.

Chapter Nine

The dog woke him with a sharp bark. He blinked around sleep crusted eyes, and slowly, painfully, came to consciousness. There was now a pounding accompanying the barking. After a time, he realized someone was knocking at the door.

He climbed from bed in the same clothes he wore last night. The light was streaming through the still open curtains, and judging from the sun's position, he guessed it to be near afternoon. He had been asleep for twelve hours.

He grabbed his heavy coat, slipped into his moccasins, and opened the bedroom door. The dog raced past him to the front, barking all the while. It gave Frank a jolt of confidence to hear its deep woof, like angry thunder.

"All right, all right" he said, pushing the dog back with a leg and thinking he needed to give it a name soon. He carefully opened the door a crack, the dog thrusting his nose in the space and sniffing the air noisily.

It was the sheriff.

"Frank."

"Sheriff."

"Got yourself a new friend, I see," said the sheriff, his frame reduced to a thin line of camel coat and hat brim, pulled low and hiding his eyes.

"What brings you out this way, Sheriff?" asked Frank, straining to keep the dog from pushing open the door.

"Afraid this is an official visit."

A vision of the journal, still lying on the cardboard box by his bed, flashed across Frank's mind, and he felt a cold, clammy rush of guilty adrenaline. Then he remembered the wing and its dark secrets. *Did this justify his taking the journal? Would the sheriff and judge overlook the petty theft he showed them the tools?*

Somehow, he didn't think so.

"Pardon?" he asked, stalling for time. The dog whined, and made another rush at the crack.

"Might be easier for all of us if you let your friend out," said the sheriff.

"I don't know what he's going to do. He might bite."

"Is the tail down?"

"No. As a matter of fact, it's wagging." He shared a wry grin with the sheriff.

"I'll take my chances."

Frank opened the door, the dog bursting through like a shot.

For a moment he thought it might bite, it seemed so eager to get at the sheriff. Instead, it raced around the big man, sniffing his leg and trying to reach the basket now held high out of reach. The sheriff handed the basket across, the dog watching the exchange carefully.

Frank was slightly put off by how quick it happened, but suddenly the sheriff was rubbing the dog around the neck and pulling gently on the flesh behind the ears.

"This looks like one of Red Barton's dogs," said the sheriff. "He keeps a whole mess of 'em on his farm. They're always running away."

It was not a complete surprise to Frank. The dog was housebroken, after all, and too comfortable around people to be wild. Still, the idea that he might have to give it up was a blow.

"Claire told me you didn't get around to dropping off the basket yesterday," said the sheriff, still playing with the dog and not looking at Frank. "I told her you were probably snowed in, and promised to run up and check on you. She sent the new basket. We can have an exchange of prisoners if you like."

"That was thoughtful," said Frank. "Please, tell Claire thanks."

"I will." The sheriff released the dog and stood. The dog immediately ran off to pee on a tree. "But you can thank her yourself, too. The road's clear."

Frank looked doubtfully to the edge of the hill and the heavy snow.

"I sent the plow up your route this morning," said the sheriff, lifting his head slightly. "You must have heard it."

"No," said Frank slowly. "Out like a light. What time is it?"

"About 11," answered the sheriff without looking at his watch.

"I guess I was fast asleep."

The dog rushed back inside, bringing with it a cold winter wind. "I'm sorry," said Frank. "Where's my manners? Would you like to come in? I can make a cup of coffee and get that basket."

The low brim dipped once. "That sounds good."

The sheriff stomped his boots on the side of the house to clear them of snow and followed Frank in.

"The basket is in here," he said. He led the way into the dining room as the sheriff shed his gloves and scarf. He kept his coat on for a time, though. The fire had long since died, and the big room was cold.

"I'll start a fire and pour some coffee," said Frank.

"I'll get the fire," answered the sheriff, bending down to get at the wood. "You get that coffee. There's a new thermos in the basket"

Frank retrieved two cups from the kitchen, frowning at the lockers, wondering if they, too, had some dark secret from the Captain's past.

He returned to the dining room, poured two cups of coffee from the new thermos, and watched the sheriff stir the fire back to life.

A moment later, the two men sat across the corner of the dining room table closest to the fire.

The sheriff looked around. "You've been cleaning up."

Frank nodded, and then, in part because he was thinking about the kitchen, and in part because he was nervous, he said, "I'm going to have those meat lockers in the kitchen hauled away and replaced."

"So you're still determined to stay?"

The sheriff leaned back in his chair, stretched his long legs, and held his coffee sitting precariously on his lap.

"I think so," said Frank, putting more certainty in his voice than he felt.

"That would explain the mattress."

Frank looked at him in confusion.

"Emil was belly aching this morning about some mattress he's keeping for you down at the store. He's not going to deliver it, so you'll have to arrange some other means to get it up here."

"I forgot about the mattress. I didn't really think he'd order it." He smiled to himself. "Poor Emil."

The sheriff frowned, shook his head. "You don't want to start up a blood feud with the Mundts. You're badly out numbered."

"I didn't start anything," countered Frank.

The sheriff raised his eyebrows, as if he had a point. He looked to the fireplace, the newly washed floor.

"This room's almost livable with a fire," he said. Then he carefully turned in his chair to look at the ugly scar along the back wall. "Almost."

Frank looked to the wall as well, thinking again of the journal and the children's quarters. "Sheriff..."

"I think we can use Cal when it's just us, Frank."

"Cal," he said, then sipped quickly at his coffee to hide his mixed reaction. He desperately wanted the sheriff to be on his side, but he still had reservations. "When we first met, you started to say something about the Captain."

The sheriff nodded slowly. "I did."

"Care to elaborate now?"

"I think the judge would be a better source on that front, than me."

"I heard he had a sister," said Frank determinedly. The sheriff turned his coffee cup on his lap. "That's true enough."

Frank waited him out.

"Don't know much about her," said the sheriff finally. "She came with the Captain. Lived in the house. Died here, too."

"Did she have any children?"

"I guess so. The judge traces his lineage from her."

"But not Emil and Henrik?"

"No. They claim the Captain."

"Were there any rumors about...the sister?"

The sheriff lifted his head another fraction, looked at Frank, the crinkles around his eyes drawing close. "What kind of rumors?"

It was Frank's turn to be implacable. "I just wondered. You said that night at Claire's, a man brings his own evil. I wondered what you meant by that."

The sheriff finished his coffee, sat up and put the cup down on the table. "Who you been talking to, Frank?"

"Why? What does that matter?"

"I guess it doesn't *matter*," said the sheriff slowly, casually. He leaned on the table with his arms, looked down at his hands. "Mundts don't have a lot of friends outside the family. You'll hear a lot of nasty rumors if you want to listen to them, Frank."

He leaned back again, looked to Frank. "Of course, that don't mean there's no truth in them."

"Like?"

The sheriff shook his head. "I don't spread rumors, Frank. I gotta work with the judge, and everyone else in this town, most of them related in some way to the woman you're talking about. A sheriff sees and hears a lot of things in a small town. In my experience, he says a lot less if he wants to keep his job."

"You told the judge about my wife."

The sheriff winced. "Yes, I did. But that was special circumstances—and not a rumor. Because of the roles we play, we have to keep each other informed, especially about new arrivals. For what it's worth, the judge is a discreet man."

Frank saw the logic, even if it left a bitter taste in his mouth. He knew, too, that he would have to risk much more than idle speculation about the past if he wanted the sheriff to take him seriously.

He was on the edge of retrieving the book, of showing the tools in the wing, when he caught the sheriff watching him, waiting. He couldn't say why, there was nothing menacing or suspicious about the act, but it put him off. *Another time maybe, when I know for sure where the sheriff stands.*

The sheriff stood slowly as if sensing the decision. "Well, I guess I better get going," he said, pulling his hat down. "I'm on your payroll, after all. You'll be writing letters."

He shook Frank's hand. "Thanks for the coffee. I'll take that basket money down to Claire if you like?"

"Thanks, but if the road is clear enough, I like to go pay her myself."

The sheriff nodded, looked to the fireplace. "I'll ask Red about that dog. Wouldn't do to harbor someone else's dog. That's a capital offense in Torview. Maybe you'd like me to hold on to him, until we find out?"

Frank felt a rush of panic. He didn't want to lose the dog, even for a moment.

"I was hoping it could stay here," he said. "I mean, of course ask this Red if it is his. But, well, even if it is, I'd like to buy it off him."

"You sure you want to keep a dog like that in the house?"

"He looks comfortable enough," said Frank, looking to the dog who was still sitting in front of the fire.

"She," corrected the sheriff with a smile. "She does look comfortable at that. Well, I guess it will be okay. Don't get too attached. If it is Red's, he'll want her back."

"Like I said, I'll pay for...her."

"I'll tell him. Tell him he'll get a good price, too. But Red likes his dogs. Don't get your hopes up."

They shook hands again, and the sheriff gave the dog another playful pull on the neck on the way out.

Frank watched him leave from the doorway. At least the sheriff hadn't asked him to leave again. Maybe he was getting used to the idea that Frank was staying.

The trouble was, after last night's discovery, he wondered if he should.

* * *

After a wash and shave, he pulled the last of his clean underwear, shirt, and pants from his temporary closet (one of his moving boxes). He'd have to do something about the dirty laundry soon. Maybe he could run a clothesline over the big kitchen stove for drying, and wash the clothes by hand in his industrial bucket. He couldn't ask Claire to do it if he was determined to free himself from her cooking, could he?

He had decided, after the sheriff's visit, to bring both baskets back. He needed to cut this line of dependence, if he was going to make a real go of it in the house. But he wanted to thank Claire in person, and talk to her.

He let the dog out before he left, and watched her from the porch steps chase a squirrel up a tree. Despite his first night's real sleep, he still felt off balance, caught in a whirlwind. *Stay in the house, prove a point; leave the house and end an uncomfortable situation for everyone. Cut off one dependence on Claire; take on a new one with the laundry? Tell the sheriff about what he learned in the journal, the tools; don't. Confront the Mundts with their past...?*

The dog finished her business, and raced back to the comfort of the fire in the dining room. He followed her, still mulling his options. Standing over her, he distractedly reached out to rub her neck, just as he'd seen the sheriff do. But she'd have none of that from him, scuttling playfully out of reach.

"I suppose you think I forgot about your consorting with the enemy?" he asked, standing with his hands on his hips, trying to look serious. The dog barked playfully once in return, and ran in a quick circle around the table.

"Yes, yes, I know," he said, watching her with a smile. "Enemy might be a bit harsh. The sheriff, your new friend and mine, *Cal*, comes off like something from an old Western. But the question is which hat does he wear: black or white? I can't get a read on him."

The dog stopped suddenly at his feet, barked again, tail wagging like a metronome.

"Oh, I know how *you* feel about him," he teased. Then he reached out to pet her, which she allowed briefly for a time, until she fell with a thump to the floor in front of the fire.

"I want him to be a good guy, too," he said quietly. "I need him to be."

He put out a plate with some of the meatloaf from the latest basket, and set it down in the front of the dog. He ate the rest with some mash potatoes and cold milk from a mason jar (cutting Claire off was going to be hard).

He packed the two baskets and set them by the front door to take with him to the car. He then put another log on the fire, and carefully arranged the screen around it. The dog watched him all the while, her head on her front paws, sighing contentedly by the fire.

"Well, you're forgiven," he whispered, rubbing her ears one last time. "Though I think a bath is still in order."

He told himself he was keeping her inside because of the cold, but in truth it was because he was afraid she would run away. He was tired of losing things that mattered to him.

At the last minute, he walked back upstairs and grabbed the journal. He had no clear plans to how he would use it, but he took it just the same.

The drive down the road was not as difficult or frightening as he'd imagined. The plow had cleared most of the snow, pushing it down the hill line, and pouring salt on the blacktop. The chains made a funny but reassuring crunch as he went down the twisting road. Maybe he should have taken them off?

Main Street was almost deserted when he pulled into town. He wondered what day it was. *Sunday? Was everyone at home, or at church? Did they even have a church here? And when did I lose track of the days?* He'd have to get a calendar or a watch with the day and date.

He went directly to Claire's this time, not wanting a repeat of the Jenny and her son, or any other odd Mundt run-ins.

Claire was dressed in a new apron today, but it covered the same conservative dress, and her hair was still in the lifeless bun.

"Mr. Henning," she said, as she opened the door. "Been wondering about that basket."

"Sorry about that," he said, showing her both baskets. "I'm afraid the snow…"

"That's what Cal said," she interrupted. She looked curiously at the second basket. "You didn't like the meatloaf?"

"Love it. I just wanted to bring you the baskets back. Just in case, you know, it snows again. And you don't have to send the sheriff up with anymore. I'm going to try and do some of my own cooking for a change. Not that your cooking wasn't a godsend."

He faltered over the last bit, knowing he sounded like an ass. This was not starting off well.

She took the money, put it in her apron pocket without counting. If she was disappointed by his words, he couldn't tell. Nothing broke through that hard face but determination.

He stood in the doorway, wishing he had thought this through a little more. Her perpetual frown took on a shade of curiosity as the moment dragged on.

"You want to come in?" she asked.

"If you have some time," he answered, hearing the relief in his own voice.

She grimaced and nodded slowly, as if she long suspected this day would come. She picked up the baskets. "Come in, then."

He closed the door behind him, offered to carry the baskets. She shook him off and indicated the living room off the hallway. "I'll be there in just a moment."

He was surprised to find a small fire in the hearth. It did help, he decided, but only just. He sat in one of the padded chairs across from the fire, tapping his fingers on the arm. The room grew still as the moments dragged on and she didn't return.

He heard a voice in the kitchen, followed by the sound of plastic on plastic. *A phone receiver being put back on its cradle?* He hadn't heard the phone ring. *Who was she calling?*

She returned a moment later, minus the apron, and settled in the opposite chair with her legs carefully tucked against each other. A thin, overworked hand pushed the plain dress down repeatedly, like a seamstress on a press. She didn't quite meet his eye, but she didn't look away either. She waited for him, lips pressed in a tight line of anticipation.

"I guess I should explain," he started. "I didn't come just to return the baskets and pay you. And I want to say again, it's nothing against you or your cooking, my wanting to go on my own."

It still sounded off, and he watched her mouth grow smaller and smaller. He sighed, started again.

"You've been very kind to me. I just need to know I can make it on my own for a time. I'm sure I'll be enjoying your food again soon enough."

She continued to watch him, the line just above her nose deepening in concentration, but otherwise giving nothing away.

She has green eyes, he thought. *Eyes so light and washed out, they look like pieces of lime candy in milk.*

"You're staying in that house?" she asked suddenly, bringing him back.

He struggled. There was no way to approach this delicately, not with her, not with this context. In the end, he just said it. "Mrs. Mundt, I know why you don't go back to that house."

The lines deepened. *Any deeper, and her forehead will just collapse in on itself.*

"Why?" she asked, her voice trembling slightly.

Her reaction surprised him. Her question wasn't a matter of doubt, or a test of his knowledge, but one of fearful curiosity, as if she assumed he might know something she didn't.

He reached carefully for the right words.

"The Captain and his sister were..."

What? Sick? Monsters? There would be no forgiveness for a misstep here.

"Wrong," he finished.

She winced, turned slowly to the fire. The room filled with awkward silence.

Then, almost in a whisper, she said, "They thought Philo weak."

He felt his pulse quicken, forced himself to remain still as another pregnant moment dragged on. Until, with more force, she added, "He was weak."

She turned, the glint of fire lighting the pale, unfocused reflection of her eyes. "But he was strong, too. The gambling was just a means to an end. And not the one they all thought. It was a way to finally free himself. Philo was a sensitive soul. Philo was weak. But he was strong, too."

She blinked, turned to him as if only now remembering suddenly he was there and who he was.

"Mr. Henning..."

"Frank."

"Mr. Henning," she insisted, "quit playing the fool and get out of that house. Get out of Torview. Take that girl with you. You don't belong here, either one of you."

"Do you mean, Liz?"

"Of course I do."

He didn't know what to say, his mind racing in all directions. *How did she know that he'd even met Liz?*

"Do you care for Liz?"

The hard lines relaxed for just a moment, and the Claire that might have been, that most likely was all those years ago with Philo, flickered briefly across her expression. But then, just as quickly it fell away again, and the hard, bitter lines returned in force.

"She's not of Torview," she said flatly, as if this explained everything.

"But Philo was," he countered softly.

She looked away.

"Mrs. Mundt, why did Philo leave?"

Her hands twitched slightly, and her voice took on more force, weighed down now by misery. "Because he could." A bitter pause. "And he didn't take me."

The twitching hands now curled in on themselves, making two white knuckled fists. "Now, Mr. Henning, I think you should leave."

She stood up and he did as well. He took a step to the doorway, stopped, and turned back to her. He gently took her clenched hands in his, watching the worry line grow impossibly deeper. But she didn't take away her hand.

"Mrs. Mundt. Claire. I didn't mean to bring you more pain. I hope...I hope you find peace somehow."

He slowly let go of her. The hands stood there where he left them, now unclenched, but somehow removed, as if they no longer belonged to her. The hard worry lines now had new companions around the eyes, but these were marked with confusion, and maybe a struggle to remember something long forgotten.

He turned and left. Just before he closed the door behind him though, he heard her repeat the words, but now in tones of shocked sadness, "He didn't take me with him."

As he walked down to his car, he wondered what had really become of Philo.

Maybe, he thought with a chill, *it wasn't a case of Philo forgetting his wife. Maybe where he went she couldn't go.*

* * *

He thought about going down to see the judge next, but changed his mind as he stood by the car outside Claire's. The journal was tucked in his jacket, but it wasn't much to work with. He wasn't even sure, at this point, what he would accuse the Captain and his sister of, or how it could help him in his own struggle with the Mundts.

Too, if started making accusations, his next meeting with the judge would probably be his last. He needed more information, more proof. Vague suspicions and a weathered, cryptic journal were not enough. He'd hoped to find some answers from Claire. Now he would have to look somewhere else.

Besides, he was fairly certain the judge knew the contents of the journal already.

The sound of excited children voices drew his attention across the street. The fenced-in school yard was suddenly alive with children. It looked, to Frank, like any other school during recess. The swing set, roundabout, and jungle gym of the yard were left untouched, the metal apparently too cold to use today despite the sunshine. Some of the older students stood huddled in little pockets against the cold, but the younger ones were making snowmen or angels in the snow covered field. A few had even started a snowball fight. A well-wrapped adult figure in scarf, hat and gloves stood nearby watching over the lot.

He remembered Sol saying something about a library in the school. Maybe he could get some answers there. He walked across the street, watching the children and their caretaker carefully, wondering how he could approach the issue without setting off alarm bells.

A rusty pickup truck, a pair of dirty Dalmatians in the back, passed behind him as he crossed the street. He turned back to see a tiny, wrinkled man in a toboggan hunched over the wheel, his lower jaw thrust out like a doorstop. The dogs gave Frank a bored stare, but stayed close together against the cold. The man turned his rudder-like chin in his direction, nodded.

Frank returned the man's nod reflexively, temporarily distracted by the common act of courtesy. The normalcy of the act was almost surreal to him now. Was his caution becoming paranoia? Was he projecting too much on the town of Torview?

He turned back to the school, walked slowly to the front. He made sure the well-wrapped figure was looking the other way, and quickly slipped through the front door.

A young girl at the front desk looked up at the sound of his steps. The loose, crooked lips and high forehead told him her family name without his having to ask. She pushed back an enormous pair of glasses that did nothing to hide the close-set eyes, or a face ravaged by acne. She smiled, completing the picture with a set of bad teeth.

"Hi there," he said brightly.

"Miss May is outside," she answered, pushing her glasses back again reflexively. Frank guessed her to be in her late teens.

"Yes," he said, trying to assume an air of confidence and familiarity. "Well, maybe you can help me. I'm thinking about writing up the town of Torview. Freelance article, the leaves, that sort of thing, you know what I'm talking about I'm sure."

The lie came easily to him.

"Cal—Sheriff Miller—told me to go ask around town, and maybe check with some authorities on the subject. I guess that would be this place. I guess that would be you."

"Miss May is outside," repeated the girl, giving the glasses another push.

"Oh, I'll want to speak to Miss May, too," he said. "What's your name?"

"Mary."

"Hi, Mary. Frank Henning."

He offered a hand which she shook automatically. He wished he thought to bring a notepad and pen, but he was making this up as he went along. It occurred to him that he had changed a great deal since arrival in Torview. What he was doing now he would never have considered before.

"Mary, Cal told me the library is to the right, third room down..." He waved in the general direction of the circular hallway that apparently ran around the building.

"No it's that way," she said, pointing to the left and then quickly pushing her glasses up again.

He noted only one of her eyes appeared to focus on him, the other strayed off to an angle.

"Right. Cal—sorry, Sheriff Miller—probably said left. I get confused. Part of getting old." He winked, and she giggled. "Would you mind showing me, Mary?"

"I can't leave the desk."

"Right. Stupid of me." He smiled at his error, which she returned by showing all of her crooked teeth at once. "Well, maybe I can just go back there and get started while I wait for Miss May."

A flush of red crept along her neck. "I don't know."

"Well, I suppose I could wait outside."

He looked with a grimace to the frosted glass of the door. There was a perfectly good bench across from the desk, but he deliberately ignored that. Mary looked as if she was about to suggest it anyway, so he beat her to the punch with a heavy sigh.

"Well, thanks for your help, Mary. Maybe next time." He turned slowly to the door.

"I suppose it would be okay if you just waited for her in the library," she said. "They'll be back inside in about twenty minutes."

Frank, feeling guilty, turned with a smile.

The library was little more than a large closet, with books along three walls, and two obsolete desktops on a small table. He ignored the computers as they were currently off and he assumed would require a password.

The books were arranged by subject and author's last name. There was a large section on agriculture, a slightly smaller section on the Sciences, and two short shelves of "classic" literature—minus all the controversial bits he remembered from school. He found the history section near the top (*out of reach of smaller hands?*). There were a few well- thumbed textbooks on American and European history, and a copy of Well's *Short History of the World.* There was also a thin ledger with a taped on title: *Torview: An Account.*

He pulled this down, and began leafing through its stiff, waxy pages. Most of it was little more than an idealized version of the Captain's discovery of Torview and its development as a town. Missing where all the Captain's personal reflections and any details of the house or its occupants. A brief history of the mine was given on one page and an essay on the importance of agriculture to the community on another. There was a short list of the founding fathers' offspring (without the Captain's personal assessments). Interestingly, there was no mention of his sister or her kin. Theodore was listed, as was Fredrick, and Han. Even Nina was given a line. Of Thaddeus, however, there was nothing.

He put the ledger back, gave the shelves another cursory glance, and then gave it up. As he turned the corner outside the door, he ran into a small bundle of winter coat, scarf, and hat. A mitten covered hand removed the scarf, revealing a pinched nose and a prim expression.

"What are you doing here?"

"Miss May?"

"Who are you?" There was a bitter quality to the mouth, and though the tightly pressed lips had a hint of the Mundt crookedness, it was impossible for him to be sure without seeing more of her face and head.

"Frank Henning," he said, offering a hand. He saw no reason to lie. He had done nothing wrong.

"What are you doing on school property?" She ignored his hand.

"I came to see the library. I thought..."

"This is a private school. You have no right to be here." Her voice had the nervous ring of someone used to adolescent audiences, audiences she could send to the corner or silence with a hard look.

"I'll be leaving, then."

"I know who you are. You're that man. There are laws against people trespassing on school grounds during hours. Those laws are to protect the children."

She lifted her little chin defiantly. Some of the children she was speaking of were even now coming through the door from the playground.

He started to apologize, but stopped in midsentence, distracted by the sight of the students watching them.

They ranged in age and size, some clearly almost adults, others hardly more than toddlers. Many were dressed in overalls and jeans, big-boned, healthy children with curious expressions. Near the front, however, stood a young boy with a cleft lip. A girl, about Mary's age, was holding a tissue and absentmindedly wiping the drool from his chin. The girl's right shoe was a reinforced platform boot. Behind her, another boy, also young and obviously congenitally blind, was holding her skirt. Beside him, a short girl with pigtails stared back at Frank with eyes that didn't blink and didn't register. And behind her, another boy looked to be on an oxygen mask.

There were more like this, crippled in limp or mind, many dependent on one of the others for support of some kind.

But this was not what stopped Frank.

All of the children, all of the ones that were touched with some deformity, had the Mundt tuft of hair and features, even the girls, including the loose-lipped, crooked mouths.

He looked closer, noting here a nose turned up like a snout; there an ear shorter than the other, or missing altogether. Eyes were crossed or lazy, or worse. Everyone with skin like white paste, some with wine-colored birthmarks across their faces or necks.

He heard someone hiss behind him, turned back to Miss May, lost in thought. Her glare intensified at his obvious discomfort, took on a protective, judgmental anger. He felt the blood rush to his face. But before he could explain himself, she interrupted:

"I'm going to call the law now! Children to class!"

The older ones took the lead, shuffling off to the first room in the circular hall with the young trailing like ducklings, some holding on to shirts or elbows.

He watched them leave, heartbroken, feeling his bile rise with guilt and revulsion at the same time. The sound of a phone clattering in a cradle brought him back to the present.

Miss May was making good her threat.

It occurred to him then, that there just might be laws against grown men on school grounds. He quickly walked to the front door as Miss May's reedy voice trilled over the phone behind him.

"Constance, get me Cal."

As he passed Mary, her fingers busily picking at the back of her hands in mortification, he whispered, "Sorry." But she only hung her head, and the glasses slipped unnoticed down her nose.

Outside, he turned down the street. He didn't look where he was going, his feelings of guilt and anxiety still wrestling with a deeper sense of horror.

He heard the distant bell of a shop door open, but didn't bother to look up. His imagination was too busy reeling from the recent images, and the implications that were even now starting to surface in his fevered mind.

The shoulder took him by surprise. It was hard and heavy and sent him spinning. He missed his step, and slipped on a piece of ice. He fell down on the cold and wet sidewalk, scraping the palm of his hand as he tried to break his fall. He looked up at the shadow in the weak sun that had sent him falling, waited for the apology.

"Get up." The shadow focused into Henrik Mundt.

At first he could only stare in disbelief. But as he realized there would be no apology, that the shoulder that struck him was deliberate, an upsurge of hot indignation turned his face red and set his hands shaking.

"What is your problem?" he asked, glaring up at the other man.

Henrik sneered, his crooked mouth twitching in anticipation. "You." Then, malicious pleasure dancing in his eyes, he reached down and poked Frank in the shoulder with two enormous fingers sending him reeling again against the pavement.

"Do something about it," said Henrik, his face now inches from Frank's. Sweet stink of tobacco and body odor fell from the large man like a foul cloud.

Frank glared back at Henrik in muted shock. He had never raised his hand against another, or had one raised against him. He found his anger mitigated now with a sense of distress.

As if knowing his mind, Henrik chuckled in derisive scorn and poked him again, then made a fist of his massive hand.

They both heard the sound of approaching steps at the same time. For one moment he thought Henrik would act anyway, his fist like a cocked hammer ready to fall.

"Henrik," said the calm, familiar voice of the sheriff.

Henrik's eyes glared at Frank, becoming two points of hot hatred, refusing to look to the approaching sheriff. Frank watched the fist shake with unconscious, animalistic rage.

"Henrik..." repeated the sheriff, coming closer now.

An unnatural twitch passed over Henrik's face, his eyes drawing in on themselves like retreating spots. He breathed heavily.

"Henrik."

With a visible effort the eyes returned to awareness, the fist slowly unclenched. Henrik retreated, but not before he spat in Frank's face. The brown mucous of saliva and tobacco ran down his cheek and nose like hot puss.

Only then did the sheriff's shadow fall across Frank's sprawled form. "What's going on?" he asked, looking from one man to another.

"He fell," said Henrik and he walked away. The sheriff watched him for a moment, then turned to offer Frank a hand up.

Frank waved him off, found a lump of relatively clean snow and used it to wash his face, retching as his fingers brushed the sputum and tobacco from his cheeks and eyes.

* * *

He stood shakily, this time accepting the sheriff's help. Then he turned to glare at his rescuer. "I suppose he just gets away with that?"

"With what?" asked the sheriff, his brim-shadowed eyes measuring Frank carefully.

"You didn't see that?"

"I saw Henrik standing over you from down the street. As I was heading this way anyway, I thought I'd see if everything was okay. Why? Something happen?"

"Yeah, something happened. The man assaulted me."

The sheriff cocked his head. "You want to make an official charge?"

Frank looked down the street at the retreating Henrik, turned to stare at the faces watching him from the barber shop window. *No one had run out to offer me help*, he thought. *Were they any more likely to be witnesses, and if so, for who?*

"Forget it," he said bitterly. "He'd just claim it was an accident. He *accidently* knocked me over. He *accidentally* spit in my face. And you didn't see that either, I suppose, so what does it matter?"

The sheriff chewed his lip in thought. "Likely that is what Henrik will claim."

Frank felt flushed, confused, and somehow dirty. He was furious at the sheriff, furious at himself. *Why didn't he just stand up to Henrik, consequences be damned? What did logic and pragmatics have to do with a fight?* He was shaking with post-adrenaline. He needed a shower. He needed to get away.

"I'm going home now."

"Just a moment, Mr. Henning."

Something of the hardness that kept the Mundts at bay was in the sheriff's voice again, but now it was directed at him.

"I just got a call from Miss May," he continued. "The principal of the school. I think you better come with me, and we have ourselves a talk."

"You're kidding," Frank whispered, disbelief and confused guilt setting him reeling in another wave of panic.

The sheriff's mouth grew taught as a fishing line. "No, sir. I'm not."

Stunned, Frank blinked back at those unrelenting eyes, tried to see something of the friend he thought he had made that morning.

Something wet and hard struck his head, then his shoulders. He looked up at the sunless sky.

It   was   starting   to   rain.

Chapter Ten

They sat across the sheriff's desk, a shabby twin of the judge's, with a coffee-stained blotter, and a nest of pens and yellow legal pads scattered across the surface. The sheriff pulled up one of the pads, found a blank page, and took Frank's statement.

At first, he answered all the questions with a sense of numb disbelief. The whole thing had the sense of surreal. He was no criminal. *Yes, he'd gone into the school. No, he didn't talk to any of the children, apart from Mary. Yes, Mary had told him to speak to Miss May at first. But then she said he could wait in the library. No, he didn't stay long. He looked at a few books, and then was leaving when May found him. His purpose? To find out more about the Mundts.*

These questions were asked with simple, official efficiency. The sheriff listened without comment to the answers, made careful notes on the paper. Then the questions took another, darker turn and Frank felt the floor fall out from under him.

Have you ever been convicted of a felony?

Have you ever been accused of stalking or any predator behavior?

Do you have any pornographic material of children?

Have you ever molested or wanted to molest a child?

Frank answered each questions with a horrified "no," staring incredulously across the desk at the sheriff, head down, writing the answers like he was taking an order at Sol's.

When it was done, the sheriff had Frank read the notes and sign them, then put the record in a standing file cabinet.

My name, and those questions forever linked, thought he in horror, *to stay god knows how long in the town offices of Torview*. He wanted to throw up.

The sheriff was leaning back in his office chair now, watching Frank from under his hat. He offered Frank some coffee.

He couldn't find the strength to voice even a simple rejection.

"There just standard questions, Frank," said the sheriff quietly.

So, we're back to first name basis.

The sheriff stood up, poured two Styrofoam cups of coffee and put one on the desk by Frank. "I don't think you were there to hurt anyone. I just have to be careful, especially where the school is concerned. And this way, your side of the story is on record, too."

The words *predators* and *record* kept running through Frank's mind and he found it hard to concentrate on what the sheriff was saying. He ignored the coffee and continued to stare at the sheriff as though he was looking at a stranger.

"This isn't right," he said finally, his voice a hollow whisper of confusion and hurt. "I've never hurt anyone in my life."

The sheriff sat on the corner of his desk, one long leg on the floor, the other straddled over the edge. He picked up Frank's coffee and made him take it.

"We know that, Frank," he said calmly. "We did a background check on you a while back." He sipped his own coffee, meeting Frank's eyes with no sense of embarrassment or apology.

"You did the right thing coming in here when I asked," he continued. "May called the Judge after me. He wanted me to pull you in, arrest you on trespassing charges. This way is better, believe me. This way the misunderstanding can be worked as a misunderstanding.

No charges or lawyers. I don't think that's necessary in this case. Do you?"

"I just wanted to look at the books," said Frank, again the words barely audible.

"Best you use the public library from now on," answered the sheriff, as if clarifying directions. "It's here in the Municipal building. I'm surprised you didn't know that, seeing as how you went by it on the way to the judge's office."

The cold ball of emptiness in Frank's stomach stirred again as he realized the interview was not over. Despite his calm dismissive manner, the sheriff was still working. *Would always be working*, he thought. He tried to swallow, but his mouth was as dry as sand. He watched the cup shake in his hand as he finally took a drink. He burned his mouth trying to swallow too much too fast, and spit most of the coffee back in the cup.

The sheriff just watched him, his expression registering nothing. But Frank suspected he was noting every gesture, every tic and blush—and judging. He took a deep breath, tried to focus, tried to find a sense of strength.

"I think I should have had a lawyer present, Sheriff," he said, looking the man in the eye, trying not blink. "And you didn't read me rights. I'd like you to make a note of that as well. Put that in your drawer."

The sheriff made a small sound with his tongue, sighed. "You're not listening, Frank. You're not being charged with anything. I'll talk to May."

"Like you talked to Henrik? That worked out really well." The implacable eyes held his for a moment, but he went on, losing himself to bitter resentment, "Maybe, I should skip you doing the *talking*, and press my own charges. Starting with Henrik, but maybe not ending there."

If the sheriff heard the implied threat to himself, he didn't bother to acknowledge it. "I'll take your statement, Frank. We'll see how it goes."

"I think we both know how it will go, Sheriff," he said, dropping his eyes.

"I think we do," agreed the sheriff matter-of-factly. "You don't have much of a case without witnesses, Frank. At best, the judge would put a restraining order on Henrik. That is if he is convinced by your story."

Frank snorted.

The sheriff stood up, took Frank's coffee and dumped in a sink near the wall, poured a fresh cup and handed it to Frank.

This time, he managed to hold it steady and sip slowly. "Well, why don't you pull Henrik in here and write him up?" he asked. He tried to match the sheriff's calm demeanor, but failed miserably.

"You're still upset. I can understand that. But you have nothing to worry about, with May or the school, or the judge, as long as there are no more... misunderstandings. And as to Henrik, I will have another talk with him." The hardness of the eyes flickered briefly a moment as the sheriff stared off into space, then turned back to Frank. "And this time it will stick, believe me."

Frank frowned into his cup. It was the crux of his problem here in Torview: who to believe? Who could he trust? He had no doubts that statement in the sheriff's drawer was the start of another campaign to get him out of Torview. *Probably the judge's idea.* It sounded like the sheriff forced a compromise with the judge on actual charges, for which, on second thought, maybe he should be grateful. But it was just like everything else with the sheriff: too many questions, too many possibilities, too few answers.

"I got some more bad news to share with you," said the sheriff, breaking his train of thought. "That dog is Red's. He wants it back. He won't take money for it."

Frank looked hopelessly around the office, as if searching for some sense of normalcy, some small sign or gesture that the world was not totally against him.

"I'll follow you up to the house," said the sheriff, but not unkindly. "I'll take her in my SUV. I'm sorry about that, Frank."

He wasn't ready to go home just yet. It seemed too much like giving in, as if he were admitting to the sheriff some sense of guilt; or just as bad, that what he approved in some way of the whole mess.

"If you don't mind," he said, looking down at the floor, "I'd like to go get something to eat first. How about we meet up at my place in an hour or so?" He didn't want the sheriff's company. He wanted to reestablish his independence, and send a message, however feeble, of his own.

The sheriff took his time in answering, as if not completely happy with the thought of letting Frank on his own.

"Ok. In about an hour."

He left the sheriff sitting on his desk. He couldn't bring himself to say goodbye.

* * *

Sol, sensing his mood, brought his food and let him eat in peace, for which he was grateful. He barely remembered tasting the food, eating mechanically and trying not to think of his recent humiliation and trouble, focusing instead on what to do next.

He heard the bell ring over the door, and turned to see a short, muffled figure enter. For a moment, he thought May had come to denounce him in front of Sol, run him out of town with vile accusations of predator.

But it was Liz, not May, hiding under the fringed parka hood. She sat beside him and ordered a soda from Sol, drank it with a twisted straw.

"Hey," she said, when Sol left again to check on the kitchen.

"Hi."

"I saw you walking across the street. I've been keeping an eye out for you."

He turned to look at her. She still had her hood on. All he could see of her was the tip of her nose.

"I'm not sure you should be seen talking to me just now," he said.

"Why?" Her voice was muffled by the extended hood of the parka.

"I'm definitely persona non grata here now."

"Well, don't give up. I overheard Uncle talking the other day," she said. "He said there was little chance they could get you out of the house in under a year. He said you called their bluff."

"Yeah, well, they're working on another plan now."

"What plan?"

He shook his head. He couldn't talk about that with her.

"Uncle Del said you lost your wife recently."

"That's right."

"I'm sorry."

"Thanks."

She fidgeted with her straw for a time. "Uncle says that's why you're fighting so hard. Nothing's more obstinate than grief, he says."

He lifted his mouth in a bitter half-smile. "He might be right."

"What was she like, your wife?"

To his surprise, he told her. "She was quiet most of the time, at least around me."

"Was she pretty?"

"Very. And kind. Very patient, and kind." He looked up from his plate, stared ahead. "She had a soft sense of irony. You could see it in her eyes, if you knew where to look. She was always finding something funny in life, always smiling in a secret kind of way."

"She sounds nice," said Liz after a time, breaking in on his thoughts. How long had he stopped talking?

"She was."

"I hope I find someone like that someday. I'm glad to hear there are people who actually make their dreams come true."

He blinked, smiling at his reflection in the back wall. It had been a dream. Tara was always saying he lived in the clouds... *No, that wasn't it. How did it go? 'When you don't have your head in the clouds, it's straight under the sand.'*

And then, often as not, she would turn, and he would see that odd, ironic smile that left so much unsaid—that he never dared ask her to explain. And in those times, the skies were brutally open, and no sand was at hand or deep enough, and he consoled himself that he needed neither, and that to each person is granted a certain mystery that no other can know. This is what he told himself. But another part knew doubt, and he wondered why the smile was tinged at times with sadness.

"It wasn't always perfect," he said quietly, remembering.

In many ways, the discovery of her illness restored something lost. Toward the end, before the discovery, Tara had seemed distant, tired, the smile a constant, now openly wistful presence. She took up sudden hobbies and dropped them almost the next week. She spent more time away from the house, took on new friends, friends she did not believe he would care to know. *There was that silly ballroom instructor, who kept demanding more and more of her time, even calling her at home.* She grew tired of talking about their retirement plans. She took to falling asleep before he came to bed.

Then came the day she called him at the office. She was crying, and wanted him to come home. She met him at the door, took him by the hand and led him to the bedroom, and told him she was going to die.

After that there were no more ballroom dancing sessions, no more calls. They went through that final, terrible ordeal together, clinging to each other like wise children, hopeless lovers. And it was as if the years had rolled back to the beginning, but better, and worse; because they knew it was going to end.

They never spoke of that other time, the time before. She tried once, but he stopped her with a gentle, self-effacing insistence. He brushed the recent past over like a spell of bad weather. They had more important things to focus on, he insisted, like her recovery. She accepted his position, but there was a look of sad wisdom in her eyes as she kissed him gently on the cheek.

"You mean the cancer?" said Liz, again interrupting his thoughts. "I guess that must have been hard."

"Yes," he agreed, thinking of Tara's ironic smile.

"You have to work on it," he added lamely, sensing Liz's concern at his withdraw.

Sol came by and topped him off. Frank gave him a grateful nod. He refilled Liz's soda as well, and waved her off when she went to pay.

"Going out of business sale," he whispered to Frank, with a wink. He wandered back to his register and paper.

"It's sad, his leaving," said Liz. "But nobody comes here much. Uncle says the town's not ready yet."

"How are things with you and your uncle, Liz?" he asked, careful to keep his voice even.

"Oh, he has all these great plans. Wants me to go to the town dance this weekend. You going?"

"No. I didn't even know there was a dance."

"Yeah," she said. "I don't want to go either."

"You don't like to dance?"

She snorted. "I like to dance, but that's not what they do here. It's all country songs, slow songs, and line dancing."

"You don't like that kind of music?"

"No." The cynicism was clear even through the parka.

He smiled. "Well, you don't have to dance. You can meet people. People your own age."

"You mean like Michalus? Yeah, Uncle Emil would like that. He's always pushing the boy on me, saying we should be friends seeing as how we're distantly related. Michalus is a creep."

He remembered she used a similar expression to describe her mother's old boyfriend.

"Well, it's not so bad having a friend," he said.

"Michalus? Pah-leeze. Besides, he doesn't want to be just friends."

"All right," he said, fighting down a disturbing reference to the Captain's journal. "But Michalus is not the only boy in town. And there are girls too."

"The other boys are just like Michalus. The girls are worse."

He remembered then the school yard faces, and wondered how much that played a role in Liz's assessment.

"Really? Everyone?"

The parka shrugged. "Well, I guess Erik Barton's okay. But he always smells like pig shit."

Barton, not a Mundt. Red Barton's son? That would be a coincidence. Could he use Liz to keep the dog? He looked to the pink nose poking out of the parka. He guessed Liz to be about sixteen, maybe seventeen. Given her history he supposed it was only natural for her to be reluctant to start dating, especially if the choices were between Michalus and pig shit.

"I hope you're going to stay...Frank." It was the first time she'd used his name. It sounded strange, as if she were testing it on her tongue.

"I'm trying, Liz."

"Cheers," she said, raising her glass.

He considered his options as they drank the toast. He decided he would have to enlist Liz to his cause. She was the only one who might help him that he could trust. But he wasn't comfortable about it, particularly after his run in with May and the sheriff.

"Liz, I wonder if you would do me a favor."

"Sure." Her eagerness to help almost made him change his mind.

"There's a couple of ledgers in the Judge's office. I want to take a look at them."

"You want me to get them for you?" she asked.

"No. No. But maybe you can help me get in the judge's office when he's not there. It won't take me long. I just want to take a quick look. It could help me."

"What are they about?"

"That's what I want to find out. I think there are records about the house. They're old. Maybe they can help me persuade the Judge to leave me alone." While this *was* a possibility, it was so remote that he felt guilty suggesting it as his motivation. What he really hoped was that it would give him more evidence to confront the judge.

Behind the parka, Liz appeared to have similar doubts. "I don't know, Frank. It seems kinda...sneaky."

She was right of course. He could, maybe should, just ask the judge to see them. But the deck was being stacked against him, and he didn't think taking the high ground would serve him well. Not with the Mundts. Not even with the judge. He couldn't tell Liz that, of course.

"You know, the judge and I are not seeing eye to eye just now," he said. "I just want to know what he knows. If I have some more information, I might be able to call his other bluff. Then, maybe they'll give up and I can stay, and everyone can get along with each other."

This is too much like the school, he thought, picturing Mary's crushed face as he left. He could see another session coming with the sheriff should he get caught, another document added to the pile of mounting evidence against Frank Henning, stalker of schools and burglar of township luminaries. Worse, this time he was involving the judge's niece.

"Ok," she said. "I'll try."

He held his second thoughts to himself, wondering if he was any better than the Mundts.

Yes, he thought stubbornly, *I am. I'm not threatening anyone in the streets with physical violence. I'm not trumping up charges for a kangaroo court. I didn't go looking for this fight.*

And it was a fight; a dirty one. No matter how detached the sheriff may appear about the incident, it was no small matter, that record in his files. And Henrik's threat was more tangible still.

I'm going to have to get a lawyer, he thought. *Maybe I should get a gun.*

The absurdity of the situation was suddenly too much to bear. All over a stupid house. He felt like laughing, or crying, or shouting.

"I guess I gotta go now," said Liz, turning to him. He saw more of her face now, and realized the hood was serving double duty, hiding a very large pimple along the side of her nose. She surprised him by reaching out to squeeze his hand. "You're all right, Frank. See you soon."

She was out the door before he could think to answer.

Oh lord.

"I think you have a friend there," said Sol, sliding up and offering coffee. Frank waved it off.

"That makes two," he said. "If you're willing to take the title."

"Of course, amigo." Sol looked to the door. "She's been in here a couple of times. Next to Henrik, my best customer. Talked to my oldest boy once when he was here. She always seemed a little lonely." He gave Frank a considerate look, grinned. "Until today. You know, a kind stranger with recent heartache, standing up to the Mundts...you could be in trouble, my friend."

"Christ, she could be my daughter."

Sol nodded. "I'm just saying."

Buy what will you be saying (or thinking) when news of the school incident gets around? Frank felt a flutter of despair tickle his stomach as he saw how easy it would be to become public enemy number one around here, without even trying. Even Sol might turn on him.

Maybe I should tell Sol.

But sitting there in one of the few safe spaces he knew in Torview, with one of the few people who did not hold a bad opinion of him yet, he couldn't bring himself to do it. It was just so vile to even think about the implied accusations, much less talk about them.

Instead, he chatted for a time about the weather until it was time for him to go.

He walked out the door thinking it was a mistake not to tell Sol. It would look bad. It would look like he was hiding something. *Remember me well, Sol*, he thought, *when you hear the worse.*

He walked to his car, thinking he was losing the fight already.

Chapter Eleven

The sheriff was waiting in the SUV by the gate. The rain had washed most of the dirty snow off the road, but there was still a soggy layer on the ground around the hill.

"Let's leave your car here," suggested the sheriff, looking at the muddy road. Frank climbed into the SUV passenger side. The interior smelled of coffee, leather, and deodorant. It was a pleasant combination, mixing well with the warm air from the heater.

They did not speak about the incident with the school on the way up. They did not talk at all. The sheriff, as always, didn't appear to care one way or the other. But Frank felt the unnatural silence like another blow in his losing war with the town of Torview. It didn't help that it was his own anger and stubbornness that kept him from speaking.

At the top of the hill, they parked in front of the house and the sheriff reached behind the seat to grab a leash.

Seeing it, Frank experienced another wave of bitter futility. He didn't want to lose the dog, wondered why it was so necessary. *How do I know the sheriff offered Barton money for the dog, or that he even spoke to Barton? What if it wasn't Barton's dog, and that this was just a way to get the dog out of the house?*

He looked out of the corner of his eye to the implacable sheriff waiting patiently by his car, digging a toe in the ground to test its resiliency. The thought of voicing these questions was no more possible than striking Henrik in the street. Only the degree and position of authority was different, the results would be the same.

Holding his doubts like a secret, he led the way up the steps, unlocked the door, and opened it a fraction, expecting the dog to come bounding out. The sheriff stood behind him with the leash in hand.

There was no rush of heavy nails along the floor, no bark or sound of any kind. He opened the door completely, and stepped in. The sheriff followed. There was an odd smell in the air, like something had been left burning. The house was perfectly still.

"Must be sleeping," he said, breaking his silence at last. He started to move through the foyer, but the sheriff stopped him with a gesture.

"What?" Then he looked to the floor where the sheriff was staring.

A small line, like the edge of a shoe print, was etched on the floor beside Frank. It was red and sticky. More prints could be seen coming from the stairwell, growing more distinct closer to the steps.

"Stay here," said the sheriff. He pushed his coat back over his gun, released the strap holding it down. He walked quietly to the back and the wicket door, careful to avoid any of the footprints. He turned the handle and opened the door slowly, glanced inside, his hand on his gun. He stood a long time that way, but did not go in. Finally, he turned back, motioned for Frank to stay put. He checked the kitchen the same way, then the right wing, then headed to the stairwell.

Frank heard the soft creak of his step on the bad stair, saw the sheriff pause, then start up again, one slow, careful step at a time until he disappeared behind the turn. Then there was a long, and to Frank, impossible silence.

"Mr. Henning." The sheriff's call traveled down the stairs in the same no-nonsense tone he used in the questioning earlier.

Frank rushed across the floor, glancing quickly first through the open wicket door. The dining room was a mess, the chairs overturned, the food from the cooler thrown around the room, something plastic burned beyond recognition in the fireplace and making the foul stink—maybe the cooler.

He vaulted up the steps, noting the increasingly clear bloody prints. It was just one print, the right shoe, but it went up and down the steps. He reached the top, ran through the small room and stopped just inside the bedroom door.

The dog lay at the foot of the back wall, a puddle of drying blood around its still, broken form. More blood was splattered on the bed and his shredded sleeping bag. On the back wall, above the headboard was a message, written in the same blood. It took a moment to make out, the gore distorting the smeared, giant letters:

GET OUT.

He took a shaken step inside, then another, stopping only when the sheriff took him by the arm as he drew near the dog. From this distance he could see the dog's throat had been ripped open. He looked to the now lifeless brown eyes staring at nothing, the black, rubbery lips pulled back across the teeth in an unnatural snarl. There was nothing familiar about the dog, nothing to remind him of the brief companion he had made. Instead he was looking at something obscene, something butchered for no discernible purpose but the gory message.

He swayed, his head suddenly grown light, his eyes unfocused. He staggered to the corner of the room and retched.

* * *

The sheriff took his time investigating, letting Frank trail behind him as long as he stayed out of the way. They started on the first floor.

Like the dining room, the kitchen was a mess. Everything Frank bought was broken or ripped or thrown on the floor. Only the right wing looked the untouched, the bed stands in place, and the back panel door still closed. The sheriff barely gave it a look.

For half a moment, Frank wrestled with telling the sheriff about the tools, making him walk to the back and opening up the panel door. But what would they find? Would they be there? And what could he say if they were? There was no connection with some arcane tools and what happened to the dog.

In the end he let it go, wanting, perhaps irrationally, to the keep the tools his secret, a kind of backup for future confrontations with the judge. *If there even there,* he thought again.

Finally, they went back upstairs.

The small bedroom and bathroom were relatively untouched, apart from the mirror above the sink, which was completely shattered.

It was the master bedroom where all the damage had been done, and where the killer left his message, and his mark.

The original footprint was in the puddle where the dog had lain. The print was big, and judging from the imprint, a boot of some kind. The sheriff traced the single step from the puddle to the top of the stairwell, then came back to the mess in and around the bed.

In addition to his sleeping bag, the paperbacks were torn and scattered around the room, the box Frank used for a bedside table ripped to shreds. As he watched the sheriff go through the books and box, turning over each item carefully with a pen, he felt an odd mix of relief and anxiety. The journal was still in his coat pocket; a happy coincidence of a last minute decision that morning to bring it with him. Like the tools, he kept his secret.

The sheriff studied the dog for a time on the floor, checking the stage of rigor mortis, examining the ripped throat. The dog's neck had been broken, he reported, probably before the throat was ripped. There was no sign of any knife or other cutting tool in the room.

"It would take a strong man to kill a dog like that," said Frank, fighting to keep his voice level. "Particularly that dog. A twisted man. Maybe two."

The sheriff looked to Frank.

"You know goddam well what I mean," he continued. "Or do you plan on just giving the Mundt brothers another talking to?"

The sheriff remained implacable as ever. "That dog has been dead for at least an hour, maybe two, maybe more."

"So?"

"So, Henrik spent most of the morning in Albert's—before you ran into him on the street. And I was with Emil."

"That doesn't mean they couldn't get up here to do it. You didn't see Henrik in the bar the whole time, did you?"

"No. But the timing would be difficult."

"Then another Mundt," said Frank angrily. "Another monster I haven't met yet. Maybe my peeking-tom neighbor, Granger."

The sheriff looked again to the print. "What size shoe do you wear, Mr. Henning?"

"Jesus God! Do you think I did this?"

"The timing says it's possible." He held up a hand. "Let's just say I want to remove you from the equation. Put your foot near the print, but be careful not to step in the blood."

Frank shook his head incredulously but did as he was told. The print dwarfed his own.

"Satisfied?" he asked bitterly.

"The print does not appear to be yours," agreed the sheriff. He scratched the back of his head. "Unless you wore boots to disguise yourself."

"I suppose I made a mess of my bedroom and wrote that threat on the wall as well?"

The sheriff seemed to consider the idea.

"Come on, Cal! Why on earth would I do that?"

"I keep an open mind when I'm investigating, Frank. I suggest you do the same, and not rush to conclusions."

"Right. I'll *try* not to jump to the conclusion that you know as well as I do what this is about. I'll *try* not to think that you're going to let them get away with it. I'll try not to believe you and the judge were, in some way, part of it."

The sheriff bit the right half of his lower lip. "You've had a shock, Frank, and a rough month. I'm going to let that go. But be careful."

But he was tired of being careful, tired of waiting on the sheriff's implacability.

"No," he said.

The other raised his head a fraction of an inch, caught for once in surprise.

"You hold yourself out to be a man, Cal. A law man. Well, be a man with me now. Do you honestly mean to tell me you think I did this? Do you honestly think for one moment this isn't about the Mundts sending me a message? I'm asking you, man to man."

The sheriff's eyes became two small points of light amid a sea of thin, spiraling wrinkles. He pushed his hat back along his head with a finger, looked Frank sideways. When he eventually answered it was in the same neutral monotone, but now tinged with the hint of something ready to spill over, like the most distant of thunder from an approaching storm

"Man to man, Frank? Ok. Man to man, I know the Mundts. Man to man, I know everyone in this town. Henrik is a piece of shit in most ways, but he'd never hurt an animal. I can't see Granger doing it either, for the same reason. Both might open you up like this, but never a dog."

He rolled his jaw around as if tasting the truth of his words. "Emil might; he has no love of animals. But he was with me."

He looked Frank in the eyes. "Man to man, you're the unknown, Frank. And just in case you didn't notice, that door was locked, which argues for someone inside."

"So they have another key. Big surprise."

"There were no footprints but ours outside the door, much less signs of blood. I checked."

He had noticed this as well. Once more he considered telling the sheriff of his late night experiences and suspicions. Someone *might* have a way into the house that didn't require the front door; someone who had been steps away from his bedroom that first night.

Someone, he thought, *who wailed in the night...and I have never actually seen.*

He had a vision then of another session at the sheriff's desk, another report filed in the cabinet, detailing the fragile, perhaps disturbed delusions of recently widowed Frank Henning, stranger to the town of Torview.

He said instead, "You still didn't answer my question, Sheriff. Do you really think I did this? You think I *could* do that?" He pointed to the ravaged body, the gory message.

He watched the sheriff take a deep, slow breath, the edges of his nose compressed to two white lines of impatience. The storm was almost on him now, but Frank was reckless with his own sense of indignation.

"I didn't say that," said the sheriff tightly. The next moment, he seemed to gather himself, the gray eyes falling into inscrutability with a blink. "I'm just trying to keep an open mind," he repeated calmly. "I haven't eliminated anyone from the equation yet. All right?"

Frank looked to the ground as if searching for his next accusation. It was not all right, but what could he do?

It's the school all over again, he thought, *the sheriff hiding behind protocol, leaving me blowing in the wind between open accusation and freedom.*

But there was nothing of Emil's cold animosity, or the even judge's calculation, in the sheriff. He remained an enigma to Frank. He tried to follow the sheriff's example, swallow his anger.

"Let me do this my way, Frank," said the sheriff thoughtfully, as if reading his confusion.

Frank looked up. "So, what happens next?"

"I'll take you down to Claire's or follow you if you want to bring your car."

The words made no sense to him. "Claire's?"

"You can't stay here tonight." The sheriff looked around the bloody room.

"Don't worry. I'll clean it up."

"No you won't. Not till I've had Doc Stevens up here from Summerset. He's the closest thing we have to forensics around here. This is a crime scene, Frank."

"It's my house."

"And we'll work as fast as possible knowing that. The town will pay for the room at Claire's. I'll see to it personally."

It was impossible to know what to make of this. The Mundts, the judge, maybe even the sheriff were finally going to have their way. He was going to have to leave the house.

He thought again about the tools in the right wing, the journal pressed against his chest in his jacket pocket. If the sheriff was about to do a thorough investigation of the house *should* he tell him everything? Surely they would find the tools. They would see that the cabinet door had been recently broken. Would hiding what he knew (and most of what he suspected) help or hurt him? There was no way the sheriff or judge could link him to the tools and the dog. Was there?

No, he thought cynically, *most likely the tools would simply disappear and he would lose one more round in the fight.*

He looked to the sheriff waiting patiently.

It all came back to the sheriff. Holding him off at arm's length was a risk; telling him everything another.

In the past, there would be no question of telling the law everything. He would have done so with willing naiveté, a self-effacing smile on his face, trusting the sheriff as a representative of order and the higher good, to justice.

Now...now he didn't know. Now he looked to the sheriff with suspicions born of deeper disappointments than his forgiving clouds and comforting sands. Now he didn't believe, blindly or otherwise.

He wondered suddenly what Tara would make of him now. Would she think him weak, or stronger? Would she recognize him?

"I'm going to need some help with this," said the sheriff, looking to the remains.

He nodded, the fight going out of him for a time in the painful resignation of the immediate.

They put the dog in two heavy trash bags sealed across the middle with duct tape, and put it in the sheriff's car. *Her*, he thought, looking at the pathetic bag.

He wanted to bury it on the hill, but the sheriff pointed out it wasn't his dog to bury.

Chapter Twelve

The room was done in exaggerated Americana, overstuffed pillows on overstuffed chairs, the bed three feet off the floor and covered in layers of quilts, throw pillows, and comforters. Bric-a-brac perched like pieces to some elaborate three dimensional chess game from bedside tables, dresser drawers, and window sills. The windows were covered in layers of green and white curtains, each layer somehow softer and more translucent then the last. The canopy over the bed done in similar colors to tie it all together.

It was like walking into a catalogue picture; everything just so, full of light and comfort. It couldn't be more different than his red house on the hill.

Claire put him on the second floor. He had the hall to himself, she said, standing with him in the bedroom doorway, the whole house in fact. It was a Tuesday, and what guests she got offseason, generally came on the weekends.

She was still dressed in the same muted dress, the apron back in place. She didn't mention their conversation regarding Philo, or ask him why he was here. She didn't talk at all, except to tell Frank the hours for breakfast and the house rules. Then she nodded to the room as if it spoke for itself, and left him to it.

He put his hastily packed suitcase under the bed. It was nearly empty, most of his possessions, including his clothes, were hopelessly ruined. He sat on the bed, like a man falling into a dream. After the red house mattress, it was like sitting on a cloud.

He tried not to think about the dog. Failed.

He'd asked the sheriff what he was going to do with the body. They stood outside his car, just before he drove to town, and Claire's.

The sheriff shook his head. "I don't relish telling Red. He gets particular about his dogs...and you've got enough trouble as it is." He fiddled with his belt. "I tell you what, I'm going to keep this a closed investigation for now. You stay quiet at Claire's. Tell anyone who asks you just needed a break from the house, they'll understand, believe me. If he asks, I'll tell Red the dog got out and is running wild again. He may go look for him but he won't go up to house. Okay with you?"

"Okay."

"Not a word to anyone about the dog, Frank. If someone comes asking suspicious questions, you let me know. Maybe someone will give themselves away."

He agreed. They drove to Claire's. No one watched him from the road; no one was in town waiting. He parked in back of Claire's as if he'd been born to it. The sheriff stopped for a short conversation with Claire, then had a quick final word with Frank.

"She thinks you're staying here for a time while the house is getting fixed up," he said. Neither man mentioned what would happen next. Neither man looked to the school yard across the way.

"I guess I was a bit short up there," added the sheriff a moment later. "For what it is worth, I'd like to think you didn't do it, Frank. I'm sure things will sort themselves out."

He sounds like he almost means it, he thought. *And why not, things did sort themselves out.*

I'm out of the house.

* * *

And now he sat on Claire's bed, trying, as the sheriff said, to keep quiet, trying to think what to do next.

He couldn't just hole up in Claire's, eating his meals in bed, making the occasional furtive trip to Sol's. Why should he hide out? Why should he feel ashamed? He'd done nothing wrong.

He got up and paced the room, walking back and forth between the brightly painted figurines and plump decor. Suddenly he wanted to pick up one of the pieces, smash it against the wall, send a message of his own. But a message to who? Claire? That made no sense. She had done him no wrong, may in fact be sympathetic to his plight. Hadn't she told him to leave?

Everything is so twisted, so backward, he thought. *I don't know where or how to strike back.*

He went back to bed and lay down, still dressed in his clothes. He kicked off his shoes. The sun was going down outside the frilly curtain window. He hated the curtains, the window, hated the same sun that set outside his own miserable windows on the hill.

God he wanted a drink. He wondered if Claire stocked beer or something stronger in the house. He couldn't remember her mentioning it. Maybe Sol carried beer?

But the thought of leaving the house and running into Henrik, or worse, Miss May, was almost too much to bear.

There was one place in town he was certain carried a drink: Albert's Tavern.

Maybe I could get Henrik to buy me a drink...after he beat my head against the bar. A vision of the bloody warning on his wall made the back of his neck cold and clammy against the overstuffed pillow.

He didn't remember closing his eyes, or falling asleep.

* * *

Somewhere in the dead of night he woke, disoriented and frightened by the images of his dreams. He took a deep, shaky breath, again surprised by the clean, slightly fragrant air. Then he remembered he was at Claire's, and why.

He shed his clothes and crawled under the covers. There was a stillness to this house, as well. But it was a stillness wrapped in blankets of normalcy and comfort. He felt the cool of the sheets against the back of his feet, heard the mindless drawl of crickets outside the window. He sprawled out across the bed, enjoying the absence of stale air and urine. A car drove by outside the window.

But no dog, he thought a moment later; *no dog to lick the back of my hand.*

A warm rush of emotion swallowed his chest, and hot tears raced down his cheek.

It's odd. I didn't cry at Tara's funeral, or after.

Eventually he got up, walked quietly across the hall to the bathroom and washed his face, then went back to bed, and fell right back to sleep.

It was a deep, undisturbed colossus of sleep. No unnatural cries woke him in the night, no creaking steps set his teeth on edge, no dark words from a twisted journal tainted his subconscious. Just sleep, deep and bottomless and empty.

* * *

He woke late. He'd missed breakfast. That much he remembered from yesterday's instructions. He took a long, hot, decadent shower, enjoying the experience of being more than just clean, of being relaxed.

Too much comfort, he thought with a tinge of guilt. *I'll never go back to the house. Emil or the Judge couldn't have planned this any better...Maybe they did.*

He found a note addressed to "Mr. Henning" outside his door: his breakfast was under a tray in the kitchen. There was fresh coffee in the thermos, and cold milk in the refrigerator.

He ate at the small high table in the kitchen, sitting on a stool, watching the late morning sunlight's crawl across the bright linoleum floor pattern.

He tried to understand what was different. After a time, he knew it was more than just a good night's sleep. He felt safe.

He washed his dishes, stacked them to dry in the rack beside the sink, noting how the stainless steel gleaned in the sunlight from the little dormer window above the table. Grudgingly he recognized he was close to losing another round to the Mundts.

He walked through the open portions of the house, finding it just as contrived and clean and pampered, and yet somehow comforting, as the living room. Claire was nowhere to be found. He wondered if she was staying away on purpose, or busy in town.

Back upstairs, he helped himself to a complimentary toothbrush, toothpaste, and razor from a wicker basket by the sink. Shaved, brushed, and rinsed, he studied the results in the mirror

Despite his efforts, he looked a mess. He could use a haircut, for one. And more than a night's good sleep. His eyes were sunk in dark circles and puffy red ridges, made all the more prominent by his sickly pallor and pinched, almost colorless lips. His shirt was wrinkled. When he lifted the collar to his nose, it smelled of the red house.

So what now? A trip to his friends at the barbers? No, he wasn't ready for that yet.

He could go see Emil about the mattress...

He rolled the idea around for a time, surprised that it grew traction. It would be an effort, a small counter punch to the body blows he'd been taking. Something for the dog.

Before he could make up his mind, he heard the front door open. He waited, assuming it was Claire. He was startled a moment later when a soft voice called his name outside his door.

He opened it, and found Liz standing in the hall. The pimple had been addressed, and was now covered with makeup. She was dressed in blue jeans and a turtleneck, and her hair was in a ponytail, poking through the back of a White Sox ball cap. She looked older today, and more confident. She was holding something behind her back.

"I got it!" she breathed excitedly.

"Got what?" he asked, unsure whether to ask her in or step outside. He compromised and stood in the doorway pulling the door close behind him.

She made a dramatic gesture and brought two leather bound ledgers from behind her back, smiling.

"Hey!" he said, reaching out slowly to take them. "This is great."

"Wait a minute," he added a moment later, looking at her with a frown. "You were supposed to let me get these."

She cocked her head proudly to one side. "Saw the opportunity and took it, boy. Uncle Del left me in the office for a bit to talk with the sheriff outside the door."

He tried to look grateful, but was already feeling the rat teeth of doubt. *Have I made Liz an accessory now?*

Liz was watching him, obviously confused by his reaction. She looked curiously to the half-closed door.

"How did you know I was here?" he asked.

"I told you. I heard the sheriff talking to the judge about you."

"You didn't say they were talking about me. Did the sheriff tell the judge why I was staring here now?"

"No. Maybe. I didn't hear everything they said." She waited expectantly for him to fill her in.

He ignored her interest. "Did anyone see you come here?"

She dropped her smile, hearing the anxiousness in his voice. "No, no one saw me. I waited until Claire left to do her shopping. She always leaves the door open for me because I come in here sometimes, help clean up for a free meal or coke."

But the school and Miss May are across the street, he thought, *and you wouldn't necessarily know if she saw you come here or not.*

"This is great...thank you, Liz." He held up the journals and gave her a big smile. "You better get going now. And let's keep this between us, right?"

"Of course." She seemed just a little disappointed to be sent away. "Let me know how it turns out, or if there is anything else I can do."

"I will. You earned it."

That cheered her up a bit and she bounced off down the hall.

"Wait!" he called after her. She scuttled back. "How do I get ahold of you?" he asked.

She pulled out a cell phone. "Give me your cell number."

"I don't have a cell anymore."

"Well, I'll give you mine and you could use Claire's house phone…or leave a message with Sol!" Her eyes were bright with conspiratorial excitement, and the rat teeth tore another hole.

"Okay." He went back inside and picked up a pen and paper from the bedside table. There was a logo on the top that read *Claire's Bed and Breakfast*, and listed the address and phone number. No email. Apparently Claire did not use the net for marketing.

He turned to find Liz now standing in the bedroom behind him. *What would Miss May make of her being here alone in his bedroom? What would her uncle?*

"Here," he said, thrusting the paper at her. "Write your number down."

Finished, she handed him the paper with a wink. "That's priceless, that is. Michalus would kill for it."

His smile fell away quickly with images of another awkward round in the sheriff's office.

"Okay," he said. "See you soon."

She gave him another wink, her eyes laughing. Was she playing with him, knowing her flirting made him uncomfortable? How experienced was she in these matters? He'd have to warn her soon about what the judge might make of such teasing, even if, as he sincerely hoped, it was just in fun.

* * *

Holding the ledgers in his hand tempered the sunlight through the lacey curtains and his temporary peace. *Get Out.* An image of the dog lying in the blood darkened the room still further.

He opened the first ledger. It was a listing of births, all male, sometimes with small notations besides the name. The names were grouped in sets, sometimes pairs, sometimes four or more. He guessed the groupings indicated a family, brothers. The listing started with the Captain's sons. There was an "h" beside Fredrick's name, which Frank took to mean heir. Thaddeus had an "s," again, presumably for scion. *Why differentiate the two and use such arcane titles?*

The number "1" followed Han's name. Some of the names were crossed out, though it was impossible to say what this meant. Like the one in the Captain's journal, none of the listings had the actual birth date or date of death, or the parentage.

But this was not the work of the Captain. It was not his handwriting. In fact, the handwriting changed from generation to generation. Nor was there any extended exposition or historical notes. Just the names and the small notations.

He picked up the second ledger and gave it a quick glance. He flipped to the back and felt a chill as he recognized a name: Michalus. He assumed this was Emil's son and not a namesake. But he couldn't be certain, the parentage remained unlisted. Michalus had the number "2" and a question mark behind his name.

He then discovered the set he was most familiar with, one generation up from the group with Michalus. Someone had altered the listing in the past, but there they were, his nightmares.

Aldarich (s) *stillborn*
Philo (h)
Emil (1)
Henrik (2)

There was no doubt that this was the same Emil, Henrik, and Philo. Aldarich, however was new to him. No one, not Claire, the sheriff, Sol, or the Judge, had mentioned that name. He was sure of it.

If he read the notations correctly, then the s stood for "scion," not stillborn. *Or maybe, in this case, both?*

He looked through the other sets of names again. One page back was another group with similar listings of h, s, and the numbers 1 and 2. The word stillborn was written in the same hand behind the s and the name, Franz, was scratched out, just like Aldarich. In fact, every listing of (s) was followed by the word stillborn, all in the same handwriting, and all the names scratched out.

He pulled the journal from his coat and reread the passages concerning Thaddeus. There was no mention of a stillborn birth by his name of course. He consulted the first ledger again. There was no addition of stillborn behind any of these listings either.

Why not? What had changed between the first and second ledger? Had someone just not gotten around to it, or did they think it didn't matter? Or was there another, darker reason?

He idly flipped through both ledgers for a time, noting the number of different sets, the repetition of certain names (never a Junior or III behind them), the listing of numbers, always 1 or 2. *There must be four, five generations of an extended family here*, he thought.

And no girls. No parentage. No dates.

He set the ledgers aside. He had more information now, but no more actual proof of wrong doing. Even if the family continued the Captain and Sister's tradition of "training" for a generation or two, there was no evidence that it still went on today.

And what does the training entail, anyway, he thought? *It is only my suspicion, based on the nature of the tools and a few brief passages in the Captain's journal. What would the sheriff and judge make of that? Conjecture? Slander?*

Evidence. Records. He needed hard proof. There was a building here in town with records. What would he find in the town's listings? Surely the town kept a census of some sort, a listing of birth and death certificates. Should he try to match the official records up with what he found in the ledger? Was there a listing for a stillborn Aldarich? But again, what would it prove? Listings were not evidence of a crime.

But they might clear up one matter.

He saw again the children standing in the school lobby, felt his heart race at the dark implications they raised. Would the town dare to list the dangerous marriages he suspected must be at the root of deformities he'd seen at school? What about the town doctor? The sheriff had mentioned a doctor. No, that was in Summerset, about an hour away, a forensic specialist. Did Torview have a town doctor? A hospital, with records? Surely there was a local general practitioner of some kind. If he wasn't a Mundt, would he know the truth, talk about it?

But again, again again, what good would it do? Was inbreeding a crime? He wasn't sure. He thought it might be. But how did that help him secure his place in the house? He didn't see how he could blackmail a whole town into accepting him, especially on that basis. He would have to go public, outside of the town, to make the blackmail stick. No matter what result, he would remain an outcast to much of Torview afterward, and now with cause.

Besides, he didn't think he could bring himself to do it. The children were not to blame, and yet they would probably suffer the most.

And, in truth, he thought bitterly, *the incident with the school threatened to undermine any accusations I might make in any direction, blackmail or no, here in town or otherwise.*

He shook his head. If only the Mundts had come at him with violence, like Henrik wanted, maybe he could bring in the outside law (he still had doubts about the sheriff.) He had no delusions of what a day in court would be like over the school incident. Even the dog might be used against him. *Was that whole point of making it an official investigation*, he thought, new doubts of the sheriff rising?

Even if he was eventually vindicated, and surely he would have to be no matter what the judge threw at him (he held on to that like a man clutching his last coin before the taxman), he would forever be tainted by suspicion and doubt. Any accusations he raised would be seen in the light of revenge or self-service.

And then there was the other thing, the reality. He was a recent widower, torn up by the sudden and heartbreaking loss of his wife to cancer, living alone in on an isolated former mining shaft. *Enough garbage around the house ruined the property value no matter how nice it was inside.*

He was in the last rounds, but the fight was fixed, the judges bought, the crowd against him.

There was only one place to go. But how to get there unnoticed? Because that would be the key, and he couldn't be certain he wasn't being watched. The sheriff's suggestion of Claire's was becoming more suspicious by the moment.

He sat for a time thinking through possibilities, but it all came back to one person.

He put his coat on and tucked the journal inside. He debated hiding the ledgers under the mattress, but remembered Claire left her door open. He had a vision of Emil casually searching his room while he was out. Instead, he put the ledgers in a bag, went downstairs, and hid the bag under the couch in the living room.

He found the phone in the kitchen and dialed the number.

"Liz, do you drive?"

Chapter Thirteen

He walked out the door of Claire's, leaving his car conspicuously parked in the front near the street. He didn't try to hide his efforts, but walked straight to Emil's Hardware and Feed Store.

He passed a vaguely familiar truck in front of the Feed gate, and saw a young man behind the wheel. He remembered where he'd seen the truck before, in front of the school, with the Dalmatians. The young man, dressed in overalls and a ball cap, appeared to be watching him from under the bill of the cap, but didn't move or indicate Frank in anyway.

He kept walking.

He found Emil at the counter, hands down the front of his pants, talking to a customer. He rocked back on his heels when he saw Frank, and said something to the customer. The customer turned, the jutting chin identifying him as the owner of the truck. He picked up a brown paper bag from the counter and walked to the door.

"Evening," he said as he passed Frank, the jaw opening and closing like a trap.

"Evening," replied Frank, again caught off guard. The door closed behind the man before he could decide if he was being toyed with, or over reacting.

"Mr. Henning," said Emil from behind the counter, clearly in a good mood. Frank had no doubts of Emil's intentions.

"Mr. Mundt. I understand you have a mattress for me."

The smile was replaced by a confused frown, and he guessed Emil was trying to figure out what to say to this. By now, Emil must know he'd spent the night at Claire's. He may even know about the dog, and Frank's temporary eviction from his house. But if he brought it up, he'd have to tell Frank how he knew. Either the sheriff told him, or Emil was involved. Either way, Frank would learn something about the forces against him.

"That's right, I do," said Emil, finally. "I guess we need to arrange to have it hauled up?" He let the question hang in the air with all the feigned innocence of a used car salesman.

"I guess so." He enjoyed watching Emil squirm a bit in frustration.

"And when would you like it brought up?" Emil rolled back on his heels, the hands down his pants lifting the crotch up, down, up, down.

He pretended to consider the question, then went a different direction. "You have somebody that can haul it up?"

Emil smirked. "I think I can find someone."

"It's just the sheriff said you couldn't be bothered with it."

"Not for free," whined Emil, his smirk growing by the minute.

"How much?"

"Oh, I'd say fifty dollars would cover gas and labor. Not easy to take a mattress up that hill, or those steps."

He took twenty five dollars out of his wallet. "They get the rest when they bring it up."

"Which is when?" insisted Emil, his eyes growing bright.

He knows, he thought. *He knows and is happy to let me know he knows.*

"I'm painting the room just now," he said, using the line he had rehearsed before leaving Claire's. "Soon though. I'll let you know."

"You do that, Mr. Henning. And if you change your mind, you can always have the twenty five back. Heck, I'll even buy the mattress from you." Emil was now practically dancing on his toes, the front of his pants looking like an angry bellows.

"No chance of that," he said quietly, meeting Emil's eye. "I'm here to stay in that house, come hell or high water."

The light was still in Emil's eyes, but now it held more malice than glee. "Come hell or high water, Mr. Henning."

Outside the store, he thought he might have split that round, though Emil got the last punch in.

He stepped on the street, wondering how many eyes were on him now. He considered the Municipal Building. Should he push his luck? He had no intention of confronting the judge yet, but he might find something interesting in the town records, if he could get to them. No, it was too likely he'd run into the judge, and he didn't trust himself to hold his tongue if it should get tense. Emil was one thing, the judge quite another.

He checked his watch. The plan called for him to meet Liz behind Sol's at 1:00. He had a half an hour. He went through the plan again, thinking what to do with the time he had left.

The back of Sol's was hidden from view from the street, little more than a small parking lot with a dumpster. But it had a small utility road for the dump truck and deliveries. As Sol lived in the house directly behind the lot, and the houses on either side were currently vacant (the owner's moving out shortly after learning Sol and his family were moving in), Liz thought it their best chance to get away unobserved. She would get away and meet him there in her car, leaving his out in the street in front of Claire's for any watchful eyes to see.

He was relying a great deal on the girl, and Sol's goodwill. He didn't have time to discuss the plan with the diner owner beforehand.

He had thought to return to Claire's after his deliberate run in with Emil, to establish his whereabouts, and then make his way to the diner as surreptitiously as possible. But now he changed his mind. He crossed the street, hoping the place was empty, but for Sol. It was.

He sat at his usual stool, ignored the cup of coffee in front of him, and told Sol all that had happened, including the school yard run in, including the dog, including his suspicions about the Captain and the Mundts. Finally, he told him about the plan.

There was a long pause when he finished. He watched Sol carefully, looking for signs of betrayal or trust. Finally, the man in the apron nodded slowly, as if to himself.

"Sure, Frank. I'll let you go through the kitchen. And I'll check out back first, just to be sure."

He sighed in relief and nodded gratefully. "No one can know I'm with Liz."

Sol blinked. "Okay."

Was he thinking about the school yard? Was he having second thoughts? How would I feel if a practical stranger told me this tale?

"It's like this, Sol," he said, trying to explain and assuage any doubts the other might have at the same time. "I have to get up there unseen, or I'd ask you to take me. I just don't think it would work that way. You're absence would be too noticeable. And Liz has an excuse to go up the road. She's seeing Red Barton's boy."

"Sure, Frank."

He seemed to Frank to at least be giving him a benefit of a doubt. But what he was thinking, was impossible to say.

"She will be coming back here directly. To let you know everything went okay," he added, wondering if he sounded desperate. "I'll insist on that."

Sol only blinked again, nodded his head. They heard a car pull up in back.

"So, let me check," said Sol. He was back a moment later, standing in the kitchen door and holding it open. "Okay. She's in the lot."

He walked around the counter, past Sol and into the kitchen. It was smaller than he imagined and full of pots and pans and plastic bins of vegetables. The smell of fried grease and spices was so strong it made his nose run. There was a wooden door on the back wall with a screen. The heavier door was standing open. Through closed screen, he could see Liz sitting behind the wheel of a rusty Nova. He turned and shook Sol's hands.

"Thanks," he said.

"No problem, Frank."

"If anybody asks, you say I mentioned something about the Market."

"Okay, Frank. Good luck and be careful."

"Thanks, Sol." He hesitated in the doorway. There was probably more to say, but he couldn't think of anything that didn't sound like a guilty conscience. He let the door shut behind him, walked quickly to the car and lay down in the back seat without looking back.

"This is just like a prison break," said Liz.

"No," he said, cringing in the seat. "It's nothing like that at all. Just do like we planned, okay."

"Okay, okay," she whined.

"And you probably shouldn't talk."

"Don't worry so much. If anybody sees me, they'll just think I'm singing to the radio. I usually do."

"Did you bring the flashlight?"

"Yes, I brought the flashlight. You do know its daylight, right?"

She's probably right about the talking, he thought, paying no attention to her sarcastic glances in the rear view mirror. *As long as no one saw me get in the car, she should be fine.*

According to Liz, it would not be strange for her to be seen on that road at this time of day. She often drove to the Barton's, to see Erik.

He felt the car kick into gear, and experienced the disorientation of traveling without seeing where he was going.

She ignored his request, and started talking before they even left the parking lot. The car had been a gift from her Uncle, she said. A welcome to the neighborhood concession for an obviously frustrated Liz, who found the limited opportunities in Torview stifling. She wasn't allowed to go outside the Torview area unless she got permission and took a chaperon, but the Barton boy's house was in the permitted limits. She *had* made two trips to Summerset this summer. Both trips she'd taken Claire.

"Erik and I sometimes sneak off to a place we know," she continued. He saw her adjust the rearview mirror to look at him. It was clear that despite her bravado, she was nervous.

He refused to engage with her, in part because he wanted to concentrate on the road, but also because he didn't want to encourage her in any way to think of him as something more than a passenger.

The plan, what little there was of it, was for her to drop him off near the bottom of his hill. Then she would go on alone to Erik's. She would not stay long, but head back and make sure the judge or the sheriff saw her in town. He would find his own way back to town, walking most likely. He insisted on that part, though Liz had argued she could pick him up on the way back, or come later at a prearranged time.

"I have no way of contacting you and I don't know how long I'll be," he pointed out at Claire's. "Besides, the less you have to do with this the better."

"That's a long walk in the cold."

"I'll manage. No negotiation."

"Fine. Be that way."

But now he was her captive audience, and she took full advantage of that fact.

"You know, Frank, you're not being much of a partner on this whole return trip thing. It does get cold in the hills, especially at night. This car might be old, but it's got a good heater. What's the matter, don't you trust me?"

Something in her tone set him to worrying all over again.

"Listen, Liz," he said, staring at the frayed ceiling lining of her car. "You've been great about this, and I appreciate your friendship..." He stopped. *How can I say this without sounding like a presumptuous jerk?*

He heard her giggling from the front seat. "Relax, Frank. I'm just teasing you. I told you, I know a creep when

I see one. You're all right, or I wouldn't be within ten feet of you. And no offense, but you could be my father."

Feeling relieved that this much at least was understood, he addressed the more pressing issue. "The problem is you might be the only one that knows that." He hesitated, then took the plunge. "I think the judge would use our friendship against me. There was an incident at the school yard."

"Yeah, I heard."

"You did?" He stared incredulously at the back of her head, mortified.

"Michalus told me. Not much like that goes on in this town that people don't know."

"Just so you know, I just went to look at some books."

"I believe you. Remember: creep radar." She glanced at the rear view mirror again. "That May's wound a bit tight."

"I hope Sol believes me," he muttered.

"I'm sure he does. He wouldn't believe anything tight-ass May had to say about anyone anyway. They had some words about his boy last year. Real nasty stuff on her end."

He felt a little better. "Just the same, keep our friendship a secret when it comes to your Uncle."

"And the sheriff," he added a moment later.

"You don't trust Sheriff Cal?"

"I don't know what to make of the man."

"He's been decent to me."

"And to me, for the most part." *For the most part. But not always. There was still the record in that file.*

Long before he was ready he felt the car slow down and pull to the side of the road. He sat up and looked around. They were down a bit from the road to his house, but he could see it running up the hill from here. And he could see his house. It looked colder and lonelier than ever.

"Thanks, Liz," he said, climbing from the car and putting on a wool cap. It was getting cold already and he pulled his coat close. "Just like we planned it now. Move on."

She handed him the flashlight through the window, gave him a long look. All the bravado was gone now, replaced by concern and doubt, and he thought, *she deserves better than a Michalus or the judge, or Torview. If Erik Barton had any brains at all, he'd take her out of this place and never look back.* Then he wondered why he thought Erik Barton would be any better than anyone else in Torview.

He smiled, waved her off, and turned away. He heard the car pull away behind him, and started up the hill.

Using the chimney as a marker, he picked his way up the snow-covered hill to the red house. It was more difficult than he thought. The ground was uneven, and hidden by a crust of crystallized snow. He learned to step carefully and slowly through the crust, after nearly turning his ankle on a hidden rock.

After five minutes his legs were burning from the effort of climbing and exaggerated footsteps. His breath erupted in white temporary clouds that faded as quickly as they formed, and he was soon sweating under his clothes. Occasionally, the cold air found its way down his jacket and chilled the sweat along the base of his back.

A half hour later, his legs trembling in exhaustion, he stepped onto the plateau in front of his house. The sun was now little more than a brown coin in the white-blue sky, and the light was falling fast. Despite this, he kept the flashlight in his coat pocket, guessing its light would be like a beacon on the hill at this time of day.

He approached the house carefully, listening for signs of life inside or out. The woodshed stood forlornly to his right, looking less menacing now that it was spider free. The handle of his lethal broom was still lying against the shed, like a warning post, or a shotgun in the rear window of a pickup truck.

He stepped quietly to the front door, opened it slowly, gritting his teeth at every creak and complaint of the rusty hinges. Why hadn't he oiled them when he had the chance?

The foyer was dark, which was nothing new. The back room doors were closed. *Where they shut yesterday when I left with the sheriff?* He couldn't remember.

A new odor competed with the usual stale air of the house and yesterday's burnt plastic, a pungent copper taint that drifted down from the stairwell. He looked to the second floor, knowing the blood on the floor and walls was the source.

As he looked down again, he saw that the right wing door was open.

He was certain it had not been open when he left.

Had the sheriff been back already? Somehow, he didn't think so.

He stepped inside the foyer, shutting the door quietly behind him.

He found the crowbar in the kitchen, tossed under the sink with the other wreckage. He took some comfort in its weight and held it in one hand like a club. Holding the lit flashlight in the other, he walked back to the open wing door.

He stepped through, shining the light down the length of the wing, the crowbar raised high.

The wing was empty. The back partition closed. He walked to the back and opened it. He wasn't surprised to find the tools gone, but it sent a chill down his back just the same.

He went back to the foyer, checked the backroom, and finally upstairs. Everything remained a mess, the blood now congealed, the smell rising from the wall and mattress rank and overwhelming.

The house was empty.

He went back downstairs, took out his key ring, stepped out the front door again.

Now for the cellar.

* * *

Someone had anticipated him.

The cellar door was covered in a light blanket of snow which had started to melt in the afternoon but was freezing again. He brushed the snow off with the crowbar. The cellar door was made of heavy, treated pine. It looked to be more recent then the house. *A replacement?*

He found the iron latch that closed the door, and the locks that secured it. *Two locks.* He didn't remember the sheriff mentioning two locks. One looked brand new.

He used the key to pop open the older lock. It didn't fit the other. He tried to bust the latch with the crowbar, but it was too well made and mounted to get a good purchase.

Fine, he thought. He had a backup plan.

He went back in the house, swinging the crowbar in anticipation.

He delivered the first blow for the dog. The crowbar went through the back wall like butter, crumbling the plaster into dust and leaving hanging bits of hair and white chalk. He pried the bar back and forth opening up a fist-sized hole. It was messy work and he was soon covered in dust. He stopped to wrap a cloth around his mouth and nose. The flashlight was sitting on the dining room table behind him, making a shadow of his form against the wall.

He'd chosen the broken middle line for his entry point. He didn't care how much noise he made at this point. But he did stop and listen after the first few blows, for what exactly he couldn't say.

The hole was big enough now for him to see the wooden frame that supported the plaster wall. One by four boards ran from ceiling to floor with the occasional crossbar in between. He went back for the flashlight, and poked his head through the hole. He thought could just squeeze through one of the cross-sections.

Behind the plaster wall's frame was a small alley, and another, older wall. This wall was clearly the original, made by the Captain all those years ago to convert the house from mining shaft to home.

The older model was made of unbroken plaster similar to the outer wall, only much older. Only one section in the middle was different. Enormous aged pine boards reached from ceiling to floor and covered a space roughly the size, and in line with, the dining room big doors and the sealed front entrance of the house.

The opening to the mine shaft, he thought. *They brought the ore up here, then ran it right through the house.*

He pulled his head out of the hole, removed the cloth from around his face, and looked once more around the empty dining room. It remained empty, and still.

He took a quick breath, then stepped through the small opening in the wall and frame, holding the crowbar precariously in one hand and the flashlight in the other.

The alley between the two walls left just enough room for him to negotiate. A quick pass of the light down either direction of the original wall revealed no cracks or entryways, but it was difficult to be sure as the wall curved slightly on either end. He turned right, and carefully scuttled through the alley to the end.

And it was there, a simple utility door, little more than something you would find on a closet, flush against the wall with a sliding handle making the access invisible unless close up. He slid the handle back, his heart racing at its smooth, noiseless retreat, then pushed the door open, watching it swing back into pitch darkness.

Cold, damp, ancient air emanated like a piece of nightmare from the dark rectangle of the doorway. It took an effort of will not to shut the door again, to run back out down the alley and out the hole in the wall. To climb in his car and leave Torview forever.

Swallowing his fears, he slowly lifted the flashlight floor to ceiling, revealing a square railed platform just on the other side of the entry. As the light continued upward the light failed to register anything more than empty darkness and vague, shadowy outlines.

He stepped out on the platform, feeling it sway slightly under his weight. Steadying himself, he stepped to the edge of the platform and experienced a body-clenching vertigo and grabbing for the railing and nearly losing his flashlight in the process. The platform he stood on extended over a heartless, empty drop that was lost in vague contours of wet black rock and empty shadows.

Still clutching the rail, he turned carefully to his left where a slim landing extended from the platform and ran the length of the original wall. Directly across from the planked covered section of the wall was a massive head-frame, extending from the landing side on two massive support beams.

The frame was roughly rectangular and made of crisscrossed grey timber. A hoist was mounted to an immense crossbeam at the top. A rusty chain ran through and from the hoist, connecting to a rusty sheave wheel mounted on the landing.

He had guessed right, the planking blocked the original opening from the hill to the house. The frame hauled the ore from the dig with the hoist and sheave wheel, and then deposited the haul into what was now his dining room. Doubtless it was a rending or processing room before its conversion.

There appeared to be a stairway of some kind on the opposite side of the shaft. He stepped carefully to the landing, and shuffled along its length in that direction. As he drew closer, his flashlight picked out the steep, alternating flights and short landings of a floating staircase, attached to the shaft like some odd barnacle.

The staircase descended into the dark, lost to an ever-expanding bottom that his light could not reach. Looking closely at the nearest sections, he noted many of the spindles connecting the treads to the handrail were missing or hanging loose. The treads looked to relatively whole, what he could see of them. But one was missing near the top, and the dark hole it exposed sent a chill through him.

Enormous rusty chains and broken flywheels were scattered everywhere along the landing, some trailing their ends over the edge and down the hole of the open shaft. The other end of the chain around the hoist disappeared down the hole in a straight, rusty plumb line.

He could see some of the stone had been chiseled and shaped around the shaft, stairwell, and landing. But wherever possible the architects had taken advantage of the many natural fissures and edges of the rough hillside interior. He leaned as far as he dared, and saw far, far below, an extension running from the stairs to one of these natural openings.

The staircase appeared to be the only way down to the extension, and down was where he knew he had to go.

He put a tentative foot on the first tread, felt the whole stairwell sway lightly, and waited with his heart in his throat for it to stop again. He took another step down, and heard the protesting creak of the long unused tread like a klaxon alarm. He thought about the dog lying broken and torn in a puddle of blood, and took another step. He thought about Emil's supercilious sneer, and took another. He thought about the campaign against him, the humiliating interview with the sheriff, all the ugly and manipulative efforts to make him leave, all, most likely, orchestrated by the judge, maybe with the sheriff's help. He thought about being pushed down, spat on.

And with each thought, he took another step down.

But the way was too long, and his anger too frail, to sustain him more than a few minutes. It burned out soon enough, like a piece of paper in fire. He thought then of Tara, first refeeding his anger, than moving to bitterness, and finally misery.

But this, too, soon failed.

By then he was well below the top, the shaft now lost in shadow, but nowhere near the bottom. He stopped for a moment, standing on a frail step, lost in the dark, empty recess, with only his feeble light and a stubborn determination to support him.

It wasn't fear that stopped him. He knew anxiety. How could he not, standing so precariously close to death? *And god knows what below,* he added. But the fear was so common now, so familiar, that even the sense of vertigo had lost its crippling sting.

No, he stopped because he realized something had changed. He had exhausted all of his emotional resources, even the loss of Tara...But he would go on. He would continue to the end because he simply didn't care anymore. He was tired of being lonely and frightened and angry and bitter. He wanted to end the matter, once and for all. No more sleepless nights, no more howls, no more guilt, no more secrets.

And if I do fall, he thought, continuing down the steps and sending the stairwell swaying precariously again, *I'll at least save the good town of Torview the cost of a funeral and coffin.*

Chapter Fourteen

At times he felt like a suspended spider, hanging perilously on a thin web over a deep, unforgiving well. At other times, he lost track of time and seemed to descend into a dark dream. Occasionally he would see thin fissures and ledges in the walls nearest him (the light didn't reach far enough now to discern anything beyond his immediate space), and he wondered if they were man-made or natural.

It was cool now but not cold, as if the hill insulated the lower regions from the outside world. *Or maybe, I'm descending to a ring of hell.*

The wood treads of the steps creaked from time to time, and he still tested each one carefully before he put his full weight down, always ready to spring back or forward should he hear the unforgiving crack of splintered wood. But no screams from the depths or wails of despair. Just the echo of his creaking steps, bouncing off the distant cave walls.

It felt like hours, but eventually he arrived at the extension. It was not what he expected.

A triangular bridge of ropes, two about hand high, and one at foot level, spanned the gap between the short stair landing and an extension of rock jutting from the interior like an extended black tongue. Beyond the rock was a dark entrance, possibly another cave.

He didn't trust himself to hold the flashlight, crowbar, and the guide ropes at the same time, so he tucked the crowbar under his belt near the hip like a sword. He considered turning off the flashlight and putting it in his inner coat pocket as well, but couldn't bring himself to face the tightrope walk with no light at all. Instead, he tucked it upside down in his outer pocket, still on, with the lens sticking out the top at an angle and shining up through the gloom. He moved the light around until the residual radiance let him see a few feet in front of him. But as he started along the bridge, clinging to both guide ropes and stepping gingerly onto the single tightrope beneath them, the flashlight bounced against his body making crazy shadows and distractive flickers.

The rope bent and swayed under his feet, and his hands soon ached from the tightness of his grip. The worst part was in the middle, when the foot rope dipped perilously under his weight and he heard the distinct sound of something snap. Fortunately, whatever snapped wasn't critical to the bridge and he eventually made it across.

He pulled the flashlight from his pocket and hurriedly stepped along the extension and under the overhanging arch, not daring to look back or down from the jutting ledge. Inside (it was a cave of sorts) he swallowed around a dry throat, and leaned against the cool and comfortingly solid walls to catch his breath. There was no natural light to the recess but his flashlight provided enough illumination to see by in the relatively close space.

The flooring was smooth, as were the walls. He guessed he was in a man-made excavation. Tunnels continued in all directions, including up and down. He considered for a moment taking one up, to see where it led, but that could wait. Down would be where he would find his answers, if anywhere. He took the crowbar out of his belt, picked the steepest decline, and headed to what he hoped would be the bottom.

As he descended, he noted little nooks and recesses branching off the time worn passageway, some natural, others obviously man made. Many of these alcoves were large enough for a group to stand under, but a few so small only a child or very small adult could crawl within. Above each opening, even the tiniest, were markings. Many were done in faded chalk, arcane symbols that he didn't recognize, but others gleamed in ominous, pasty crimson under the beam of his light.

The descent seemed to follow natural channels, sometimes turning back on itself for a time, and then back again in the original direction. Other times someone had clearly excavated earth and rock for ease of passage. There were carved steps in steeper descents, and short wooden ladders for the straight drops. Occasionally, the tunnel would take him near the open center, and he would see the empty shadows above and below.

He explored the most promising run-offs, particularly the ones marked in what he assumed was blood. Most looped back to the original path after a brief passage to a small natural alcove. Inside, on the smoother rock sections, were more hand drawings and symbols, a few appeared to be done by the hand of a child. Occasionally, he found odd pieces from the past on the floor: the stub of a candle, a broken piece of crockery, a rusted tin cup, a pile of burned twigs, a crumbled piece of paper, a clutch of barbwire wrapped around a stick. Once he found the skeleton of a small animal, most likely a bird, but the wings were missing.

One of the blood marked recesses opened into a much larger cave and appeared to be a room of some kind. In the center of the cave were three broken stools sitting before a natural dais of sandstone. The dais rose a foot above the floor, and on it lay a pair of rotted bedrolls, bits of stuffing hanging out where the vermin had been at them. Next to the bedrolls was an old wood easel, supporting a writing slate. At the bottom of the slate, along the easel's support bar, was a row of candle stubs.

He stepped closer, shining the flashlight across the gray-black of the slate. There was a neat series of what looked to be handwritten lines running across the board, but the words were now faded and impossible to read. He looked again to the mattresses, wondering why they were there. *Was this one of the Captain's hideaways? Were the faded lines bits of his recorded thought?*

He left the room and continued on.

He almost missed the small reliquary (or so he assumed it to be) as it was partially hidden by a turn in the passage. Only a chance reflection of his beam on the small crimson symbol, like an upside down fishhook with a triangle at the bottom, alerted him to the cutback.

Inside the deep fissure was a closet-size space, with a low pressing ceiling and rough rock walls that he could touch on both sides simply by lifting his arms. In a natural niche was a photograph with an antique black wooden frame, again surrounded by fat white candles.

But this time, some of the candles were almost whole, and matches, modern day matches, lay scattered on the floor. He felt his heart race as he realized some of the matches were only recently used.

The photograph was of a tall, oddly familiar bald man with a full but neatly trimmed beard. He was standing next to a woman, who sat in a plain wooden chair in front of a fireplace. His heart raced again as he recognized the fireplace as the one in the red house dining room.

The man was dressed in a dark formal coat, shoe string tie, straight collar, white shirt, and black wool pants. She wore a plain smock and a small black hat. The hat sat like the lid of a fat tea pot over her piled mass of dark hair. She was a big woman, and even sitting down you could tell she would be nearly as tall as the man.

They stared back at the camera with hard, humorless eyes. There was a noticeable resemblance between the two. The man's right hand rested on the woman's shoulder. She held hers tightly in her lap.

The Captain and his Sister, he thought.

He stared at the image, trying to see in it the people and the natures he suspected from his readings. There was something ominously compelling about their severe expressions, despite the normalcy of their attire and poses. A trick of photography or imagination made it seem as if they were watching him in turn.

He looked to freshest candles on the small ledge of the niche, the recently burnt matches on the floor, and shuddered. Who had come to pay homage to the patriarch and his sister? And why?

He stepped closer to the picture, drawn by those black, hard judgments, and stepped on something, heard it snap under his foot. The flashlight revealed a bit of corroded barbwire now ground to dust under his shoe. The light also revealed another recess, only visible from his close proximity to the photograph. It was little more than a thin fissure, a long crack from floor to ceiling, hidden behind a fold in the reliquary wall.

Stepping carefully, and watching the floor, he turned his body sideways and slid through. The way was short, and opened up into an even smaller space than the one he just left. Now the ceiling was too low for him to stand up in, and he squatted to move completely inside.

A wooden, child-sized chair sat in the middle of the small alcove facing away from the entrance. There were worn leather straps on the arms, and the legs were bolted into the floor. Small dark stains spread out from all four legs, and the seat was covered in sticky, congealed blood. On the far side of the room, directly across from the chair's perspective, was a small mirror.

He shuffled next to the chair until he could see his reflection in the mirror. He felt the walls and ceiling pressing down and around him. The air was lifeless, unnaturally still, stale. It was like being buried alive in a box deep under the earth, a box or coffin.

Instinctively, he turned his flashlight off to get the full effect.

The world went away and he was left alone, trapped in walls of darkness, deep, deep beneath layers of rock and soil. It couldn't have been more than a minute, but even in that time he began to imagine unidentifiable sounds, whispers of movement real or imagined, just on the edge of hearing. He was certain of a presence behind him, watching, reaching out to touch him, grab him.

Was this one of the tests, he thought with a shudder? *Had the Captain dragged his young sons down here to sit bound to a small chair in the dark inside his precious hill?*

He turned the flashlight back on, and almost dropped it, startled by the face that looked back at him.

But of course it was his own, still reflected in the mirror.

He looked to his flashlight, tried not to think about the battery's strength. Tried not to think of finding his way back up through those twisting passages in the dark. He shuffled out of the hole, then out of the reliquary, and continued on downward.

But all the while he felt the hard, black, merciless eyes watching him.

Chapter Fifteen

The end arrived after a long descent through a
deep fissure with steps cut into the rock floor and enclosed
on either side by walls of rough earth and stone. The air was
close in the chimney-like shaft, damp and earthy and chill.
He was glad to be free of it when he finally reached the last
step.

The stairwell opened up into a circular cavern, the
floor and walls worn marble smooth over time by countless
feet and hands. Close to the stairs, an elaborate arched
facade guarded more descending steps that disappeared into
stygian darkness. At the back of the cavern, stood what
could only be an altar.

On the altar were four fat black candles, one on each
corner. Cryptic designs and symbols were etched along
the altar top and sides, all done in the now familiar dark
stain of blood. And in the center of the altar, laid out like
ritual trappings, were the missing tools from the right
wing.

He ignored the altar for now, and walked slowly to
the dark archway. The stonework was of white marble,
filigreed and scrolled like something out of a Greek
temple. The images carved along the capitals, front, and
pillared sides were worn, suggesting great age, but he could
just make out heraldic figures and symbols that might be
similar to the ones in the caves. There was a small domed
ceiling behind the archway, also done in white marble, or
at least painted to look that way.

The steps were cut into the rock floor, and were
broader at the top than bottom, creating a sense of depth.
The illusion was enhanced by clever etchings along the
walls, each decreasing in size as they descended to the

bottom. In reality it was only a few steps to the bottom. An imposing white stone door sat across the length of the small landing.

He took the steps slowly, watching the door all the while. When he reached the bottom, he turned around again. He could just make out the top of the altar above the stairwell. Turning back again, he studied the white door.

The door had two access points, a small spyhole grille near the top, and a larger pull-out drawer at the bottom. The spyhole grille was shut from inside the door. There was a bin to the right with a small pile of firewood, similar to the pile he had standing by his house.

But there were no handles to the door, beyond a bar across the lower drawer. The drawer pulled down halfway, making a chute. A person, a small person, might be able to squeeze inside. But it would be a very tight fit. Hardly a day to day means of access.

For the firewood, then, he thought. *Or other supplies.*

But why make a door that doesn't open?

His thoughts were interrupted by the bark of a man's voice, followed by the trill of a laughing woman. At first he thought the voices were coming from behind the white stone door, but a moment later realized the sounds were above him.

He turned quickly and raced up the steps. The voices were coming closer now, as was a glow of light from the top of the natural stairwell. He looked around for a place to hide. It was no good running behind the altar.

He quickly tiptoed back to the archway where he found a small recess behind the pillars. There was just enough room for him to hide in the shadow created by the wall and pillar angle. He ducked behind the pillar and into the recess, extinguished his flashlight, put it on the floor, and held the crowbar tightly in both hands.

The voices grew clearer, as well as the approach of steps. Light suddenly flooded beyond the archway. A short crack between the pillar and the natural wall, exposed by the intense light, showed Emil, Henrik, and Jenny entering the cavern.

Each carried a lantern in one hand and a bundle of clothing in the other. They carefully arranged the lanterns on the floor and altar to provide the most lighting, and put the bundles on the altar without disturbing the tools.

His vision was limited, as the crack was small and the three kept moving in and out of his sightline. But he could hear them clearly enough, and their casual banter sent chills running down his spine.

The three were now grouped around the altar, drawn by some instinct or ritual. He watched Henrik casually unroll his bundle. It was a wrinkled and dirty purple robe with a large cowl.

Henrik took his greasy ball cap off, revealing a perfectly bald dome and the singular Mundt tuft at the back of his head. The long, dirty locks that fell to his shoulders started only just above his ear line. He quickly pulled the robe on, and pulled the cowl up to cover his head.

Jenny climbed into her robes more slowly, being careful to keep them straight and smooth. Her robe was obviously better tended than Henrik's, and was the color of forest green, not purple. Frank could smell her heavy perfume through the crack now.

Emil ignored his robe for a time, standing in his street clothes, watching the others in idle distraction. Finally, at Jenny's insistence, he donned his robe, similar in color to Henrik's. Unlike Henrik, he left his cowl down, and Frank felt his heart fall as Emil turned to look at the archway.

"I thought for a moment," said Emil, still staring at the archway but not moving, "we'd find him here."

"The lock was on the cellar," said Henrik bluntly.

"I told you," said Jenny, brushing her hair under her cowl. "Delphus has him nicely tucked away now at Claire's."

"The Judge had nothing to do with it," said Emil pointedly. He looked again at the archway, lowered his voice. "The dog was a mistake."

"Yes," said Jenny, matching his tone but with a shade more tension. "But a fortunate one for us, don't you think?" She reached out and brushed her thick fingers down his arm.

"The mistake was getting the wrong one," snarled Henrik. His big cowl turned in Emil's direction. "He's alone, with no family," he continued. "Accidents happen."

Emil frowned. "And accidents get investigated. We don't need the attention. You heard the Judge."

"Who's going to investigate?" said Henrik, crossing his massive arms over his chest. "Guy falls down a hole here, just like the Thomas kid. It's even safer this time. This Henning's got no one to come around asking after him."

"Do you really think so?" asked Emil, his voice now full of muted frustration. "Do you know how much work the Judge had to do over the Thomas kid? And he was local. How do we know what connections this Henning has? Don't be stupid, Henrik."

"I'm not stupid," barked Henrik defensively.

"Now, boys," said Jenny, stepping between the two men and putting her arm around each. "Let's not waste this time over silly arguments. Let Delphus handle it. He'll have Henning sorted out soon enough." She giggled. "He might even turn him around. We can always use new blood, Scion preserve us."

Emil shrugged her arm off. "Uncle Del is too worried about his precious niece to handle Henning."

"Not to worry," chuckled Jenny. "*I'll* turn her out soon enough. They're always curious at that age, and she's no innocent you can be sure." She turned with another giggle to her husband. "Henrik's got his eye on her, don't you, dear?"

Henrik grunted.

"She's for Michalus," said Emil in a flat tone.

"She's for the family," said Henrik, pulling the cowl down to glare at his brother.

"Of course, dear," said Jenny, running a hand up and down Henrik now. "Emil knows that. And Michalus is part of the family."

Emil, who was looking at the archway again, frowned at this, but the others couldn't see it. He glanced to his brother and his wife, then back to the archway. "The judge said the old ways might not be for her."

"The judge is not heir," said Henrik. "No matter what he pretends otherwise. You are heir, now."

Emil shifted on his toes. "I don't want it."

"That doesn't matter," said Jenny, her voice suddenly hard. "You must take a hand."

"You said the judge could handle it."

She scoffed. "Handle Henning, yes. But as to the family, you must be the voice of tradition. The girl will have the old ways...or she will see the Scion."

"The Thomas boy all over again," said Emil.

"Better that, than another Philo," countered Jenny. "The others are already suspicious enough of our line. Claire hasn't been down here since Philo disappeared, and her heart was never in it anyway. Granger is talking about another meeting. You know what he'll suggest. You stepping down will only make matters worse."

"He can have it," said Emil bitterly.

"You don't mean that." She stepped close to Emil, took his arm in hers. She glanced nervously at the archway, dropped her voice. "You're not thinking about what it will mean to you, to Henrik, to our boys. We'll be out of every decision."

Emil's eyes twitched.

"If you want what's best for Michalus, you have to be heir in more than name," she insisted.

Henrik was watching them carefully. "She's right."

Emil sighed, nodded. "I know." He looked to the ground. "I just wanted..." He shook his head. "Michalus is so enamored with the girl."

"I know what Michalus is," said Jenny with a deliberate smile. "He's a boy with the fever to be a man. You need to bring him down here. You were wrong to stop his training. I'd get him to think about something besides that girl. And who knows, maybe I might add to the line one more time. We need a new Scion. Michalus needs to know..."

"Michalus knows his legacy," interrupted Emil.

"But not the whole truth of that legacy. He's a student with just book learning, he needs a more practical appreciation."

"He'll find that out soon enough." Emil turned to face her. "Besides, you know the judge's thoughts on that. We're not getting what we need from the old ways, and he's right. The blood is tainted. Walden...."

"Is our son," said Jenny fiercely. "He's a fine boy."

Emil looked away. "The Scion is not getting younger, and neither Walden, nor Michalus, nor any of the others are fit to take the role." He glanced to the shadowed arch, and with a mumble. "He would not accept them anyway. He's told me as much. We need new blood."

"And you think that's the girl?" laughed Jenny bitterly. "You know what her mother was." She looked to Henrik for support, then back to Emil. "And quit bringing up the judge. He's past his use. Philo coddled him too much."

Emil ran a distracted hand across his head. "If I am heir, then I will have it my way. Michalus will marry that girl and we'll leave them alone—in everything. That's final. As to the judge..." He chewed his lower lip. "I agree. His time is done."

Jenny met her husband's eyes behind Emil's back, gave him a small, knowing nod. "As you say, Emil. If you change your mind later about the girl..."

"I won't."

Jenny waved her Henrik's protest off behind Emil's back. "As you say," she repeated. "You're the heir."

Emil nodded brusquely. "I am." But unlike Frank, Emil didn't see Jenny wink to her husband, or Henrik's sneer.

"It's time," said Emil, turning back to the others. "Light the candles."

"Should we wait for the others?"

"No. They're busy, or won't come."

"We're losing them," said Jenny, looking meaningfully to Emil.

"We'll get them back," said Emil confidently. "Or will start another line, and it won't matter."

"With Michalus and Walden," she said with a smile.

"And the girl," added Henrik.

"For the tradition," added Jenny quickly, before Emil could ask him what he meant by that. "For the family."

He nodded slowly. "For the family."

Henrik lit the candles as Emil stepped toward the arch.

For a moment Emil was out of Frank's line of sight. He tightened his grip around the crowbar, readying himself.

But Emil must have stopped just short of the pillared entrance.

"Scion," he called in loud, ritualistic tones. "The Heir and family greet you and send our goodwill. We ask yours in return. If there is any need or any desire you have, let it be said and we will answer it. For the Family, and in the Name of the Family, and the One who gave us both."

Frank turned to look down to the white door, which was only just illuminated by the light of the lanterns in the other room. Nothing stirred.

"C'mon," said a hungry voice behind him. It was Henrik.

Frank turned to the crack again. Jenny was shedding her robes and the rest of her clothing. Henrik was pulling off his boots to get at his pants. Emil returned and soon disrobed as well.

He was not really surprised by what followed. He had expected it ever since he saw the way Jenny looked at Emil, and Henrik ignored it.

There was nothing erotic about the act, at least not for Frank. Instead, he began to grow ill. It was not just the taboo nature of their lust, nor the almost ludicrous familiarity each took with the other, going from one permutation to another like a determined but jaded dance troupe. It was revolting because of everything it was not, for everything it mirrored darkly, a parody of something wholly intimate and private, shared with Tara time and time again over the years.

Now that was ruined, forever juxtaposed with the animalistic grunting and thrusting and utter depravity of the figures seen through the crack. Like a terrible accident passed on the roadside, he couldn't look away.

Until it became too much, too real, and then he turned away with a convulsion, fighting to keep from screaming, from running out and beating them off each other like dogs with the crowbar. He stood there shaking in the dark corner, trying desperately to hold onto the image of Tara, sublime and beautiful in their bed—only to have it wretched away by the mounting animal sounds, Tara's image now superimposed with Jenny's lust-ridden laughing fat face and Emil's mounting, frantic wheeze.

He looked up from to the floor to the white door, searching for some distraction, some way to block the noises and images from the other side of the wall.

And then he did scream.

The face looking back at him behind the now open upper grille was horrifically deformed. The mouth was twisted in an unnatural snarl, the upper lip severely cleft at the top and exposing a maw of brittle, crooked teeth. The nose was little more than slits with twin spars of bone near the bottom, and the white, pasty skin, was stretched over the elongated skull like a piece of tissue. And the eyes.... *My god, those eyes!* The eyes were red and milky white, like strawberry currant ice cream. And they were staring back at him.

The grille closed with a sudden bang. The debauchery behind him stopped. Someone called out and he heard the rush of feet in his direction.

He didn't think to use crowbar. He just let the naked, sweating Henrik take it from his hands. Emil joined them, then Jenny, all naked, all staring at him and the now closed grille.

Jenny laughed, breaking the spell. With a snarl Henrik swung the crowbar, even as Emil cried, "No!"

***

He woke once, briefly. He was being dragged across the floor by the shoulders. He smelled the foul, tobacco-ridden breath of Henrik, and heard the words, "For the Scion," or something to that affect.

Someone was lifting him, squeezing him into a box or hole. He remembered falling backwards, landing hard. Strong hands grabbed him again, and he was assaulted by a new odor, something moldy, stale, and nauseating. Then he passed out completely.

Chapter Sixteen

When he woke again, he was lying in an iron bed, very similar to the ones in the right wing. He was bound to the bedrails by leather straps. His head hurt terribly, and there was a bitter, coppery taste to his tongue. It was difficult to focus or move, each time he tried, he felt a searing pain along the top of his head. Eventually he gave up and just lay still with his eyes closed, futilely willing the pain in his head to go away.

There was music playing somewhere.

After a time, he tried again. Something danced in the corner of his right eye. A small fire in a red stone hearth was burning brightly to his right. The fire provided the only light in the room, reflected across a dark marble floor and casting complex shadows on whitewashed walls and ceiling. To his left was a small open doorway. Lifting his head for a moment, he saw an old overstuffed Victorian near the edge of his bed.

He had to lay back and close his eyes again then, his head feeling like it was splitting open like an overripe melon. Eventually, he was able to open his eyes again and take a better look around.

Above the fireplace hearth was a strange seascape painting. It appeared to be of a boat traversing storm-tossed seas, lightning etched in the background against a roiling black sky. But the perspectives were off, the waves too broad at the top, the sky too narrow for the open sea, the boat unnaturally square. It might have been done by a child, but for the evident control.

Also on the hearth was a candelabra and two small iron figures of men holding lanterns. The figurines stood on either end of the hearth. The candles were unlit.

The music made an abrupt stop with a scratch, and started again a moment later. He recognized the tune: Vivaldi's *The Four Seasons*.

He heard someone moving beyond the door to his right, gently rolled his head in that direction. Heavy, shuffling steps seemed to hesitate just outside the doorway, their source still lost in the shadows. He tried again to sit up, but stopped with another sudden spasm of pain along his head.

Then the sickly-sweet stale odor of before permeated the room, overcoming even the wood smoke from the fireplace. He heard a soft rattle of difficulty breathing and watched the doorway expectantly, blinking rapidly to clear his pain-rattled vision.

He waited for what seemed an eternity, his own breath growing heavier in anticipation and fear, his head pounding with every new breath. He blinked once, and it was there in the doorway, the ravaged face from the spyhole.

The face returned his stare for a time, filling up the entire doorway. The man was easily a foot taller than the sheriff, and broader and stouter than Henrik. He wore an old black tweed coat with missing buttons and loose strings hanging from the button holes. Under the coat was a yellowed white shirt with a short round collar and ebony round buttons. His heavy trousers were worn shiny at the knees and frayed at the cuffs, which rode hide above the black boots with missing shoe strings. The foul odor was emanating from the giant. He was holding something in his hands that Frank couldn't make out.

The giant twisted its long, unnatural head in a rolling spasm, the terrible mouth clicking like some kind of broken nutcracker. The red-milky eyes returned to stare at Frank for a moment, then the giant stepped through the archway and up to the bed.

Frank twitched in his bindings, tried to meet those red-milky eyes, but was drawn instead to the knife now clearly visible in the giant's hands. It was a rounded blade, and the edge winked in the firelight.

The two stared at each other for a time, the twisted features of the giant twitching from time to time in unnatural spasms. Then without warning, the giant grabbed Frank's arm in one massive hand, and quickly slit the bond along his wrist. He stretched across the bed, the smell threatening to gag the prostrate Frank, and did the same for the other wrist.

Then the giant turned, and with slow, almost painful steps walked to the Victorian. It folded its big frame in the chair with a sigh.

Frank sat up on the bed, his vision blurring for a moment from the effort. He rubbed his wrists for a time, and then carefully felt along the top of his head, discovering a deep gash.

He turned to the giant. It appeared to be watching him carefully, but its face was partially hidden now in the shadow of the Victorian wings.

"I'm sorry," said a voice from the chair, sounding like crumpled paper. The words erupted in broken bits and whistles, and it took Frank an effort to understand.

"I think I scared you," continued the giant, "and gave you away earlier, at the door."

There was no malice or ill intent in the broken voice, just pain and an almost impossible sorrow. With an effort, Frank ignored the pounding in his head, stared at the shadowed figure.

"Aldarich?" he guessed tentatively.

The giant nodded, leaning a little into the firelight.

Frank saw the half-rotted mouth remained open even after it was finished, and watched in slight revulsion as the spotted purple tongue moved slowing from one broken set of teeth to the other, like a distended worm writhing on a summer sidewalk. *Spring's* allegro filled the shadows with ironic illusions of light and air.

"Why was I bound?" he asked, swinging his feet over the side, but not daring to stand up yet.

"You kept falling off the bed," said Aldarich. "You had some kind of fit. It seemed safer to tie you when I had to leave the room." His head rolled again in spasm. "To check on them."

He didn't have to ask who the giant meant.

"Where are we?"

"The Captain's underground home. The Scion's home. My home." This last was said with just a trace of bitterness. "You know who I am. How?"

"I guessed. I came across the name in a ledger. You are Philo's brother." He met the red-milky eyes, trying to ignore the ravaged face. "And Emil's and Henrik's."

"Yes."

"You're listed as stillborn."

A sound like dry leaves being blown over concrete was coming from the chair now. It took a moment before he realized Aldarich was laughing.

"If only," said the other, and now the bitterness was full of irony. After a time, the laughing noises stopped. "So you know everything."

"Not everything," he said. "I read the Captain's journal. I know you are the scion. I think."

This brought no response from the chair, just the painful rasp of awkward breathing.

"Why am I here?" he asked finally, when the chair remained silent. "I mean, as opposed to down somewhere in a big hole, dead?"

"Emil thinks he's clever," answered Aldarich.

Each time the other spoke, Frank thought the ruined jaw would fall off. *It's like watching a door come off its hinges.*

"This way, there are no remains," finished Aldarich.

Frank started to nod, stopped at the pain, and said, "I'm behind the white door."

"Yes."

"The door doesn't open, does it?"

"No. They used the chute. I tried to soften your fall, but I was late. It seems I am always late now." He made a clicking noise with his tongue, turned to the fire.

"I'm sorry about the dog," he said after a time, his head rolling in another spasm. He put his big pale hands on the arms of the chair and Frank saw that many of the nails were black. "I didn't hear it happening until too late."

"Who was it?" asked Frank.

"Jenny's boy. Walden. Walden's come to the house many times, always leaving some small animal behind." The head fell. "Once a young boy. I was too late for that as well." There was a long, awkward pause. "There are a number of monsters in my family. I'm just one of the uglier versions."

Frank searched for something to say to this, failed.

"So it was Walden who wrote the message; the one telling me to get out?"

"Yes."

Frank looked down at his hands. There was blood on them. The sight made his throat itch, and he started to cough.

Aldarich climbed slowly from the chair and walked out of the room. He brought back a tin cup full of cold water, which Frank took gratefully.

"I have some wine," said Aldarich. "But I don't think you should drink it now in your condition."

"This is fine."

The cold of the water made his head ache again, but it also relieved some of his discomfort. He looked to Aldarich, hesitated. The other waved him on.

"Ask," he said around another broken chuckle. "You cannot ask me anything that will disturb me more than my own conscience."

"Michalus is Jenny's boy," said Frank slowly.

"Yes."

"They...." He hesitated again, searching for a way to say it. "They share each other?"

"Yes."

Frank was on the edge of some understanding, but his throbbing head made it difficult to think. "The grille," he said, struggling with his thoughts out loud. It looks out on the altar. Emil called you. You can talk to them. You...you watch them?"

Aldarich paused before answering, the jaw moving slowly from side to side again. "It is part of the ritual," he said with a dry, rasping sigh. "The blessing of the scion's gaze on the fertility ritual is tradition."

He hung his awkward head. "And if I don't watch, they will stop bringing food, water, wood for the fire."

When he spoke again, it was in slow, muted tones, the words still breaking but now coming more often. "If there is a healthy birth, sometimes I get gifts: soap, a new cup, a bowl. If it is a boy, I might get a bottle of wine. A new record for the gramophone. A book." This last he said almost reverently. "I like books best of all." A pause. "Though my eyes cannot see the small print now."

Again Frank struggled between propriety and his need to know, but he was too far along now to quit.

"Does the judge come down here?"

"Not for the fertility ritual. But he presides over the initiations. Sometimes they hold meetings down here." Aldarich looked to the fire. "And sometimes Delphus comes just to visit, to see how I am doing. He always brings a small gift. Usually wine. But he hasn't come in such a long time now."

There was another pause.

"Initiations?" prodded Frank.

"The children."

"They take the children down here?"

"Not as much now. It used to be a very important part of the process to bring the children before my door to have the scion look upon them. Some are trying to move away from that tradition." He paused. "But they still use the house."

"For what? Use the house for what?"

"To teach them. To teach the children their family history, their heritage. To educate them into what it means to be a Mundt. To prepare them for the rituals and initiations that will come later."

The head rolled again.

"The sheriff is part of this?"

"I have only seen the sheriff in the house, though he has never seen me. He has never been below that I know of. Philo said there was an arrangement. It is possible the sheriff doesn't know everything that goes on, but I doubt that." The head rolled again. "It doesn't matter, as he has no children."

Frank started to respond to that, but changed his mind. "Philo is gone," he said instead. "Disappeared."

"I know." A long pause as the head rolled again from side to side. "I know where he is. Someone killed him and shoved him through the chute like you. I was sleeping at the time so I didn't find the body until later."

"Henrik?"

"I believe so. Emil may have ordered it, though. He wasn't terribly surprised when I told him about finding Philo dead. Emil said that it was probably for the best; Philo had broken the tradition. They were angry about the house...and other things." Aldarich looked to the fire again, whether in reflection or anger or some physical tic, it was impossible to tell.

"I should have known something would happen," continued Aldarich, turning back to Frank. "I told Philo to be careful. They were asking questions."

"About the gambling?"

"No." The big man sat up straighter, leaned forward in the chair and sending a waft of his odor in Frank's direction. "No," he repeated. "About our plan. We had a plan."

"You and Philo?"

"Yes. We wanted an end to it, to everything. I was to be the last scion, and he would be the last heir. We told no one, not even Claire. Philo would sell the house. I was going to seal off the underground, permanently. He was going to bring me what I needed."

Aldarich's head was now dancing in all directions in obvious excitement, his words becoming more broken and forced. "I think Henrik or Emil suspected Philo was up to something, but they didn't know about me. They didn't know we were working together."

"What happened?"

Aldarich hesitated. "I don't know. We were going to bring the judge in on our plan. Philo believed he could convince the rest with the judge's help, especially after I sealed the lower regions. We knew Henrik and some of others would never come around, but Philo had hopes for Emil. Maybe he spoke to him, or the judge, and they betrayed him. But I don't know. We didn't have a chance to talk before he was killed."

Aldarich leaned back in his chair. "But it might be that one of them confronted Philo when you bought the house. Or maybe Henrik just acted on his own."

"If I had anything to do with it, I'm sorry."

The shadowed head danced again, but the other remained silent.

"Are you in danger?" asked Frank.

"I don't think so. I don't think Philo told them of my involvement."

There was a long pause as both men thought on what this revealed of Aldarich's brother.

"Can you get out of here?" asked Frank finally, looking toward up to the ceiling.

Aldarich nodded. "The Captain had secrets which he passed on only to the scions," he said, spitting the words out as if each syllable cost him. "The others don't know, not even the heir, not even the judge. We—the scions—were always careful not to show ourselves. But yes, I can get out."

"If you can leave, why stay here?"

The big man laughed again in that strange, rough cough. "And where would I go?" he said. "The only place I belong expects me to stay here."

"You've...you've never been outside?"

The broken jaw worked slowly around the question for a time.

"Once," he said finally, his voice barely reaching Frank just a few feet away. The fire cracked and Aldarich turned to look at it as he spoke.

"Before I became the scion, I saw the world outside Torview. We were young, Philo, myself, Emil and Jenny. Our father took us to another town, a small place with a little diner. A rare treat. Our father was unusual in that way for a Mundt. Philo, I think took after him."

There was a pause as Aldarich drew a deep, rattled breath before continuing.

"The others didn't like leaving home, but Philo and I were excited. It was only a small town, but we both took it as a grand adventure. I wore a hood that hid my face. But it was hot that day, and Philo told me I could take it off once we were inside, and father wasn't looking." Another long pause. "The waitress saw me."

Frank saw something glean along Aldarich's cheek, a tiny glitter caught in the glow of the firelight.

"I'll never forget the look on her face, or the way she wouldn't look at me again. She said something to my father, and we left quickly before there was a scene. We returned to Torview and the house, and a week later I was name scion." He looked down at his hands. "I was glad to go inside. My uncle, the current scion, took me in and showed me a world where I could exist without...." But he didn't or couldn't finish the thought, his head rolling to one side. "He died a month later."

"There are places you can go besides Torview," said Frank after a time, forcing himself to look directly at the ravaged face. It helped that it was still lost in shadows. "There are people who would take you in."

"No. I have grown used to this place, this life. It would be too much of a change."

He sat up again, ignoring Frank's protest. "Besides, it is almost my time. Emil and the judge suspect I am nearing my end, though I have been careful to hide how close it is from them. They will elect a new scion soon anyway. They would have before now, but they are unsure if they have a proper candidate. I'd hoped to end things before that."

"How did you plan to end things? What was your plan?"

Aldarich looked distractedly at his hands. "It was not very complicated, I'm afraid. Philo would resign, take Claire and himself away. I don't think he really believed he could end things that simply, but he put a lot of faith in my part."

"Which was?"

"I would seal the underground and the house once and for all. Philo was to bring me explosives." The big man stood to his feet slowly. "How do you feel?" he asked, looking down on Frank. "Care for the tour?"

Chapter Seventeen

"We're very near the bottom of the shaft."

Aldarich led him through the house, pointing out different rooms and sights. Both men moved slowly, each carrying their pain and thoughts with muted expressions. "Much of this is built into a natural recess," continued Aldarich, his voice as broken as his steps.

Each of the underground rooms was done in white and framed in colonnades and tracery, as if the Captain were making a Greek temple to his dark god of the underground. But no Mediterranean sun ever touched the hard, lifeless spiraled architecture, and the effect was lost to gloomy eeriness.

They walked through the small library, which held the gramophone, and a fireplace which provided the only light. Vivaldi had moved on to *Summer*, doing little to offset the cold of the bone white walls and shadowed corners.

Three of the library walls were covered with bookshelves, the fourth presented an archway to the next room. The books along the shelves were old, the spines faded with age, use, and bad air. But sitting on the arm of a ratty chair was a familiar paperback, the back cover torn off.

Aldarich must have noted Frank's surprise, because he shuffled his feet in embarrassment.

"Yes," he said. "I'm afraid I borrowed one of your books. It was lying on the floor...after Weldon had at it." He picked up the book, handed it to Frank. "I didn't think you'd miss it."

"No," said Frank, waving him off. "You keep it."

"I can't read it anyway," said Aldarich. "My eyes." He looked around sadly at all the books on the shelves.

Beyond the library was a kitchen of sorts. A tin chute, twin to the one above but now in the ceiling, opened above a large wood crate. Aldarich confirmed that the chute was the same. It was used in the early days to send food and sometimes messages to the Captain and the scions.

"It was a bad idea," he added a moment later. "At least for food. Things would get stuck from time to time, and the rats would get at it. They started bringing the food down directly when one of the scions got sick and they almost lost him. We don't use it now, of course."

The bedroom was simple, though large, and oddly similar in lay out to the main bedroom in the red house. There was a wood stove in the corner, next to the big canopied bed, a bathroom off to one side.

But unlike the upstairs bedroom, this room had closets, some full of dated and worn clothes, but others holding tools. Not the ominous tools of the right wing, but implements of carpentry and basic home improvement, including paint brushes and an assortment of paint.

"We have to do all our home repairs, of course," said Aldarich, pointing out the tools. "But these are precious to the scions for another reason." He then led Frank to a small alcove, opening the ornately carved wood door with a shy sense of pride.

Inside was a tiny domed chamber, a reliquary with a short pew and small altar. The shrine's ceiling was painted in brightest blue, with cotton white clouds and black distant birds on the wing carefully added to create a sense of open sky.

"The second scion did this," said Aldarich, pointing to the ceiling. "Originally, the ceiling was covered in the Captain's verses." Aldarich paused. "I don't know what possessed him to paint over the founder's words, but I'm glad he did. It freed us in a way. After the second scion, we all tried, in some small way, to make our world more livable. Some covered up the past, others created something."

"Did you try as well?" asked Frank.

Aldarich looked to the floor. "I tried to paint pictures from the books I read."

"That was your work over the fire?"

"Yes. I'm afraid is not very good, or accurate. I have never seen the ocean, or a boat for that matter. Is it close?"

Frank hesitated, remembering the odd shapes and layout of the painting. "I don't know," he said. "I don't think that matters. There's something about it. I think its art."

Aldarich seemed to consider this, his eyes looking once more to the ceiling. Then he turned and continued the tour.

Frank was surprised to discover there was a second story to the underground house. Many of the rooms on this floor were used for storage, including food preserves, water barrels, and wood. There were more signs of scion work, as well, including a mosaic and a room full of tapestries. All of the work explored themes of outdoors and light, sometimes of animals or people.

But the years of mildew and earth, and the stink of human bodies in a confined space, still tainted the atmosphere, and even the works were like lonely, hopeless flowers in a landfill. It wasn't long before Frank felt depressed and claustrophobic. He tried to hide his discomfort from Aldarich, who seemed to be taking great pleasure in the tour, particularly in showing the scion artifacts.

But he must have seen something in Frank's face, because he stopped eventually and said, "But perhaps this is not of interest to you?"

"No," said Frank quickly. "I'm just tired. Maybe it is the knock on the head."

"You were lucky there," said Aldarich. "I think Emil blocked most of the blow. Come, I will take you back."

Sitting in the first room again, Frank did feel better.

"I noticed signs of the Captain, or his sister," he said, broaching the subject again.

"No. They have been removed completely over the years, at least inside our house. We don't dare touch the other places, the education rooms."

"Those caves with the odd markings?"

"Yes."

They sat in silence for a time. Frank was thinking about the cave with the mattresses and the chalk board.

"What exactly do they teach in this education, Aldarich?"

The scion shook his head. "No. I will not speak of that."

But after a time, he added. "I still have the Captain's Precepts, if you would like to see it."

"*Would* I like to see it?" asked Frank.

Again Aldarich shook his elongated head. "No." He stood. "But you should read it just the same."

Later, his mind reeling from the implications of what he read, Frank followed Aldarich to the top most room. It was little more than a closet with a ladder rising up through a hole in the ceiling.

"This leads to the house," said Aldarich. "But it is a long climb. You should rest before you try it."

Frank nodded agreement and they went to a nearby room with chairs to rest for the climb.

Aldarich didn't speak for a time, looking instead at a picture on the wall of a bird, another artifact from a previous scion.

"So, now you know," he said eventually, turning back to Frank and looking at the Captain's Precepts in his lap.

"Yes," said Frank. "Now I know."

"It is...not right, this existence."

"No," agreed Frank.

Aldarich took a long, rattling breath. "I am nearing my end. I would like to leave knowing I put an end to..." He gestured around the room, then back to the Precepts. "All this."

Frank nodded, waited.

"Will you help me?" asked Aldarich quietly.

"Yes."

The broken giant sighed, his head rolling slowly to one side in relief.

"And you will leave with me," added Frank a moment later. "Whatever time you have left should not be spent in this place."

Aldarich looked away. When he looked back he stared softly at Frank. "I don't know your name. I've watched you sleep, and I heard you call out a woman's name at night, but I don't know your proper name. I overheard Emil say Henning once."

"Frank Henning." He stood up and offered his hand. Aldarich, surprised, took Frank's hand carefully in his own. The skin of the giant's palm was like dusty paper, but the grip, as Frank suspected, was strong.

When he was seated again, he found Aldarich still staring at his hand as if in a dream.

"Frank Henning," he said in that strange, broken whisper. Then he looked to Frank. "I appreciate your concern, Frank Henning."

"Just Frank."

Another pause. "Frank..."

Then the scion took a sad, deep breath, looked away. "I don't think I should leave this place, Frank. I'm not...suited for the outside."

"I told you there are people who won't care what you look like."

"I'm not just talking about my appearance," interrupted the other.

Frank looked to the Aldarich who was still looking away. "What are you afraid of?"

"I'm afraid of what they will do to me," said Aldarich. Then, more softly, he added, "I'm afraid of what I might do."

"I don't think you're...a monster," argued Frank, using Aldarich's word.

"But you don't know me," said the other, turning finally to face Frank. "I have seen things, done things, far worse than presiding over a fertility rite." He pointed at the Precepts. "I went through that. It is part of me." He looked down at his hands. "I know guilt."

Frank considered the Precepts again, a ritualistic credo whose purpose was systematic indoctrination to the

Captain's twisted vision. There had been dark implications to the words, particularly in regards to the children's education and the role the scion would play.

Aldarich nodded as if reading Frank's mind, looked to the picture again. "I told you I watch them because I'm required to. But that's not true. Somewhere it became something I...wanted to do."

Frank didn't answer right away. "We're all human, Aldarich. You've lived most of your life in a tomb made by a madman. And this..." He held the Precepts up. "Is not you. It's the Captain. I just met you, that's true. But I don't think you are evil."

"You don't?" Aldarich's milky red eyes searched Frank's, his odd head cocked to one side. "That first night," he said, "when you slept in the master bedroom, I was suddenly overcome with an urge to kill you. You were an intruder in my family's house. My house. I could, you know. Kill you. These hands are strong. Is that someone you want out in the world, Frank?"

Frank swallowed. "So you were there that night. I heard you on the steps."

"Yes. I watched you from the stairway."

Frank met the others stare, searching for signs of anger or threat.

"But you didn't kill me," he said finally, finding nothing in the red eyes but pain and doubt.

"No," admitted Aldarich. Then, after a long pause. "I was curious."

The silence dragged on again, until Aldarich broke it with a cough. "Will you bring me the explosives, Frank?"

"Yes," he answered around another dry swallow, dropping the subject of Aldarich leaving as well. "Yes, I will help you," he said firmly. He tried to stand, but a sudden wave of nausea sent him reeling back in his seat. "But I think I better rest some more, first."

Aldarich's jaw was doing its crazy dance again, and the red eyes seemed to be looking at Frank with some concern. When the giant spoke, it was in the same raspy, broken inflections, but now strangely removed, as if spoken from a great distance. "Thank you, Frank Henning. You are a good man." A pause. "Frank, are you okay?"

But Frank had lost the struggle for consciousness. His last impression—or was it a dream?—was of two strong arms picking him up like a baby.

Then it all went dark.

* * *

He woke to find himself on a musty couch, a blanket drawn over him. He sat up. His coat was folded neatly over couch's arm, his shoes were on the floor beside him. His head still ached, but he wasn't falling apart with the pain now. He saw that the Captain's Precepts was now in Aldarich's hands.

Aldarich was sitting across from him watching him. "I brought you something to eat and drink," he said as Frank sat up. He nodded to a tray beside Frank. On an old piece of china was hard bread, some cold water, and a piece of cheese. Frank ate slowly as each bite brought a little fresh spasm in the back of his head.

"Better," he said, when he finished the plate.

"Can you climb?" asked Aldarich.

"I think so. Anyway, I have to start sometime." He looked to the Precepts. "I was hoping to take that with me. For evidence."

Aldarich hesitated. "There are many things wrong with my family. But it is still my family. Help me stop them my way, Frank. That will be enough."

The climb proved more difficult than he imagined. Aldarich made him go first, to catch him should he fall.

Frank's head was ringing after five minutes, and his arms and legs were soon shaking. He had to stop frequently. Then, after about ten minutes of this slow climb, the lights went out again.

He woke once more to find himself being carried like a sack over Aldarich's massive shoulder. His head ached with every jarring step, but it was the overpowering smell of the scion that almost set him to retching. He controlled the urge, but just barely.

A few moments later they arrived at a small ledge, and Aldarich set him down gently.

"Stay here," he said. "Don't move."

The big man continued up the ladder slowly, his ragged breaths growing fainter as he disappeared in the shadows above. A short time later, he returned. Frank sat up to give Aldarich room on the short ledge.

"The ladder goes up to the main bedroom," said Aldarich, after catching his breath. "I checked. We're alone. But be quiet. There may be someone just outside the house."

Frank nodded.

He saw Aldarich move to the near wall, just to the right of the ladder. He heard a latch being lifted, felt a draft as something opened to let in the cold air. The shadow of Aldarich moved off the ledge and through a dark doorway. Frank stood up and followed after.

They stood in a small closet, almost too tight for both of them. Aldarich's smell was again overpowering. Frank could just make out the figure of Aldarich by the tiny circular glow coming from the wall. Aldarich blocked the light temporarily with his head, and Frank realized it was a peephole. He heard a click, and then Aldarich opened a panel door on soundless hinges. Aldarich stepped through, ducking his head. Frank again followed.

They were now in the main dining hall. Aldarich closed the paneling carefully behind them. Curious, Frank looked, but couldn't see any outline or sign of the door. Aldarich pointed out a knot about shoulder height. He pressed it and the paneling snapped open again.

"The Captain liked to keep an eye on others," he explained. "He was very careful to keep the passages a secret, even to his heirs."

Aldarich spoke in harsh, broken whispers and blinked continuously, as if even the dim light of the dining room were more than he could stand. Then he stopped suddenly, his whole body flinching in shock. He was staring at the hole Frank created in the back wall.

"Sorry," said Frank. "I didn't know any other way."

"I thought you came by the cellar entrance," said Aldarich, still staring with disbelief at the hole.

"It's locked."

Frank could see that the sight of the torn wall bothered Aldarich. He tried to imagine the conflicting emotions the other must be feeling. But before he could express his concerns, Aldarich turned abruptly and waved him to the front door. "I'll wait here." Then in softer tones, "The light hurts my eyes."

Frank hesitated. He wanted to say something. Instead he offered a hand again. The other shook it with the same hesitant wonder.

Chapter Eighteen

He was careful with the front door, opening it slowly and looking to be sure no one was waiting outside. He then ran to the shelter of the tree line as fast as he could.

It was afternoon now. The weather was warmer, most of the snow melted off. But the ground was still wet. There was no one he could see on the hill, or down by the gate. He climbed down the rutted path and over the gate, then down to the main road.

He had no choice but to use the road; the hill was too steep to manage for any distance. But the road meant going by Granger's. Maybe he would get lucky and his nosy neighbor would be in town.

Not five minutes later, he heard the sound he'd been dreading: the distant hum of an approaching vehicle. It was coming from behind him. He stepped off the road and tried to hide behind a tree.

It was a truck, vaguely familiar. His heart fell as it pulled up beside his tree. The truck was Red Barton's. The young man he'd seen outside Emil's store stuck his head out the driver side window.

"Hey, get in," he said.

Frank stepped around the tree but didn't move any further.

"It's okay. Liz sent me after you. I'm Erik."

Frank could hear the truck's heater blasting from where he stood, and the slightly softer sound of rock music. He considered his potential ally from the safety of the hill. A mess of dirty-blonde hair poked under a ball cap and framed a face still clinging to the last vestiges of baby fat. It was a handsome face, with bright blue eyes twinkling between humor and confidence. The boy wore a faded *Linkin Park* t-shirt that hung tightly on his broad chest and arms. He seemed impatient, but relatively harmless.

Frank climbed down the hill and went around to the passenger side. Erik was busily tossing old cans, cigarette boxes, and a few tools in the small cab behind his seat.

"I've been watching the house from my room all day," explained Erik, "playing sick."

His voice was changing, but hadn't quite caught up with the rest of his body. It made an odd contrast with the biceps straining the sleeves of the t-shirt. "I can just make out the car park from my room with my binoculars. I saw you climbing down. I would've got here sooner, but I had to give my dad a story for the truck. Told him I was feeling better and wanted to run into town to see Liz. Sorry about the mess." He glanced to the floor, holding the wheel under one wrist as he adjusted the volume of the radio down some more. The cab was toasty warm, and smelled of coffee and cigarettes and stale French fries.

"Where's Liz?" asked Frank.

"She went back to town yesterday, like you told her to. But she was worried, so she made me promise to keep an eye out for you. She thought it would be a good idea for me to pick you up if saw you come down." There was a sense of pride to Erik's voice, and Frank had a sense of deja-vu and a vague image of his first days with Tara. "Hey, you okay? You look a bit pale."

"I'm all right."

"You should have someone look at that cut."

"I will."

"Here," said Erik a moment later, handing Frank a greasy ball cap. "Better put this on and sit a little low in the seat until we get to town. We'll hope people think you're my old man."

Frank took the hat. It smelled of oil and cigarettes. He put it gingerly on his head, ignoring the pain, and carefully pulled it down. Erik put the truck in gear and took off with a low growl from the engine.

"So what's the plan?" asked Erik.

"You can drop me off just outside town," said Frank. He had no intention of getting Erik involved any more than he had to.

The boy looked disappointed. "You don't want me to take you to the bed and breakfast? Liz said she'd watch for us there."

"No. That won't be necessary."

They drove in silence for a time, Erik clearly not satisfied with that answer and trying to think of another way to get to Claire's. To put him off, Frank asked his own question.

"How old are you, Erik?"

"Sixteen. But I've been driving this thing for two years now so don't worry about that."

"You like Liz."

"That's obvious. Better get down a bit now."

They were nearing Granger's. Frank scrunched down in the seat and kept his head down.

He watched Erik from beneath the brim of his hat. Was this how the sheriff saw the world? One focused, ceilinged, limited perspective after another? And speaking of limited perspective, if he told Erik what he intended to do, would he still take him back to town? He had no doubt Erik meant him no harm personally, but he also suspected the boy was acting mostly for Liz. Young love was a fickle motivator.

And then there was the dog...It was Red Barton's dog, and presumably, Erik's as well. He could let it be, as the sheriff had suggested, but it was a shabby way to treat someone who was taking risks for him.

"About the dog..." he started.

"We'll find her," said Erik confidently.

Frank's heart broke a little more. "No you won't."

Erik looked at him sideways for a moment, then turned back to the road.

"It was..." started Frank, "she was killed. Butchered."

"Why?"

"To leave me a message."

The boy's handsome face twisted in anger and confusion. "What message? Who?"

Did he dare tell the boy? Would it serve a purpose, or lead to more trouble?

"Walden," he said.

A dark blush crept along Erik's neck. "What was the message?"

"Basically for me to get out of town."

"Goddam Mundts. Dad says they've ruined this town for everyone. He's going to be furious."

Frank was surprised to hear of another potential ally, albeit an unintended one. Had he made a mistake not going to see Barton himself? It was the sheriff who advised him not to. But how many other faces had he seen in town and lumped in with the Mundts? How many other decent, kind people had he cut himself off from simply because he assumed everyone was out to get him?

"I'm not sure telling your dad will do any good," said Frank. "I think the sheriff wants to run a quiet investigation for a time."

"Huh," muttered Erik. "He just doesn't want any trouble."

"You don't trust the sheriff?"

Erik shrugged. "He's all right, I guess. But when it comes to the Mundts, he tends to do a lot of quiet investigations."

"Maybe that's not such a bad idea," said Frank, remembering the look on Henrik's face just before he swung the crowbar.

"Dad's not afraid of the Mundts," said Erik. Then, as if to show he wasn't either, he added, "You can sit up now."

He did, but he kept the hat on. They drove in silence for a time. They were nearing the edge of town, and Frank was thinking over everything. Things would happen fast now, one way or the other, and there was no guarantee they would go his way.

"Erik," he said, finally. "I'm going to try to take Liz away from here if I can."

The deep raced up the boy's neck again, this time reaching his cheeks. "You don't have to worry about Liz, Mr. Henning. I'm going to marry her. The hell with her uncle, and the rest of them. Dad will let us stay with him until I get my place. Maybe I'll take her out here myself."

"The Judge will never let it get that far. He means to marry her off, and soon. They'll ruin her, Erick."

"Marry her? To who? That twit Michalus? Please, Liz can't stand him."

"She won't have a choice in the matter." *And that's not the worst of it*, he thought, remembering the Mundts' conversation by the altar.

"He can't force her to marry." But the boy's anger was stronger than his certainty. "Goddam Mundts!"

"I understand your frustration," said Frank. "But listen to me. It's important."

He waited until he had the boy's full attention.

"I'm going to take her away...No, don't argue. I'm going to take her away, and later, when it is safe, we'll get a hold of you. You can see her then; pick up where you left off."

He wasn't sure he would contact Erik. It would be better for Liz all around, if she assumed a whole new identity and life. The Mundts, the Judge in particular, would not simply let Liz walk away. Contacting Erik would be dangerous. Besides, Liz hadn't exactly indicated feeling about Erik the same way as he obviously did about her. Maybe she wouldn't want to see him again. Too, they were young and things might change, including Erik's youthful passion.

I feel guilty about lying to boy, he thought. But he didn't change his mind.

"Erik, if I should fail, you need to promise me you'll tell Liz to get out of here. You don't have to go with her, or if you do go, stay with her." He held up a hand to stifle another interruption. "I can't lay any of that on you. You just have to make sure she goes. Promise me."

"No problem." The red patches on Erik's face made the tiny blonde hairs of his complexion stand out.

It will have to do, he thought. At least there was a desperate last hope now, even if he should lose this final round to the Mundts.

A short time later, Erik ignored Frank's instructions and drove past the Main Street intersection.

"Let me do this much for you, Mr. Henning," he explained. "There's a place up the road a bit where I can turn off and park. It's hidden by some trees. I use it when I want to see Liz without anyone knowing. You can walk right up to Mrs. Claire's backyard from there." The blush crept up his neck again, but he looked obstinately out the window.

They soon pulled into the turn off, and Erik pointed out the small path to Claire's.

"Don't forget your promise," said Frank, climbing out of the car.

"I won't."

"And don't go near Claire's, or Liz, for a time. They may be watching them to get to me."

"Okay," said Erik more reluctantly. "I'll be at the barber shop if you need me."

"Thanks, Erik," he said, taking a moment to shake the boy's hand. "Tell your Dad, I'm very sorry about the dog. It was a good companion to me in a bad time."

The boy looked uncomfortable, as if not sure how to respond to this. "Don't judge the rest of us by the Mundts," he answered finally, as if that explained everything. He put the truck in gear, waved, and took off.

Frank watched the boy drive away. *How many more people are you going to bring in this mess?* But he was thinking Erik was right, *God damn the Mundts.*

Chapter Nineteen

He followed Erik's path to Claire's, keeping behind the trees whenever possible. Liz's car was parked in the back lot. When he walked in through the backdoor, he heard voices in the living room. He drew close, and peeked around the door frame.

Claire was holding Liz's hand in her own, a pained, desperate expression on both their faces. Liz turned when he stepped into the room. She smiled and jumped up to hug him.

"I was so worried," she said.

He pulled off the greasy cap.

"Jeez, what happened to you?"

He squeezed her shoulder, looked to Claire. "I'm okay."

"Did Erik find you?" asked Liz, making him turn to her again.

He nodded. "Liz, I need a moment to talk to Claire. But stay close. I need to talk to you as well."

"Whatever you have to say to me, you can say in front of the girl," said Claire.

She was wearing her hair down today. It stopped just above her shoulders, softening some of the age in her bearing, but not the lines in her face.

"Claire's been telling me about the town," said Liz, her voice low and apprehensive.

"I told her this town is no place for the likes of her," explained Claire, answering Frank's questioning look. "I told her she needs to leave before it's too late. Both of you need to leave, now, and never come back."

"All right," he said, meeting her eyes. He took a deep breath. "But you're coming too."

"No." But the word was small and desperate on her lips.

"There's something you need to know," he said.

Claire flinched, looked to the floor, wrung her hands once, then looked to the sunlit window.

"Philo didn't leave you behind, Claire."

Something pensive, something that had been hanging like fire for too long, stirred and set her hard eyes dancing. She turned slowly from the window.

"Philo is dead," he said, glancing to Liz. "Killed by his brother, Henrik, and probably at Emil's bidding."

Claire threw her head back as if he had slapped her, and sudden tears ran hot and fast down her face. He watched her eyes revolve from anger to pain and back again. Liz ran to her. The two held each other like mother and daughter.

He tried to meet Claire's eyes over Liz's shoulder. There was no shock in those washed out pools of green, just resignation, as if she had known all along that this would be the answer to her hope and despair.

"There's no reason for you to stay now, Claire," he said gently. "He's not coming back."

Liz, still holding Claire, looked to Frank, confused and worried and upset.

Claire seemed to come to herself, looked down at the girl in her arms. "He is dead then," she said, not looking up again.

"Yes," said Frank. He let the two comfort each other a moment longer, then, "Liz, give me that minute now."

Claire let her go and Liz walked out slowly, looking from one to the other expectantly.

When Frank was sure she was out of earshot he stepped close to Claire, took her hand in his as he did the other afternoon, made her meet his eyes. "I went down there." She flinched again, as if his words had physical impact. "I saw a ritual. Emil, Henrik, Jenny. I know there have been others. They..."

But before he could go on Claire's face almost broke apart with emotion, and she wretched her hand away.

Her breath ragged, her eyes two large pools of pain and loathing, she stuttered, "We had no choice! You don't understand!" Then her face shifted again, becoming dangerously close to madness. He reached out, took her hand firmly between his again.

She looked to her hand in his, and slowly the madness retreated again to the familiar, protective hardness.

When she spoke it was to the floor, avoiding his eyes, her words soft and uneven. "We couldn't have children. We were so young. Philo said there was a way..." She swallowed a sob. "I thought...and he thought...that was what he wanted."

She shuddered, as if reliving the event. "I went to that unholy space only once." She looked to him, then back to the floor. "Afterward, we could barely look at one another. I told him I was leaving him. He told me everything then. He told me about being heir, about the scion. He told me I would never have to do that again, that he would never do that again. I never did. I never went back to that house."

She shook her head, still staring at the floor. "But later, he went back. He had to as heir."

He felt her hand flutter in his.

"He said," she said, looking desperately up from the floor. "He said, he did not...did not do *that* again, though. He was weak. He would play his role. But he would not do that to me again."

The hard line between her brows deepened. "I got pregnant." She looked to him again, her voice now heated with bitter madness. "Do you know what plans they had for my baby? Do you know what they do to children here? They needed a new scion. Do you understand?"

He swallowed. "I know. I read the Captain's Precepts."

Her head made a small, unnatural twitch, reminding him of Aldarich. But after a time, the madness retreated again.

"I told Philo I lost the baby. I think he knew the truth, but he never asked. He told the others I could not have children now. After that, they left me alone."

The confession had been unexpected for both of them. The raw truth was too much to process, if ever.

Looking to her now, some instinct told him Claire, though damaged, was still fighting, still holding desperately to some final sense of life, to hope. But she was also teetering over her personal abyss, one small step away from completely losing herself to the nightmare she had long buried. It could either direction.

He squeezed her hand gently in his, searching for something to say, for some way to reach beyond that lost expression, to find that last, desperate shard of hope and give it a new resolve, a new purpose. Or at least, acknowledge her pain in some way that would serve.

He searched, and found nothing. No words. It was too much, too real, her confession and pain. It pulled too closely to his own pain and loss and doubt and the thought of broaching that with Claire, here and now, was too much.

He had only one thing he could call on, could actually express. His own raw immediate need.

But distraction had worked for him, to a point, and maybe it would work for her as well.

"They're not going to just let me take Liz and leave," he said, cringing at the incongruity of his words. *Later,* he thought, *later, I promise, Claire, I will try to find the right words, or at least the time to share.*

But that was a lie. There would be no later, and he could only continue, hoping she could see beyond his words. "I know too much," he said. "The only reason they're not here now, is they think I'm trapped with Aldarich or dead. Claire, I need your help if Liz is going to have any chance at a real life."

Her head made that unnatural twitch again. "Liz? What can I do?" Her voice was a small, harried thing, her hand fluttering like a fly in his. The washed out green eyes dilated, the abyss loomed dangerously close. "I can't help you."

"Yes, you can," he insisted. He reached out, took her chin gently but firmly in his hand, and forced her to meet his eyes.

"Aldarich and Philo had a plan," he said. "Philo was going to end everything. He was going to take you away, Claire."

Another shudder traveled the length of her body and finished with a sudden sob. Fresh, hot tears ran fast and unchecked down the hard lines of her face.

"I need what Philo was going to use," he finished.

For a long time she simply stared at him in confusion. For a moment he panicked. *Maybe Philo had never told her about the plan? Or maybe*, he thought desperately, *the revelation had been too much for her and she was retreating too far now, falling into the final abyss of despair never to fully return.*

But then her focus grew clear again, as she found something close and manageable to hold on to. His request was not beyond her; this was something she could do.

She pulled her hand free and wiped the tears from her face. "All he told me was never go near it."

He felt a warm trickle of relief run down the back of his neck.

"There's a box out back in the shed," she added a moment later.

"That's probably it," he said. "I'm going to take it, and with Aldarich's help, put an end to the house. I don't know if that will stop anything. I don't know if that will even keep Liz safe. But I promised Aldarich." He paused. "And I think, Philo deserves the effort."

"He was going to take me?" she asked, her voice trembling.

"Yes. Aldarich said as much."

He looked at her closely, searching. The hardness was still there. *It will never completely leave,* he thought. But it was touched now with the trace of something else, a small, sudden and unexpected determination. Something in what he said, whether it was Philo's intention to take her away, or his faith in her to help him with Liz, or both, or something else altogether, had let her take a step from the abyss.

He saw the effect and was moved, in no small part because it made him think of Tara and their last years together. *Would she have left me but for the cancer?* His heart fluttered as he finally admitted the possibility. A hard moment later, he realized he'd never know. He envied Claire, her small peace of mind regarding Philo, though not the cost she'd paid for it.

"The second thing I need," he continued, retreating yet again from his own abyss, though knowing now that he would eventually have to return and deal with it, just as Claire would have to deal with hers, "is for you to take Liz and leave, and never come back."

He had been thinking about this ever since he made Erik promise his help. He just couldn't leave it at that. The boy was too young, and Liz not that much older for all her hard-earned wisdom. They would never make it by themselves. It had to be Claire.

"You know what is at risk for Liz," he added. "You know, and that's why it has to be you. You know."

The words checked her first reaction. Her face showed the conflict as clearly as if she were speaking aloud: the self-doubt and recrimination; her anger, revulsion, fear; her protective feelings for Liz; the memory of Philo and all that went before...It was but a few moments, and it was not resolved completely, not even certainly, but the balance shifted finally, and something long buried took precedent, something that wanted to act out against the nightmare.

"For Liz, then," she said.

He reached out, squeezed her hand. "For everyone they hurt," he said gently. "Including Philo; including you."

She took a long, slow breath. "Yes. For everyone." She pressed his hand briefly, then took it back.

"But they won't just let me go either," she said a moment later, brushing away another round of tears. The familiar, hard expression was in place once more. *Though perhaps*, he thought, *the eyes are not so desperate or lifeless.*

"I know they watch this house when Liz is here," she continued. "The judge tolerates her coming, because he knows the girl is close to me. But he never lets her out of sight long. They don't trust me; not since Philo." This last she said with bitter pride.

"If Aldarich and I are successful, there will be a lot of confusion. In the distraction you can slip away."

She scoffed lightly, but didn't otherwise point out the feebleness of the plan.

"Where will we meet?" she asked.

"We don't."

As he said it, he realized fully for the first time he didn't really expect to come back.

"You go the first moment you can slip away unseen, and don't stop." Then, before she could argue, "How soon can you be ready?"

"I should pack some things for the road," she answered slowly, pragmatically, touching her hair.

He looked again to her. She looked a mess, her face worn and drained. But there was a release about her now, as well, as if she had dropped a weight long carried.

"I have some money in the bank," she said. "And in the house safe."

"Take the house money," he said. "Forget the bank. The judge has too many connections. Here's my credit card, and all the cash I have left. Only use the card if you have to, and then move on right away. They can trace these things now. Be careful with phones as well. Use only pay phones, and only for a short time. Take Liz's away from her," he added a moment later. "She might try to call the boy."

She raised an eyebrow. "As certain as sin."

He smiled, despite the situation. After a time, she joined him.

"If you stay at a hotel," he continued, " don't use your real name. And don't be seen checking into together if you can help it. They'll suspect you'll go to Summerset, so head elsewhere. In the last resort, go to the F.B.I. Tell them as much of the truth as you can, but..."

"The judge," she finished for him. "He'll have an answer for all of it. He'll have the authorities looking for us. Liz will be brought back, and likely I'll be thrown in jail for kidnapping." She shook her head at the impossibility of what he was asking her to do.

"I know it's a lot to ask," he said. "But I don't see another way."

"What about you?" she asked after a time. "What if you succeed? What will you do for money? How will we find each other again?"

He was thinking if the judge and other Mundts should learn he was alive and what he done, it wouldn't matter where he went or what he did for money. They would likely pull all their resources and means to stop Frank from telling his story.

For the judge, that probably meant legal measures. He didn't think the judge would try to have him arrested—that would give Frank a day in court. More likely he would try to have him temporarily, or even permanently committed, citing Frank's obvious grief over his wife's recent death to cancer, his strange behavior in buying a remote, practically untenable house far from his home, his run in at the school, and of course, the disturbing demise of the dog.

He could already imagine the reluctant testimony of the sheriff, damning Frank with every slow, careful word: *"We couldn't understand why he'd want to live in that house, all alone...Kept to himself mostly, but had a few run ins with the locals; some trouble at the school...Whoever did that to the dog didn't come from outside...."*

Even if they failed to prove him insane, the effect of the charges and testimony would undermine any stories of abuse and corruption he might offer in his defense. In fact, his version of events might even be used against him: *generations of single males living in a sealed, secret underground home? Systematic inbreeding to produce chosen heirs? Children made to grow up in a twisted madman's vision of a better reality?* It all sounded too surreal, even to him. And his proof? A few enigmatic journals, his word, and what he claimed was the word of a man (who had been stillborn according to official records) now (presumably) buried under the house Frank himself had blown up.

But it probably wouldn't come down to the judge's efforts anyway, he thought bitterly. Emil and Henrik would have something more permanent and immediate in mind. He put his chances of surviving another round with Henrik even lower than his odds of getting around the judge's formidable influence.

And if Liz were with him or even suspected of being with him...so much the worse for Liz and Claire. That couldn't happen.

But he didn't tell Claire any of this. Instead he told her he had and extra ATM card for money (which was true, though he didn't know if it was active). Then he wrote down his old phone number (now disconnected) and told her to call it in a few weeks, when they were safe. They'd arrange to get together then, he assured her.

She took the paper and folded it in her apron pocket without looking at the number. What she guessed, he couldn't say.

She gave him a funny look, then reached out and touched him lightly on the arm and said, "I'll see she gets a chance...no matter what happens." An understanding passed between them and he felt, in this much at least, he had out-maneuvered the Mundts.

"Thank you," he said.

They called Liz back. She was happy to hear Claire was going, but wanted to know why the three of them couldn't just leave now.

"I've got to go take care of one more thing," he explained, sharing a look with Claire, careful not to let Liz see his expression. "I'll be meeting you both later." Claire dropped her eyes. "Trust me," he added with a big smile at Liz. "This is for the best."

"Okay, but I'm coming back for you if you don't show."

"No!" said Frank, losing his smile. "No matter what happens Liz, don't ever come back here."

"But..."

"He's right, dear," said Claire, taking her hand again. "Now help me get ready. I'll explain everything when we get on the road." She nodded to Frank, her expression determined.

He didn't say goodbye as he didn't want Liz to get upset. Instead, he snuck out the back door, taking the key Claire gave him, and made his way to the shed.

Chapter Twenty

By the looks of things, Philo intended to take down the whole hill.

The sealed plastic crate was packed with explosives and a carefully boxed detonator. Frank had no idea what he was looking at in terms of actual firepower, but he sensed it was enough. Now it was just a matter of getting it up to the house.

He looked around the tool shed, took stock, and made his final plans. Claire and Liz needed a distraction to get away; Aldarich needed the explosives to finish the house once and for all. Despite what he told Claire, he didn't count on the explosion to be enough—and, in the end, it would only serve as distraction. When it came to freeing Liz and Claire, he had something more permanent in mind.

But what, exactly, that was, he didn't know. He looked around the shed, desperate for inspiration, fortification, or both. Standing in the corner was a grass-stained lawnmower, beside it a utility garbage can. Along one wall was a corkboard holding varying sized screwdrivers, hammers, wrenches. Considering his recent experience with the crowbar (there was one on a worktable beneath the corkboard) he decided to pass.

He looked down, surprised to find his hands shaking. Why not, he thought? He was hurt, his plan was weak, and he was no hero.

"Tara," he whispered to the dust-filled air. But there would be no answer from that direction either.

He bent down and tried to lift the explosives. The crate was made of tough but light plastic, the explosives not as heavy as he imagined. He held the crate in his arms, trying to get a sense of the task. Could he make it to the car? He thought so. He put the crate down again, feeling the effects of his effort in his head. He took a moment to let the spell pass.

It was the middle of the afternoon. Outside the open shed door, the sky was a soft blue, not a cloud in sight; the sun, a distant buttery disk removing the last signs of the snow fall. It looked to be a beautiful day.

* * *

He walked into the kitchen; put the crate carefully on the table. Claire and Liz were ready and waiting with their bags in the living room. They came into the kitchen when they heard him come back.

"Liz," he said as soon as they entered. He needed to get through this next part as quickly as possible, with no argument or discussion. He had to, or he might lose his nerve. "Can you drive your car to the place you and Eric meet, that place outside Claire's on the road?"

"Sure," she said distractedly. "But…"

"Do it now," he said with a gentle smile, but firmly. "Then come back here, but come the long way, down the street. In fact, make sure people see you go in here. After that call your uncle and tell him you want to stay with Claire a little longer."

"Okay."

He squeezed her shoulder goodbye.

"I'll see you…later?" she said questioningly.

"Yes." She hugged Claire and took off.

Claire looked to him, her arms folded across her chest and the hard determined lines once more in place, though now shifted to a more immediate purpose. "What is your plan?" she asked.

"I'm going to drop this off at the house," he said, pointing to the crate. "Then I'll come back. That should give Liz time enough to establish she's with you. If my timing is good, I'll be talking with the judge when the works go up. You and Liz should sneak off to the car and get out of here before that. She'll show you where the car is parked."

"I know where it is," said Claire with an irony that reminded him briefly of Tara. "And before you go anywhere you better let me look at that head."

She waved his protests of time off, and led him to the kitchen sink. Running warm water, she bent his head under it, and then carefully washed the cut. He watched the water turn rusty in the sink, some of the run off tickling the inside of his nose. As careful as she was it still hurt. But her touch was oddly comforting just the same. When she was done she put some salve on it.

"It could use a stitch or two," she said blandly. "But it should be okay for now."

She washed her hands, shook the water off in the sink, turned to him. Suddenly everything was awkward, and hard, and impossible, all at the same time. He knew he should leave, felt the press of time like an anchor around his head, but the brief comfort of normality, of simple human decency, was hard to abandon.

He noticed that she had changed into a simple blouse and jeans. She had a good figure, and with her hair down she looked almost approachable. He reached out a hand and brushed back a stray hair that hung along her forehead.

"I like your hair this way," he said. "You should wear it loose more often."

She didn't meet his look for long, but long enough for the faintest of ironic glimmers, like a dying ember catching life from an unexpected breeze. She turned away just as quickly, the moment going as far as it could, or needed.

"Here," she said, handing him a piece of paper. "This is my sister's number. We don't talk much now." She looked away. "Not ever, since Philo. I'll call her later, when I'm sure I'm safe. She'll know how to get ahold of me."

"It's dangerous," he said. "They could use her..."

"They can go to hell," she said firmly. Then, more gently, "I'm not going to give her anything that will get Liz in trouble. But you call her, later, if you want."

He took the paper. "Okay." He put it in his coat pocket with care, a token of forlorn hope.

Then he picked the crate up carefully, and she held the door open. He didn't look back, but walked straight to his car, not looking around. He opened the trunk, put the crate inside, had second thoughts, and sat it in the back seat instead. He put a seatbelt around the crate, then got in the car and took off.

Only as he was pulling away did he look around to see if anyone was watching. The off street was empty; no noticeable noses in the window. He was the only car on the road, and Granger, for once, was not on his porch.

He thought about Aldarich on the way up the hill. He thought about Liz, and Claire, and Tara, and the dog. He thought about the life he'd lived, and the time he had yet to live. And there was no sense to any of it, but it was impossible to think of it any other way.

Chapter Twenty-one

The carpark was empty, which was a relief. He worried he'd find the sheriff waiting for him, or worse. He opened the gate and drove up the hill, slowly, parked in the front, and sat looking at the front door through his windshield.

He had come to no new decisions or ideas about Aldarich. Part of him wanted to take him out of the house, insist he come along; another part didn't see how he could. Maybe Aldarich was right to worry about his freedom.

But to do nothing, to let him simply die in that terrible tomb of twisted history...

He looked around the car, opened the glove compartment, and went through the side panels. He found them finally, tucked away in the visor compartment: a pair of old sunglasses. He pocketed them and climbed out of the car. Again, he carefully picked up the crate and hauled it out.

The front door was still open, but Aldarich was not in the front hall. He put the crate down inside the front hall, walked through the dining room wicket door. The hidden panel was closed. Again, there was no sign of Aldarich.

"Hello," he said, his voice echoing eerily in the stifled, heightened silence. There was no answer.

He left the explosives by the door and walked around the house, moving quietly, feeling the hairs rise along the back of his neck with every empty room.

He avoided looking at the bloody mess inside his bedroom, and focused on the open, secret door instead.

Open? Had Aldarich said he'd left it open?

He looked in the small space, discovered a short ledge and the top of the ladder they climbed earlier.

No Aldarich.

Was he back in his crypt? Why? Did he change his mind?

He walked back down and out of the house. The cellar door was unlocked and standing free.

There were small wooden steps leading down to a smooth floor, dimly visible from the afternoon sun. He almost called out for Aldarich, but something stopped him. He took the steps down, wishing he brought his flashlight, which was in the car. *Should he go back and get it?*

The cellar was thin but deep, with a low earthen ceiling supported by heavy beams and a drop cloth. Shelves ran along the near wall, empty but for dust and cobwebs. The air smelled of earth and mildew.

He looked carefully along the floor that he could see; the sheriff had said something about a sinkhole. He shuffled a few more steps in, his eyes adjusting to the half-light. He would go just a little further, and then go back for his flashlight if he had to go on.

He found the lanterns on the next to last shelf with a box of matches. He took one of the lanterns, lit it with a match and turned the valve up as high as it could go. The shadows retreated, revealing a long narrow passage that ended against a brick wall. Another cleverly hidden door, built into the brick wall, was open, another dark passageway just beyond.

There were no sinkholes that he could see.

He walked through the brick door, raised his lantern. He recognized the sloping path before him. It was the same one that led eventually down to the bottom. He listened carefully for voices or sounds of movement but heard nothing but the echo of vast, empty depth.

He turned the lantern down again, so as not to draw attention, and started down. The silence, but for his footsteps, was oppressive. As he passed the small recesses, he glanced in each but did not venture off the direct path this time. He wanted to get down as quickly as possible, to find Aldarich, make sure everything was okay.

He passed the mattress room, moving faster now as he drew near the end. He was about twenty yards passed the reliquary when he heard something moving fast behind him. He whirled with the lantern, but was too late. For the second time in twenty four hours someone cracked his head and he went down.

He didn't completely lose consciousness this time, but his vision was a cloud of blurry shadows and harsh, painful flashes of light. He didn't remember dropping his lantern, but there it lay, the glass broken and a small fire burning on the ground around the bent metal container. The dancing flames shot painful pins along the back of his eyes and he rolled his head the other way.

He saw, or imagined he saw, a bizarre image of Aldarich pinned against the wall like an insect. A moment later he realized his perspective and disorientation had made the floor a wall. Aldarich was lying face down on the ground, a corona of blood extending from his massive frame like viscous, red wings. His ravaged face was a pale mask, and the eyes distant and unfocused.

Then someone was picking him up by the shoulders and dragging him across the floor. He lost consciousness, and everything went black.

* * *

He woke to find himself bound, only this time he was sitting and the bindings were painfully tight on his wrists and legs. There was no light, no sounds but his own breathing. He was wrapped in stygian darkness.

His head hurt like fire, and his body was wracked with cramps. Nausea roiled up from his belly and he turned his head, vomiting all over his arm. The smell and the ache in his head made him gag again. Cold sweat poured from every pore of his body.

He tried to stand up, but the bindings were too tight. Something was odd about the way he was sitting but he couldn't concentrate enough to figure it out.

He remembered then his delirious vision of Aldarich pinned to the floor, and knew the pin that held him was really a knife in his back.

He vomited again, his head seeming to split in two. The silence that followed grew quickly oppressive, penetrating even through his pain. He tried to listen for any sign of his captor, but there was only the sound of his own troubled breathing.

"Who are you?" he asked, meaning to shout but only able to manage a broken, feeble whisper. Even still, his question shattered the stillness, and he cringed in expectation.

But nothing answered, nothing moved. Minutes passed, became what felt like hours, his fear and delirium playing tricks with time. He felt the cold of the underground against his cheeks, smelled the earth mixed with his own vomit. He wanted to scream. He wanted to struggle. But a deeper instinct forced him to crouch and wait, knowing eventually it would come.

And as if answering his thought, he heard a soft step behind him. He twisted his head left, then right, pulling desperately at his arms and legs, but his efforts were pointless, lost in the darkness and strength of his binds.

The silence returned, the minutes passed again, his fear growing greater for the brief break and return. He felt dizzy, felt his stomach roil again. He willed himself to be still, to breathe evenly.

He (or they! god forbid) want you to panic, he told himself. *This is part of the torture.*

But knowing that didn't make it any less effective.

And a moment later, another soft shuffle, no more than a toe dragged across the rough floor, sent a shock of panic up and down his straining body, set his imagination racing.

He felt, or imagined, a presence just behind him, a hand raised to do him harm. He held his breath, sending rivers of pain along his skull. But in the immediate stillness, he thought he heard the echo of another breath drawn quickly, and then utter silence again.

He released his breath, gasping in pain, knowing he could not hold out longer than his tormentor, and believing he had already proved his point. *Someone was there! It was not is imagination.*

Slowly, his breathing returned to a more reasonable rhythm. But his head was now a bag of rusty nails, being pounded over and over again. The nausea mounted anew. For a time, the silence, the threat was stifled under the pain. But inevitably it made its presence known again, and the slow dance of silent fear started anew.

How long this went on, could go on, he couldn't say. The only consolation was that it could be worse. Whatever was coming next, he was certain, would be.

He sat breathing heavily, trying not to smell too closely his vomit and fear, his every muscle strained and cramped against the unknown.

And still it went on. And he found he was wrong. The threat, the unknown, became a tangible presence that did not become less with time, but grew stronger until it was unbearable.

He screamed. He raved. He called on his unknown assailant to act, to show himself, to do something. He cursed, he mocked, he laughed, he pleaded. He ran through every dark emotion possible. And still he remained alone, sitting in the dark, the presence imagined/real just behind him.

Exhausted, defeated he finally slumped in the chair, his head against his chest, his eyes closed. He could not completely resign himself to his fate—there was no relief even now—but the terror, like his nausea and headache, was too constant, too present, it slipped almost unnoticed into the familiar. He felt something hot and salty in the corner of his lips and realized he was crying.

There was another shift, a slight movement just behind him. He opened his eyes. The presence loomed closer, and now a hot, sweet breath tickled the back of his neck.

Suddenly there was light. In the brief vision he had before his eyes closed against the glare, he knew he was in the reliquary, sitting in the chair. He saw his own ruined face covered in blood staring back at him in the mirror.

And just behind him another face, framed in dark, tangled hair, with eyes so blue they looked unreal, looked back in his own.

He shuddered, his eyes held tightly shut against the image.

"That's the best part," said a soft voice in his ear.

With a will he opened his eyes. Walden was still squatting just behind him, his face close to his own, and those strangely beautiful eyes searched for his in the mirror.

"Dickie shit himself," said Walden.

"Dickie?" he asked, confused and struggling for some semblance of meaning.

"Dickie Thomas," said Walden. He continued to stare at Frank in the mirror, like a man watching an experiment. "He did it again when I showed him this."

Walden lifted a long curved blade and put it next to Frank's eye. Frank struggled away from the blade, as much as the chair and his bindings would let him. He watched Walden in the mirror, not daring to turn his head any closer to the sharp edge in the corner of his eye.

The light went out again.

Walden was showing him just what the strange room could do. And as he stifled the involuntary cry against the dark, he felt a deep, heartbreaking empathy for all the children who had sat there before him.

With a laugh, Walden turned the light on again. He was standing up straight now. He pulled the blade away from Frank's eye, brought it back again with another laugh. Walden's massive bulk made a surreal backdrop to Frank's terror-filled, bloody face.

Then, with care—there wasn't much room to move about in the tiny cave—Walden walked around to face Frank directly. He was holding a lantern in one hand, the knife in the other. Frank recognized it as one of the "tools" from the Sister's cupboard.

Walden moved it back and forth in front of Frank, like a conductor with a baton. He sniffed. "You stink, but I don't think you shit your pants, yet."

"Aldarich?" croaked Frank.

"You mean the shitless scion?" Walden's blue eyes were almost childlike, but for the lack of naiveté and innocence the youth hold. "He's dead."

He squatted down in front of Frank, tilted his head to one side.

"Why, Walden?"

"He broke the traditions," answered the other. "I know. My mother tells me everything, and I saw it myself when I was here." He smiled to himself, raised his head proudly. "She didn't know he could get out, though; not even my dad knew that. *I* knew he could get out. I saw him once, when he didn't know I was here." He blinked stupidly. "I overheard dad tell mom he was a weak scion anyway. Just like Uncle Philo. No big loss."

"*You* killed Philo," said Frank, making the conclusion.

"Yes. They all kept talking about him, mom, dad, Uncle Emil. Nobody knew what to do. I knew what to do." He then reached out with the blade and casually drew a line down the center of Frank's sweat stained shirt, ripping the cloth and drawing blood.

Frank could only watch in exhausted shock. The blade felt cold to the touch at first, and then burned like fire. He gasped at the delayed pain.

"I like this room," said Walden, "but it's a little small for work. I was going to take you down all the way to the altar. I haven't had a chance to use it yet, because the silly scion might have seen me." He tapped the bloody blade against Frank's knee. "I did Dickie here," he continued. "I had to gag him for the noise, of course. I don't have to gag you, though."

He put the lantern down, walked behind the chair, and grabbed Frank's head in one massive arm. He brought the blade up to Frank's eye again, looked to the mirror to see Frank's reaction. "I learned a lot from the animals, and Dickie. I know how to make it last now." He then casually cut across the bridge of Frank's nose and down his cheek.

This time Frank screamed in pain.

Walden shuffled around the chair to stand in front of Frank again. "I like to save the eyes for last," he explained. "That way you can see what happens to the rest."

He glanced at the low ceiling that kept him from standing straight. "This is really *not* the best room for this work." He sounded almost apologetic.

"It has a lot of memories though," he continued, touching the chair fondly. I didn't cry, or mind my time at all. Mom said I could have been a scion."

"You cried," he noted a moment later. "Does it hurt a lot?" He waited for Frank to answer, then smiled. "Do you want to beg now? Dickie begged, a lot."

Frank knew better. Though the cut was not deep, his nose was on fire, the blood streaming into his mouth and down his neck. He stared back at Walden, trying to meet the distant blue expression, but it was like trying to hold water in your hand.

Walden frowned. "I kind of like it when they beg. You will eventually."

He moved back behind the chair again, grabbed Frank's head as casually as a man grabbing a sack. "I guess you don't need both eyes to see." A small smile crossed his face as Frank started to struggle. "Yeah, that's better." He then looked down to see what he was doing.

Frank saw the tip of the blade approach slowly to his right eye, Walden drawing the moment out as long as he could.

He closed his eyes but Walden adjusted his grip, holding Frank's head in the crook of his arm like a vice and using his thick fingers to pry Frank's eyes open. "You have to see," he insisted. "It works better that way."

The blade tip touched the corner of Frank's eye, near the bridge of the nose. He felt the cold steel against the skin but only a small pressure against the eyeball. He was screaming again, though he hadn't realized it until Walden made hushing noises.

There was the tiniest of sharp pricks at his eye. A moment later, Frank smelled the stench of his own bowels. Walden began to laugh.

A moment later, the laugh was interrupted by a heavy grunt. The blade still pressed against Frank's eye, moved reluctantly back. Frank felt the arm around his head loosen. He saw in the mirror a massive hand grasping Walden's wrist, pulling the blade back inch by inch.

Frank turned his head to get a better view. He saw Aldarich choking Walden with one arm, pulling him back, and holding off the blade hand with his other hand still around the wrist.

Then the two figures fell out of the mirror frame, and Frank only heard the desperate, almost silent struggle, punctuated at times by deep grunts of pain and effort. A moment later, he saw Walden rise in the frame again. He was still struggling, but now he was trying to press the blade down on his adversary, who clearly was on the ground beneath him.

The descending blade, with all of Walden's bulk and determination behind it, was suddenly suspended. A large, familiar hand rose from the bottom of the mirror to choke Walden. His face turned an ugly shade of red, then purple. The mirror held the terrible tableau for a moment, an eternity.

Then, with a sudden gasp from the floor, Walden and the hand that choked him fell from view. Frank heard a body hit the ground. He strained unconsciously for a time at his ropes until the pain from his arms and legs finally made him stop.

Aldarich climbed slowly into the mirror's perspective, his ravage face even more deathly pale than usual. The big man bent again a moment later. Frank could now see a knife in his back. Not the knife Walden had threatened him with, but another. He heard the soft whisper of something sharp drawn fast across flesh. There was a slight gurgle, then silence.

Aldarich stood again, and stumbled to the chair. He kept his balance by pressing a heavy hand down on

Frank's arm. Frank watched as he cut the bindings from his wrist, the giant hands shaking with effort, his breath painful to hear.

Finished, he handed Frank the bloody blade and fell against the near wall. He tried to turn as he fell, to avoid the knife in his back, bumping his head along the ceiling as he did so.

Frank cut the bindings on his ankles as quickly as his weak hands would let him. He then tried to stand up, but fell back into the chair with a crash. His legs were asleep. He stretched them, pounded them with his fists, tried to will the blood to flow again, all the while watching Aldarich slide unnaturally down the wall. As he massaged the life back into his limbs, he glanced behind him, saw Walden sprawled along the floor, his throat cut.

When he could finally move enough, he lurched across the room to Aldarich. He tried to ease the big man to the ground, but he was too weak and Aldarich too big. The best he could do was guide the fall so that Aldarich fell face first.

"Should I take it out?" he asked, looking to the knife rising from Aldarich's back like a lamppost. "It might bleed you to death."

Aldarich started to laugh, which erupted in a paroxysm of coughing and pain.

"It doesn't matter," he said when he gained control again. "Take it out. It hurts."

Frank tried to do it in one, quick pull but it got hung briefly on a bone or rib. Aldarich's whole body reeled with pain, but he didn't make a sound. Frank threw the blade on the ground, helped Aldarich to his feet.

"Where to now?" he asked.

"Did you bring the explosives?" asked Aldarich.

"Yes."

"Bring them to me." The giant's voice was as ravaged as his face now, and Frank felt fresh hot blood pour along his back.

Somehow, they managed to get to the altar. But sensing he was about to fall for the last time, Frank helped the big man sprawl out on the altar.

"I'll rest here a bit, while you get the fireworks," said Aldarich, trying to laugh again. "Go," he said, wiping the dark blood from his mouth. "Hurry."

He made the climb in a daze, wiping his own blood from time to time out of his eye and face. He found the crate where he left it. No one was in the house. He stumbled his way back down, trying to be careful but moving at times without conscious awareness.

Aldarich was sitting up when he reached the altar room. But he looked a ghost, and made Frank open the crate for him. The giant looked at the explosives for a time, as if surprised to see them in reality.

"Philo said there was a detonator," he said.

Frank gave him the sealed box.

"This is TNT?" asked Frank, looking to the crate.

"Yes."

"And the detonator is electronic?"

Aldarich was studying the detonator. "Yes."

"It works from a signal?"

"Don't worry. Philo told me how to do it," explained Aldarich.

"Can it be triggered from up top?"

Aldarich stopped his examination, looked at Frank with a sad smile. "The signal probably wouldn't reach that far."

The two men considered each other.

"It was always going to end this way," said Aldarich. "Philo knew that. I knew it, too. One of us would have to remain below to insure it worked." He stood up, leaning against the altar. "Let me arm it, and then help me put the explosives around the house."

Frank set the crate carefully outside the swing door, leaving most but not all of the explosives. He didn't think it safe to try and get the crate through the chute.

Aldarich was now slumped against the altar base, the detonator in his massive hands. "I'll give you some time to get out," he said, coughing blood again with the effort. "But hurry."

But Frank couldn't just leave. He struggled for something to say, and like his time with Claire, found himself inadequate to the task. Finally, he reached in his coat pocket, pulled out the sunglasses. One of the frames was bent and the glass broke. "I was going to give you these," he said, "So you could come with me."

Aldarich slowly turned the broken glasses in his big, pale hands.

"People would come down here from time to time, and talk to me," he said around great gulps of painful air. "They knew their secrets were safe with me. It was part of my role, a confessor to the secret family. But they were always dark secrets, things they could hardly tell themselves." Aldarich looked up with a broken sigh. "Tell me a happy memory, Frank."

Frank squatted next to Aldarich, and after a time pulled on the first clear and happy memory that came to mind.

"I once lived for a short time in New York, the state. Up in the mountains. This was before I met...this was before. Beautiful country. There was a diner on the road side close to my place. Across the road was a small pond, a little dock extending from the side, to swim or fish off, I guess."

He looked to Aldarich, saw the red-white eyes were turned away, as if trying to see the scene.

"Everything was dark green," he continued, "even in summer. The diner wasn't much to look at, little more than a long shot-gun building. The help was teenage girls, polite and bored, full of quiet, desperate dreams of leaving. I went there every day to have a hamburger, fries and coke, sometimes steak and eggs. I'd sit by the big window, watching the sun dance off that pond. And I read the paper, and I had my coffee, and I was happy. I wasn't looking for anything or anyone, or any answers. I had my whole life ahead of me." He paused. "I still remember that sun off the pond, and that window view. I still remember the sense of time as a friend, not a competition."

When he finished, Aldarich turned back to him, nodded, tried to smile and ended up grimacing. "What will you do now?" he asked.

"Go see the judge."

"Why?"

"I have to convince him to truly end all this—and to free some friends of mine."

Aldarich didn't speak for a time. "The judge came down here to confess once, too." Then he told Frank a name, a name the Judge had told Aldarich in a moment of weakness, knowing it would never be shared with anyone else.

Frank took the remainder of the explosives with him, to set in the ugly hole in the dining room wall.

Chapter Twenty-two

The house was still, almost sad as he walked out the door for the last time. He climbed in his car and headed down the rough path. The gate was still open and no one was waiting.

He made it down to the road, and then heard the deep, distant whoop, felt or imagined a slight shudder in the ground, followed almost immediately by another, smaller explosion.

He pulled over and parked, saw a giant plume of dust erupting all around the plot where the house had stood. When it cleared there was nothing left but a collapsed pile of debris, bits of roof and stone seemingly swallowed whole by the earth.

He climbed back into his car and headed to town.

***

He turned down Main Street, driving slowly through the gathering street crowd, all looking to the hill and dust plume around it. His head was a dull, constant pain now, and his cuts burned every time he shifted in his seat. He parked in front of Sol's, climbed from the car.

A crowd was outside the barber shop across the way. A familiar heavy figure in ball cap raced across the street.

"What the hell are you doing here? How did you get out?" Henrik's face was contorted in anger and surprise.

Frank turned to him. *This one first, then*, he thought. "Your brother let me out."

"Emil?"

"No. Not that one."

"What are you talking about?" The big man interrupted with fury, his fists clenched. "I told you to leave here!"

"I plan on it," he said simply. "But not before I take care of some things." He felt no fear of Henrik now. He had no room for emotion of any kind. In fact, he was having trouble concentrating on anything but the immediate need to keep moving. *Should I tell him about Walden?* The question bothered him on multiple levels.

Henrik swore, and stepped forward. Before he could act, however, the door to Sol's opened behind Frank.

"You leave him alone, Henrik Mundt."

Henrik turned to Sol, who was standing now beside Frank. The crowd at the barber shop turned from the hill to the street confrontation.

"What you doing, Henrik?" called an old man in overalls from across the street. Frank turned to see Erik standing next to him and whispering heatedly in his ear. "You leave that man alone now."

Frank turned back to Henrik, who was now breathing heavily, his face turning a dark red. He looked from Sol to Frank, to the crowd behind him.

"Henrik, Henrik!" called Jenny, racing down the street as fast as her dress would let her. She pulled up against Henrik, looked to Frank and Sol, frowning at Frank's disheveled and bloody appearance, and gingerly reached a hand out to pull Henrik away. "Come along now," she whispered, trying to pull Henrik away. Henrik glanced at her, gave one last frustrated look at Frank, and turned to follow her. Frank heard her whispering worriedly about Walden as they walked away.

He turned to Sol, found the other watching the retreating Mundts grimly.

"Thank you," he said. He sensed he should feel more than he did, that his awareness was not completely whole. He heard the words come from his mouth, but they were strangely distant, as if they were not his own.

Sol turned to him, his expression turning to worry. "My god, Frank. What happened to you?"

"Long story. I'll tell it to you sometime, hopefully far, far away from here." Again that strange disconnect between the words and his awareness.

"You're leaving?"

"If they let me." He looked to the Municipal building.

"I'll go with you," said Sol. "To see the judge."

"No. That won't be necessary. This is something I have to do on my own."

Many of the crow were pointing again at the cloud of dust still around the hill. He wondered how long he had before they put things together.

"Have you seen the sheriff by the way?" he asked Sol. He was surprised to find Erik and the old man in overalls was now standing behind him.

"Not recently," said Sol. "What happened up there?" He pointed to the hill.

"An ending," said Frank.

"Good riddance," said the old man, spitting on the street. "Red Barton," he said offering a hand to Frank. "Don't believe we've been introduced yet, Mr. Henning." He stared openly at Frank's face and the cut on his chest, curiosity and wonder clouding his expression. "Jesus, you look a mess," he muttered.

Frank shook the hand slowly, the memory of Aldarich stretching between them. "I'm very sorry about the dog, Mr. Barton."

The older man squinted under his hat. "My boy told me about it. The goddam Mundts are more trouble than they are worth. You'll find not everyone around here goes by their ways."

There was no underlying dark assertion to this last comment, at least not that Frank could detect in his once-removed state. Barton simply didn't like the Mundts on principle.

The older man turned slowly from Frank, nodded brusquely to Sol as if he wasn't sure just how to address him. In his disconnected state, Frank wondered how many times Barton had eaten at the diner, if at all. Sol nodded back graciously.

Something pulled at Frank's sleeve. He turned and found Erik staring intently at him. The boy seemed eager to say something.

"I'll be running along now," said Erik, blushing. "I'm going to see Liz, at Claire's."

"You make sure Misses Claire is there, and preferably sitting between you two," said his father pointedly. The boy blushed deeper and took off. Barton shook his head ruefully but smiled. "Boy's got it bad for that girl."

Did that mean people still thought Liz was at Claire's? Was that what Erik was trying to tell him? And where was the sheriff? He had come too often and too quickly before with previous street scenes. His absence was noticeable. Apparently Barton shared his concern.

"Where the hell is Cal?" he asked, spitting again in the gutter. The question had the sense of being forced, and he glanced from Sol to Frank, clearly unsure of his role. He turned his head to look across the street to the small crowd of mostly old men, many of whom were looking curiously back at him. "I'll go see if anyone knows anything." He shuffled away.

Sol grunted lightly, with a small, knowing smile.

"I'd like to know where the sheriff is, too," said Frank quietly, looking to Sol.

"Last I saw him was about an hour ago, heading out of town," said Sol. He reached in his pocket and handed Frank a folded napkin. "It's clean," he said. "You're bleeding."

Frank pressed it up to his nose, felt the paper stick. *Was the sheriff chasing Claire and Liz? Had he failed after all?* He looked to his watch, but had trouble focusing on the hands. He guessed it to be almost dinner time. If they left soon after he did, then they might have an hour or so head start. He didn't think it was enough.

He turned back to Sol, struggled for something to say. The other waved him off.

"Good luck and give him hell. Come see me when you're done and we'll take care of those cuts."

He smiled grimly and nodded. He walked in a dream through the Municipal building front doors. Most of the workers stood at the front window looking up at the hill. They stared at him nervously, a man stepping forward hesitantly with a hand raised, as if to deny him entrance. He ignored the man, and took the steps to the judge's office. Someone called after him weakly but he ignored that as well.

Emil was just stepping out of the door when he reached the top of the steps. The look on Emil's face was exactly like Henrik's. And like his brother it turned quickly to angry violence.

"What are you...?"

"I'm here to see your uncle, Emil," interrupted Frank. Beyond Emil he could see the judge rising quickly from his chair, his expression also one of surprise and concern.

"Let him in, Emil," said the Judge.

But Emil only stood there, lost in shock and indecision.

Frank finally met his eyes. "You'll have a chance to start over now, Emil. Philo was right to want to end it."

"What are you talking about?" asked the other, his eyes shifting all along Frank's face and front.

"Your brother is dead," said Frank quietly. "The house is destroyed. All the remains of the Captain, except what you carry with you, are all gone." He couldn't tell if he was making sense. *Should he tell Emil about Walden?* No, he'd save that for the judge alone.

"You killed the scion?" asked Emil in disbelief.

"No."

"Then how? And how did you get out?"

"Your brother."

"Henrik?" asked Emil in disbelief.

"No," answered Frank wearily. "Aldarich let me out."

Emil stuttered insensibly for a response, a dark red creeping along is bald pate.

"It doesn't matter," said Frank, still keeping his voice low. "The point is Aldarich has given you a chance to change things, once and for all."

Emil started at him, his face reflecting the turmoil and confusion racing behind it.

"Let him by, Emil," said the hard voice of the judge from the office. Emil stepped aside slowly, automatically, watched in disbelief as Frank walked past and closed the door in his face.

The judge was talking quietly to someone on the phone, glaring at Frank standing across the desk.

"Whoever you're talking to," said Frank, "I'd let it go until you hear what I have to say."

The judge looked Frank up and down, but told the person on the phone he'd call back shortly.

"There was an explosion," said the judge, sitting back in his chair, his demeanor calm but his eyes hanging fire.

"The house is gone," said Frank.

"You did that?"

"Yes and no. It was Philo's plan originally. He was the first to see a way out this madness."

The judge glared. "I don't know what you are talking about, Mr. Henning, but it is clear that you have suffered some kind of trauma. I'm surprised you are still standing, looking at you. I think we should call a doctor, at the very least."

He felt the truth of the judge's assessment. His legs were shaking, and he was having even more trouble concentrating. But there was too much still to know, about Liz and Claire, too much to say...about everything.

"In minute," he said. "After we've had our talk."

"Then, at least, please sit before you pass out on my floor."

Frank took the chair gratefully, almost collapsing across it.

Sitting, he took an unsteady moment to frame his next line of attack. If nothing else, he had to buy some time for

Liz and Claire. But he also needed to make certain they could truly be free.

"I know all about the Captain and his Sister," he said slowly. "I read the journal. I saw the ledgers. I even looked through the Precepts."

The judge licked his lips with the point of his pink tongue. The hard, intelligent eyes calculating and patient now, some of the fire going out of them, the crooked mouth opened slightly. "Interesting reading, I am sure," he said. "But I'm not sure what this has to do with destroying my family's heirloom, if that's what you did."

"I told you, that was your nephew's idea. Sorry, nephews."

The judge sat up.

Frank shifted in his own seat, willing himself to concentrate. He looked around the office, avoiding the judge's heated stare. He stopped for a moment on the picture of the two men on the judge's desk, remembering Aldarich's last gift. "I don't understand," he said slowly. "You allowed all this...evil to go on and on, warping your family, generation after generation."

"I don't know what you are talking about."

"I'm talking about a twisted patriarch and his sister, who was may have been his lover as well. I can't be sure, as you or someone else took out the key pages in the journal. But you forgot about the Precepts, or you thought there was no way I'd ever see them."

The judge made a face and started to protest, but Frank went on determinedly. "And this sad, twisted couple forced their family to adapt to the same nightmare, the same taboos, even to the extent of burying one of their sons alive under that damned hill, living a life as a monster, relegated to playing a perverse role for the others. I'm talking about incest and abuse of children and brainwashing, Judge Delphus. Is that clear enough?"

"These are vile accusations, Mr. Henning," said the judge, his face turning an apoplectic white. "Such accusations without proof are pure, and malicious slander! Of a public official no less. I'll have you in jail before you the day is out."

"The proof is everywhere. Just go to the school."

This brought another change to the judge's demeanor. The white anger slowly retreated and the cold, hard tenor of calculation took its place. The change frightened Frank, in part because he suspected the judge was once more in control.

"I see," said the judge carefully. "You speak, of course, of our unfortunate children. It may interest you to know that Torview suffered a tragedy some time back. It is, unfortunately, an all too common occurrence with such towns. A newly developed industrial company came to Torview, promising jobs and progress. I was away for my studies at the time unfortunately, and could not participate in the decision process. Everyone was excited about the promises, of course, and welcomed the company without doing due diligence. The jobs did come, though not as many as promised, and never anything of high quality. Those were reserved for the out of town staff. Still, some here did prosper. Emil for one, did quite well."

He frowned around the memory, looked to Frank, and finished in a flurry. "They eventually discovered the company was poisoning our water source. The company shut down the factory, and left town. They went bankrupt and disbanded shortly afterward."

The judge leaned forward, caught Frank's eye. "We fixed the water, but the damage was done. Our children still pay the price."

Frank sighed, knowing now the judge had an answer for everything. "A company, you say?"

"Oh, yes."

"What company?"

"I forget their name."

"But I could look it up, surely?"

"Unfortunately," said the judge without a hint of irony, "our records, until recently, were kept in paper, and there was a fire..."

"And all the records burned up," finished Frank with a bitter smirk.

The judge nodded, his eyes dancing.

"It might work here," he admitted, trying to match the judge's confidence. "But the world's changed a lot since you kept records. It wouldn't stand a very close examination. DNA alone..."

"You have no idea what you are talking about," interrupted the judge, some of the white anger creeping back into his face and tone. "And if you think privacy laws are not strictly enforced here, then you are as mad as I suspect you to be. I would go very carefully from here on, sir."

"So, now I'm insane. I wondered when you would play that card."

The judge shrugged, ignoring the implication of blackmail. "Your actions are well-documented. I've already made some calls to friends, local and federal, to ensure they know who you are, should you start making wild and unfounded accusations. Of course, local witnesses can be called should you persist anyway."

He leaned back, and put his hand in his watch pocket, once more assuming the mantle of inviolable authority. "And I think you'll find your so-called other proofs futile, as well. I speak of the ledgers and journals, journals by the way which you stole from this office and have had in your possession for some time. I believe that constitutes theft and possession of stolen goods, Mr. Henning. They would never be admitted as evidence. But more to the point, such material is open to vast interpretation. There were missing pages, you say?"

"And the house?" asked Frank. "The secret dwelling of the scion's?"

The judge's eyebrows lifted slightly at the mention of the name, but otherwise kept his composure. "You mean the house you say is now destroyed?"

"It could be dug up again."

"Really, Mr. Henning; do you think the public will stand for the cost? Do you think the town of Torview will just roll over and let someone dig in their hills? Assuming, of course, someone actually buys this cock and bull story from a madman."

The judge sighed, leaned forward again, his voice offering a token of reason. "But all of this is pointless. You must understand, I cannot let such stories be indiscriminately cast about. It would do my family irreparable harm, regardless of their baselessness."

"What I don't understand is why you?"

"Pardon?"

"You, better than anyone, knows what it means to live a lie," said Frank, looking pointedly to the photograph. "To give up your nature to serve a warped cause."

"I don't know what you are talking about," said the judge, but the practiced self-possession slipped just a bit and the white anger was now tainted with agitation.

"William—Bill," said Frank, using the name Aldarich had given him under the hill. "You had to let him go. Because in the twisted world of your family, such a love was forbidden. You never married, and probably never participated in those rituals. This, according to the Captain's precepts and traditions, should have made you an outcast. But the Captain wasn't around to enforce his will, and you were willing to give up who you were, if the others would let you stay. A mind, a will, like yours would be too valuable to waste. But it cost you, Delphus. It must have cost a lot. Bill, too."

A deep flush worked its way up the Judge's neck and only stopped just below his cheek bones. The blow had struck home, but not fatally. Frank didn't think it would. As a man who had lived for so long with the hidden truth, the judge would hardly roll over the first time it was voiced, whatever the circumstances.

So he wasn't surprised by the judge's eventual response. "Is this then your real threat, Mr. Henning? To expose me to my family, with another baseless rumor?"

"I think we've moved beyond threats, Judge. I know yours, and I know they are real. I don't think it will be as easy as you pretend, but I know you mean it."

"It would be far easier than you think, Mr. Henning," said the judge with a cold smile. "I was just talking to a friend at the Summerset Mental Facility when you came in. A very good friend indeed."

"Okay. So it would be easy. As I said, let's call the threats a given and move on. You still haven't answered my question. How can you, of all people participate in this? I don't just mean your sacrifice. You strike me as an intelligent, reasonable human being."

Slowly the flush left the judge's face, retreating to his neck, but not disappearing altogether.

"So, you met Aldarich?"

"Yes."

"I underestimated you, Mr. Henning."

The judge leaned back in his chair, the mantle fell, replaced by reflective sadness. "Aldarich told you about William," he said.

"Yes."

The old man shook his head. "I should never have told him." He rocked slightly in his chair, studying the air, came to it slowly. "Don't think I haven't examined the subject from many angles over the years, wrestled with the...ethics. But in the end I am afraid we are all products of our environment, Mr. Henning. We see things that we want to see. We believe the truths we inherit—even when it costs us. My...sacrifices, as you call it, was for a greater need."

"That sounds like a clever rationalization," said Frank, but he was thinking about Tara as he said it. *Did I see what I wanted to see, in the end?* Then, with a shudder, he had another, more disturbing thought. *Did she stay for a greater good?*

"No, of course you're right," said the judge. "But there are times when it *is* for a greater need. I suppose it is a hopelessly subjective, moment to moment affair, but there it is: I believe it was for a greater good."

He turned to Frank with a frown, assuming some authority again. "Not everyone is able to answer that call, or weigh the scales accurately. Some people chose to turn their back on their past, or their duty. Philo, for one." The judge waved Frank's expression off. "Look where it got him: lost, a refugee, estranged from his own wife and family."

"Philo is not lost. Philo is dead. Killed by his nephew."

Genuine shock paled the judge's face. "What do you mean?"

"I mean your great nephew is—was—a psychopath."

"Who?"

"Walden."

"Impossible," sputtered the judge. "The boy is quiet, even strange, I grant you, but murder?" He shook his head I disbelief.

"He killed both his uncles. And the Thomas boy. And a dog I had grown quite fond of," he added sadly. The judge was now staring at him in horror. It might be an act, thought Frank, but he didn't think so.

"And from his account," he continued, "they weren't clean deaths. I had firsthand experience of what Walden liked to do to his victims."

The judge looked to his face. "Tell me," he said in a whisper.

So Frank told him. He told him of the torture, of the death of Walden, and finally, the sacrifice of Aldarich.

"I think you are right about one thing, Judge Delphus," he concluded. "There are times you have to sacrifice for a greater good. Aldarich is testimony to that. But I also think you're version of the good is terribly skewed."

"I didn't know…" muttered the judge, looking to his desk. "Philo. Aldarich." He shook his head. "We thought the Thomas boy was lost in sinkhole."

Frank judged the armor was cracking but still there. It was time to play his final card.

"It's not just Walden," he said. "It's the whole thing."

The judge looked up, a bit of the fire returning. "Don't conflate a psychopath with me, or my family, Mr. Henning."

"They may not have killed anyone," said Frank. *Though give Henrik time.* "But what they do is evil."

The judge's eyes grew to two small points. He started to speak, but Frank overrode him.

"Delphus, why would you do this to Liz?"

The bald head jerked, as if struck. "I will take care of my niece, Mr. Henning, thank you very much."

"You will? Do you know the plans Henrik and Jenny have for Elizabeth?"

The judge hesitated, struggling to put his answer into words. "I don't know what you are talking about."

"I heard them, outside Aldarich's…prison," he couldn't bring himself to say home. "They are going to use her like a breeding mare, to bring new blood to your precious family."

The judge snorted. "Lies. Distortion." But his expression betrayed his doubt.

Frank waited him out, everything riding on this one chance. For just a moment, he thought the judge would break. But then, slowly, he raised his ancient head, looked at Frank, and a small, knowing smile warped his crooked mouth.

"You would say anything now," said the judge. "Anything to let her escape."

Frank felt his stomach turn. "What do you mean?"

"Yes," said the judge. "I know of your plan to spirit Liz away. I took steps."

"Then undo those steps. Call whoever, tell them to let her go."

The judge dismissed this with a flop of his aged-spotted hand. "I'm sure I know what's best for my niece, Mr. Henning. Michalus is a fine boy, despite his father. They will marry. It is my will."

"Will they? Is it?" asked Frank, growing heated. "My god man, haven't you been listening? You know what they intend to do with her? What Henrik wants to do with her? Do you have so little regard for her that you would subject her to that? I *saw* what they do on the altar, Judge!" He shouted. "She'll never come back from that."

"Mr. Henning, please!" shouted the judge in return. "Control yourself."

Frank tried to respond, searched for some way to make the judge see his error, but was left with only muted frustration.

The judge, seeing his struggle, sighed. "I admit to none of your vile insinuations of my nephews and nieces, Mr. Henning," he said, carefully. "But if you must know I intend to free Liz and Michalus from any such traditions—if they exist, which they don't."

Frank shook his head. "You fool," he said. "You think the others will listen to you? Oh, they may while you're still here. Maybe. How would you know? You don't go down for the rites, do you? There just something that happens deep underground, where they can't touch your precious greater good. Maybe that lets you live with it for now, but it won't help Liz. You'll be gone someday, and then your ruling won't matter. They'll ruin her, Delphus! Michalus, too, if he's half what you say he is. Like they ruined Aldarich."

"The traditions were set in place for good reasons," started the judge distractedly, forgetting for a moment his cautious denials. "But we're changing. Emil and I..." He blushed, his voice falling off.

"Emil?" said Frank derisively. "Maybe you should talk to Jenny or Henrik about those changes. They've got plans, judge, and they don't include changes in the tradition. I don't think it will include Emil either, if he gets in their way."

The judge stared at Frank, his hands and head shaking with emotion, a bit of drool falling out the corner of his crooked lip, the last of his armor crumbling like so much rusted tin. "I will see that they do," he started, "I am...they will listen! God damn you, Henning! Why did you come here?"

He'd been asked the question a dozen times before. He'd given as many different answers to others, to himself. He knew the judge's question was rhetorical, but now, here, with the world falling apart around both men, he answered truthfully.

"Because," he said, "I thought I could run away from my own lie."

The room seemed to deflate, the judge looking from Frank to the air around his head, as if searching for some point of normalcy. He wiped the spit from his mouth. "What did you say?"

But he could go no further. Not with the judge, not now. He could barely admit he'd said it to himself.

"Never mind," he said. "It doesn't matter. What matters is what we do next. What you do next." He held the judge's response off with a shaky hand. "I'm going to make this easy for you. I'm going to give you me, for her. Let Liz—and Claire—go. I'll stay here, and keep my mouth shut. You can keep a close eye on me. Or, you could wait until Henrik or someone else takes care of the matter permanently. Either way, you are ahead."

He looked to the old man. Was there just the touch of doubt on the judge's face?

"I don't believe you really want this life for Liz," he continued. "I think you are just looking for a chance to stop the madness. You just couldn't make that last step. Fear or denial, or something else, some twisted sense of loyalty to tradition, kept you from doing what was right, really right."

The judge scowled. "Don't judge me, Frank Henning. You have no right."

"All right," said Frank, scrambling to retain his glimmer of hope. "Think of it this way then. You're still operating for the greater good. You'll have me, to protect the family. And you'll save Liz."

The scowl retreated, the judge seemed to consider the idea.

"Call," urged Frank.

He looked one last time at Frank, a dark, ugly blush across his cheeks and along his neck. He reached slowly for the phone, dialed a number.

"Do you have them?" he asked.

Frank couldn't hear the answer.

"No," said the judge, his voice regaining a vestige of authority, a reflex of habit and personality. "Let them go. Yes, I'm sure." A long pause. "No." He hung up the phone.

"Thank you," said Frank.

"I didn't do it for you," said the judge, still looking at the phone. His voice was distant and soft, lost apparently in his own thoughts. "Or the greater good," he added a moment later. "I did it for her. And for him." He looked up, his cheeks suddenly flushed with anger and regret. "I gave you everything to this family, understand. They have no right to undermine what I gave."

Frank nodded, not sure how to respond. He started to stand, swayed, and caught himself on the arm of the chair.

"Sit down, Mr. Henning," ordered the judge softly. "You need a doctor."

He sat. "Okay. You don't by chance have a drink around, do you? I think we could both use one."

The judge eyed him speculatively, and pulled a bottle and two shot glasses from his desk drawer. He poured two full shots.

The judge drank his off in one hard swallow. Frank, with less confidence, sipped his.

"This is very good," he said.

The judge muttered something he couldn't hear, staring again at the photo, then, "Now, I wish you had come twenty years earlier, or not at all." He paused, and poured himself another shot, topped Frank's up again. He looked away from the photo and back to Frank, picked up the phone.

"The doctor," he said to Frank, his hand over the mouth piece.

He poured and downed another shot after the call, and started to pour Frank another as well, but changed his mind. "Best let the doctor see you first," he said. There was a pleasant color to his cheeks now, and the crook in his mouth was a little more exaggerated.

"I'll honor my promise," said Frank, lifting his glass in salute. "I'll stay put."

The judge frowned, shook his head. "I don't know if I like what you've done, Mr. Henning," he said, turning to the bottle again. "I don't think I'll ever like you, period." He poured a slow, careful shot. "But, I'm not so far gone as to hold you to that promise. You're right about Henrik. Once he finds out about Walden, it won't matter what really happened. He'll kill you."

The judge paused, as if surprised by his own words. He tossed the shot back, took a deep breath.

"No," he continued, "you better leave Torview as soon as the doctor is done with you. I'll do what I can to put my nephews off, though it is clear they don't listen to me as they once did." He looked to Frank with bitter irony.

The doctor arrived shortly after. There were no introductions, the judge simply asked the doctor to look at Frank.

A man similar in age and dress to the Judge, the doctor carried a small black bag and was already moving in Frank's direction before the door closed behind him. He didn't say a word to Frank. He smelled of alcohol rub and cheap aftershave.

He cleaned the cuts thoroughly, using a butterfly bandage across the nose. He checked Claire's work on the original head wound, grunted, and put three stitches in before Frank knew what was happening. He put five in the new one. Then he waved a penlight in Frank's eyes, and asked him what day it was. He told the judge to bring ice and something to keep it in, spotted the bottle on the desk, and asked for one of those as well.

The judge got up, came back with a towel wrapped around some cubes and a full shot. The doctor placed the pack along Frank's latest head blow, told Frank to hold it there. Then he tossed off the shot like it was water. When he was finished he turned to the Judge.

"This man is suffering from severe concussions. The cuts should be cleaned again later, and if it matters he should see a specialist or he'll have a scar on the face. My recommendation: he should be kept in bed and under supervision for at least two days. If he wants to sleep, okay, but wake him every quarter hour for the first two hours, then every half hour for the next two. Call me if he fails to wake or shows signs of losing concentration or if the slurring gets worse."

This last surprised Frank. He wasn't aware that he'd been slurring his words.

The judge frowned. "Can he travel at all?"

The doctor blinked. "Does he have to?"

"Maybe."

"He shouldn't drive himself. And no more booze."

"Okay. Thanks, Sam."

The doctor gave Frank a quick, professional nod, and left, closing the door softly behind him. The judge, standing by the desk, was already on the phone again. "Yes," he said into the receiver, "I think I need you here." Short pause. "As soon as you can. All right."

He hung the phone up, looked to Frank, and then put the bottle away. He sat down in his chair, stared at his wall of books.

"You'll leave and never come back," he said, as if talking to himself. "You'll return everything you've stolen." He glanced at Frank. "Everything. Journals. Ledgers."

Frank started to nod, felt the stitches bind, and said "Okay," instead.

"We'll keep the records of your actions here confidential. As long as no baseless accusations are raised, they'll remain confidential."

"And Liz and Claire?"

"I will see that they are left alone. I think I can manage that much at least."

There was a long, awkward silence.

"I don't like you," said the judge, still looking at his law books.

Neither man spoke after that. Frank had trouble keeping his eyes open. He didn't remember the sheriff coming in, or helping him stand up. He heard the others talking, but couldn't make sense of what they said. He felt the sheriff's strong arm around him, guiding him to the door. Then the world went dark again.

Chapter Twenty-three

He was in the passenger side of his own car. The sheriff was driving. *How long have I been out? Where are we going?*

He turned to look at the man beside him. The familiar hat was off. The exposed salt and pepper hair closely trimmed and lying in a severe part across the front. There were deep pores in the sheriff's nose, and his brown cheeks were covered in age spots and blackheads.

The sheriff glanced over, saw Frank was conscious. He nodded. "How we doing, Frank?"

So we're back to first names again.

"Where are we going?" he asked, and this time he heard the slur in his words. Did that mean he was getting better, or worse?

"Motel in Summerset," answered the sheriff. "Liz and Claire are there."

Frank nodded, feeling sick, fearing he would pass out again. "How did you find them?"

A small smile curled the edge of the sheriff's lip. "I told you, not much happens in a small town the sheriff doesn't know about."

He looked to Frank, then out the front again. "Granger saw them heading out," he explained. "Called me. The judge sent me after them."

"My buddy Granger."

"Worked out anyway. They're free and clear now."

"What about Emil? Henrik?"

Frank saw the sheriff's eyes crinkled slightly in the dome light of the car.

"I take my orders from the judge. Liz and Claire will be left alone—so will you—by everybody. Everybody."

"But the judge won't always be around."

"Far as I'm concerned, that's a standing order." The sheriff glanced at Frank, then back to the road. "Those three aren't as important as they think they are."

Frank nodded again. Then he sat up, the significance of the words penetrating through his haze. "You said three. You mean, Jenny."

The sheriff's mouth twitched. "I guess I did."

"You knew."

The sheriff chewed his lip, said slowly, "I knew some things. Not as much as you think."

"Why?" he asked suddenly, turning to the sheriff. "Why did you let it go on?"

The other man stared out the window for a long time, so long, Frank thought he would never get that answer. Then, he got one.

"We have an understanding, the judge and I."

"An understanding that lets you look the other way?" he asked bitterly.

The eyes crinkled again. "Yes."

Frank turned to look out the window.

"Torview is a quiet town, Frank," said the sheriff, glancing at Frank. "People don't lock their cars or houses, and a woman could wall buck-naked down any alley at midnight, and not fear a thing. I keep it that way. That's my end of it. The rest..."

Frank turned at the pause.

"I don't get into the rest," finished the sheriff, staring at the road. "I stayed away from the house." He paused, and added a moment later, "And part of the understanding was that the other stuff would stop. The judge would see to that."

Frank remembered Jenny talking about losing the others, about needing to return to the old ways. *Had the judge and the sheriff made a difference?*

Then he saw Aldarich lying on the ground, the bloody wings spreading out from under him, the knife in his back. *No, it wasn't enough*, he thought. The understanding was not enough.

"He didn't stop it all," he said.

The sheriff stared straight ahead, his lips pressed in a hard line.

"But you knew that," said Frank, watching the sheriff carefully.

There was a long, awkward pause. Then, "I suspected. The judge said he was handling it, that it would take time. That there was only a few who held to the old ways..." His voice fell off.

"You knew what that they did in that house, and did nothing. You knew about and Walden..."

"No," interrupted the sheriff, his expression as hard and angry as Frank had ever seen it. "I did not know about Walden." His voice dropped to a whisper. "I missed that one."

"People died because you missed that one. Because of your...understanding."

"Yes." There was no remorse in the word, but the sheriff seemed to shrink for just a moment inside himself.

"But why?" he asked, not wanting to let go, not wanting to let the sheriff off so easily. "Why make that bargain?"

"My wife," said the other simply.

"You're wife?"

"You met her. Though, maybe not on the best terms."

It took him a moment, then, "May. Miss May. The woman at the school. She's your wife."

"Yes."

"I don't see...I don't understand."

"May is everything to me. I met her a long time ago, outside Torview, when she was at school. I followed her back here, and married her."

"She's a Mundt."

The sheriff looked to Frank slowly, much as he looked to Henrik that first day in town. "Yes, she's a Mundt."

They drove for a time in silence, the atmosphere suddenly tense and awkward. It occurred to Frank that he had only the word of the sheriff that they were heading to Somerset and freedom. He looked sideways to the big man staring out the windshield, the big jaw set, the brow furrowed.

"She didn't do...," started the sheriff, his eyes wrinkled up in concentration. "She got sick when she was young, almost died. She can't have children. You understand?"

He did. May never faced the fertility rituals; there was no point.

"But there were some," continued the sheriff, "who would have insisted she participate anyway."

"Emil, Henrik, Jenny."

"Yes."

Frank saw the knuckles of the sheriff's hand turn white on the steering wheel.

"I couldn't have that." The knuckles released slightly. "But I couldn't take on the whole town, the whole bloody tradition all by myself." He struggled for the next words. "And I would lose May."

He turned, his face hard, determined, unapologetic. "So, the understanding."

Frank turned to look out the window again. It was night, the view reduced to shadows and dark suggestions. *Like our conversation*, he thought, *shadows and dark suggestions. It's always been shadows and suggestions with the sheriff.*

"I'm sorry," he said, turning back. "I still don't understand how you can turn a blind eye. May's not enough."

The sheriff raised a brow at this, but again, took his time answering, chewing his lip as if working out each word before he said it. "It's because you don't know May."

They drove in silence for a time, Frank too argue.

"We only talked about her childhood once," said the sheriff, as if determined to make his point clear. "May didn't have the same experience as the others, because she was so sick. But she had bad memories of that house." He frowned. "She still has nightmares...a face, a monster in a window." He shook his head, glanced to Frank, then back to the road.

"She heard rumors, but they kept her out, and later I kept her out—for her protection." He stopped, looked again to Frank. "May is strong in many ways, but not that kind of strong. This was her family we're talking about. And that kind of evil is not easy for the innocent to understand. She shouldn't have to. I kept it from her."

Again, he looked to Frank, and again, Frank simply looked back, waiting, listening.

His silence seemed to bother the sheriff, who became more animated, more determined. "She's the most decent thing I know in this town, Frank. She channeled her goodness into that school, into those children. She works every day to give them a little light, a safe place. When you walked on that schoolyard, she saw you as a threat to that safety, and acted the only way she knew how. I know you wouldn't hurt those kids, but if you think about it from her perspective—all those doubts and suspicions she still carries deep inside her, without really understanding—well, you can see why she got overly protective." He paused, a sardonic smile lifting the corner of his lip. "I guess you can blame that on me, too."

"You seem pretty comfortable with the blame."

A slight blush crept up the sheriff's neck. But a moment later, he shrugged.

"You're probably right," he said quietly. "I'm not in the good on this; not completely, maybe not enough. Maybe I trusted in the judge too much. I did what I did to protect May, and that town, but I compromised myself. You've never compromised, Frank?"

He didn't meet the sheriff's eyes. *Is that what I did with Tara, compromise?*

"I told you once," continued the sheriff, "we all bring our evil with us. Maybe that's mine; a well-intended evil, but an evil just the same. I'd do anything for May. I don't offer any apologies. I did the best I could. I don't expect you to understand."

"You could've exposed the truth," said Frank, hearing an echo of self-reproach in his words. *But it's not the same,* he thought. *It's not.* "People would have believed you," he continued. "There would have been an investigation, the judge be damned."

The knuckles whitened again around the steering wheel, matched this time by the wrinkles of the sheriff's eyes. "It's not that simple. They know why I stay in Torview, why I do what I do. They'd use May against me." He shook his head slowly. "I couldn't allow that. I won't allow that from you, either."

The blue gray eyes turned to his, and Frank saw the determination and hard promise of the sheriff's threat. He looked again out his window at the dark and lonely road. It might be the road to Somerset, or it might not.

The sheriff wasn't done with his defense, or his point. "If I talked about it, if anyone talked about it," he glanced again at Frank, "the stain would touch May. No matter how innocent she was, no matter where we went, it would follow her." He sighed, almost pleaded, "I just can't allow that. Do you see that, at least? Do you see why it has to be this way?"

What way is that? Freedom and silence, or just silence? Are you taking me to Somerset, or to some off road, where I'll be found with a bullet in my head and a gun in my hand, and the whole of Torview's municipality ready to swear I was deluded and desperate. But he didn't have the courage to ask the question aloud. He just stared out the window, wondering.

"I don't expect you to approve," continued the sheriff, his tone still anxious, or as anxious as his personality would allow. "But you were married once, and the way you talk about your wife...well, you must understand a little. We'll put up with quite a lot, for the ones we love. Do you understand now?"

Frank leaned his head gently against the window, feeling the cool glass press against his forehead. He thought about Tara, about the years and the doubts, and the smiles. He thought about the late nights away, and their final short days together, his bruised and battered mind mixing everything up into a confusion of perspectives and impossible questions.

Did she stay because she loved him, or love him because she stayed?

He heard the sheriff shift in his seat. He was waiting for Frank's answer.

He could say he understood, promise his silence, and maybe insure Somerset and freedom. Maybe this is what the judge and sheriff spoke about in those last, distorted whispers outside his office. A final test. A decision to follow, one way or the other. All he had to do was say he understood, that he would be silent. He had said as much for the judge earlier.

But somehow, the question was different with the sheriff. An image of Aldarich holding the broken sunglasses in his pale hands wouldn't allow him the comfort of compromising, not this time.

"I think you do May a disservice," he said, his eyes shut against his own pain and doubt.

The other didn't answer, but Frank heard the leather of the wheel twist under the big hands.

They drove in silence the rest of the way. Somewhere along the way, he lost consciousness again.

* * *

He woke when he felt the car slow down, come to a stop. He heard, as if in a dream, the hum of nearby highway traffic. He sensed light, pristine, hard light. He opened his eyes.

They were in a motel parking lot.

The commercial lights were bright, and hurt his eyes, but Frank welcomed the glare. He opened his door, caught the smell of oil on the blacktop, and the faint hint of fast food from somewhere close by.

"Room 106," said the sheriff, coming around to help him out of the car. "Can you make it on your own? I'd like to take off now." There was no sense of ill will or threat in his voice or bearing.

"How will you get back?" asked Frank, relieved, confused, and oddly sorry, for what he couldn't say.

"I know someone on the force here. They'll give me a lift back."

The hat was back on, and the sheriff's official, stoical persona restored, as was the voice and the bearing.

No, he thought, a moment later, *not quite.* The big frame seemed to hum now with suppressed energy, and when the sheriff turned to Frank, the blue-gray eye's seemed unsettled, distracted.

"I found these in your trunk," he said, holding up the journal and ledgers for Frank to see. "I've got to take them back."

Frank nodded. "For the judge," he said. "I'll keep my end of the bargain, sheriff. Don't worry."

I can say it now, he thought. *There's no compromise.*

The hat twitched briefly, and the sheriff shook his head, looked distractedly at the pavement. "No, not for the judge. I think I'll keep them."

Frank studied the hanging head. "They're not much for evidence, anyway," he said.

The sheriff nodded, still distracted. He turned the journal over in his hands, staring at it.

"His name was, Aldarich," said Frank. "The face that haunts May. He was a decent man."

The blue-gray eyes met Frank's, the heavy jaw turning slowly.

"Maybe I'll tell her that," said the sheriff, after a time. Then he tucked the journal under his arm, tapped his hat, turned, and walked away.

A moment later, Frank heard a door open. Liz was running up to him, Claire following more slowly behind.

The End